"*Perfectly Healthy Man Drops Dead* is a gripping mystery from first page to last, a top pick for community library mystery collections."

—*Midwest Book Review*

Perfectly Healthy Man Drops Dead

Also by Bruce Hartman:

The Rules of Dreaming

The Muse of Violence

The Philosophical Detective

A Butterfly in Philadelphia

Big Data Is Watching You!

Potlatch: A Comedy

The Devil's Chaplain

PERFECTLY HEALTHY MAN DROPS DEAD

a novel by

Bruce Hartman

Swallow Tail Press

Perfectly Healthy Man Drops Dead

Tenth anniversary edition, 2018, slightly revised from the original 2008 edition published by Salvo Press.

Published by Swallow Tail Press
Philadelphia, PA, USA
www.swallowtailpress.com
Also available in ebook format

Front cover photo courtesy of Shutterstock.com

ISBN-13: 978-0-9997564-2-3

ISBN-10: 0-9997564-2-7

1.

Call me irresponsible. I promised Elena I'd never tell this story to another living soul and here I sit, crouched over a clunky keyboard reliving the moment on that rainy Tuesday night in January when I first heard the news of Babylon's demise. Exactly a year ago it was, and if I close my eyes I can almost hear the same raindrops beating down on the awning over the door. On a night like this I know I would tell the whole sordid tale to the first attractive woman who lets me buy her a drink. There's a likely candidate sitting alone at the bar. I wonder what she would say if she knew that the stiff playing the piano was once a partner in one of Philadelphia's largest law firms and the prime suspect in a capital murder case.

Don't panic. I'm not really a lawyer, at least not any more. It's been over three years since the Supreme Court stripped me of my license to split hairs. At first it was rough. My wife of ten years left me, my dog of six years bit me, my kids screamed bloody murder when I came for a visit. To keep body and soul together I made the unceremonious transition from the Bar of Philadelphia to the Piano Bar of the Pickwick Club on 19th street just south of Chestnut, where I provide nightly entertainment to a small but dedicated band of inebriates. In short, I'm a disbarred lawyer eking out a living playing cocktail piano for an assortment of drunks and misfits—and the man who did the most to put me here was Neil M. Babylon,

Esquire, age 56, who was found dead that morning in his office at the prestigious Rittenhouse law firm. Foul play was suspected and, in my opinion, richly deserved.

Of course I was the number one suspect. Peter Cloud is my name and just three years ago I was being toasted as the newest partner in the Rittenhouse firm. Then there was a certain matter involving stolen environmental inspection files, an angry Federal judge, and a valued client who had to be protected at all costs. Babylon arranged for me to take the fall, compliments of a crooked defense attorney who made a deal behind my back to request voluntary disbarment in lieu of criminal penalties. Everybody in town knows the story, but that doesn't mean I killed him. There are probably dozens of lawyers in and out of the firm who had as much reason to kill him as I did, including his co-chairman and heir apparent Art Valunos. And don't forget the usual suspects: the wife, the ex-wife, the mistress, the ex-mistress—most of whom had been his secretary at one time or another—not to mention the secretaries he didn't marry, including the one from way back that he knocked up and had to send to college. You get the idea. There are any number of people who would have jumped for joy to see him right where he ended up, sprawled like a stuffed lobster on his priceless oriental rug.

Enter Bardahl, dropping in for a friendly drink. I was expecting him. His real name is Bardolski and he's the other person I would murder if I were the murdering type. Two choruses into "Embraceable You" and he looms enormously over the far end of my piano with his huge hamlike arms, inhaling a Coors Light and what I hope will be a lethal dose of cigarette smoke. Evidently he's not on duty or he'd be drinking in his car, not in here. I ignore him and take my time finishing the song.

Scattered applause. From Bardahl's direction, a series of dull thuds like a lazy cook pounding a steak. "Sent your sympathy card yet, Cloud?"

"Not yet," I confessed. "Thought I'd wait till I felt more sympathetic."

"Better tell Hallmark not to hold the presses. Something tells me this could be a long goddam wait. Ha ha!"

Bardahl is a Philadelphia cop, Neanderthal Division. He wears a black trench coat in all kinds of weather, probably because he put it on once and now he can't find his way out of its elaborate tangle of belts and buckles. It was Bardahl's investigation—and his uncanny arrival at my office with a search warrant the morning after I'd retrieved the stolen environmental inspection files from my crooked client's warehouse—that led to my meteoric fall from grace.

He downed the rest of his beer and wandered off to visit the head, and then an amazing thing happened. A beautiful young Asian woman hurried through the door, and after peering around in the gloom for a few seconds she stepped up to the piano and wrapped her arms around me and kissed me passionately on the mouth.

"Please help me," she whispered. "This weirdo's following me and I want him to think you're my boyfriend."

Our embrace must have lasted fifteen seconds. When she pulled away I glanced toward the bar and locked eyes with a lean unshaven young man who looked like he might have been Timothy McVeigh's next of kin. "That's him over there," she said.

Not knowing who she was or who the man was or what either of them were doing there put me at a slight disadvantage. But I didn't like the looks of that guy, and the girl seemed genuinely scared. McVeigh didn't take his eyes off me as I stepped towards him. He stuck his cigarette in his mouth as if trying to keep his hands free. "Get out of here," I said quietly.

His lips formed a tight smile around the cigarette. Actually, I'm not sure you could call it a smile. If he were a dog—which is insulting to dogs—I would have said he bared his teeth. "You the bouncer?" he asked sarcastically. "Or the piano player?"

"The girl's a friend of mine. Get out."

I took a step closer. He started to reach for something in his jacket pocket, but I was on his wrists before he could get there. In no time I spun him around and had both his arms behind his back escorting him to the door. It was a little trick I remembered from my days as a college wrestler. How could he have guessed that the piano player had come within six seconds of the national championship about fifteen years before? To spare him embarrassment I kept the whole thing very discreet. If you had been ordering a drink you would hardly have noticed.

The Asian beauty sat at the piano bar contentedly sipping a drink. It was my drink. She smiled gratefully as I took my seat at the keyboard and played the opening bars of my next song. I think it was "You Took Advantage of Me."

"Now tell me," I said, "why did I just do that?"

"That weirdo followed me out of ZuLu's when I finished my shift and I needed a little help getting rid of him. You don't mind, do you?"

ZuLu's is the topless joint on the alley a couple of doors down. I've never been in there but I think they have a slightly raunchier crowd than we're used to seeing in the Pickwick Club. "Not at all," I said. "He'll probably come back and blow my brains out, but hell, it's all in a day's work."

She had a very sweet smile which went a long way toward reconciling me to my fate. "I knew as soon as I saw you that you were someone I could trust."

"What's your name?" I asked.

"Madison."

"Is that your real name?"

"Of course not."

"You don't trust me well enough to tell me your name?"

She blushed. "We just met."

I was starting to like that young lady, so I was sorely disappointed when she suddenly looked at her watch, drained the rest of my drink and stood up to leave. "I gotta run. Thanks again."

Another sweet smile and she was gone, along with the hopes and dreams of a lifetime. And across from me sat Bardahl, still splayed over the piano like a side of beef. "What's her name?" he grunted, guardedly sipping another beer.

"Madison," I said.

"Madison?"

"Sort of gives you new respect for our fourth President, doesn't it?"

Bardahl downed the rest of his Coors Light and smacked the bottle down on the piano. "You're a piece of work, Cloud." He sidled closer with a confidential air. "Now let's cut the crap. You're the number one suspect even though I personally don't think you did it."

"Did what?"

"But I'm about the only one who has that opinion."

The cocktail waitress came by to offer Bardahl another drink but he waved her off. "You lost your job, lost your ticket to practice, your wife left you—took the kids, didn't she?—and you end up playing the piano for Christ's sake in a shithole like this. And all because Babylon threw you to the dogs. Mother Teresa would have killed for a lot less."

"Is there any reason to think he was even murdered?"

Bardahl sipped his beer and chuckled knowingly. "Perfectly healthy man drops dead. Is that it?"

"Not exactly."

"Because that's what they're saying at the Rittenhouse firm. That's the party line. Nothing wrong with Babylon, he just suddenly dropped dead, that's all. Ha!"

"He was an overweight, two-pack-a-day, fifty-six year old lecher who could hardly walk up a flight of stairs without gasping for breath."

Bardahl coughed slightly.

"No offense."

"Forget it. I'm trying to do you a favor, Cloud. Don't waste your time arguing with me. There are people in City Hall who don't wait around for evidence to accumulate. They want to see action.   It won't be me.   I'm white collar crime, remember?"

"There'll be an autopsy. Let's see what it shows."

"There won't be an autopsy."

"What do you mean?"

"I've heard a certain state senator has already intervened. The medical examiner is out. Family doctor only."

That would be Senator Lou Squires, one of the most powerful politicos in the city and nominally a partner at the Rittenhouse firm. I say "nominally" because although his name graces the letterhead he never bills an hour of time but somehow manages to take home about a million dollars a year. "All right, then," I said. "No autopsy, no murder. You don't need a suspect."

Something rattled inside Bardahl's enormous throat. I think he was trying to chuckle. "You think it's that simple, huh?"

"Seems pretty simple to me."

He chose his words carefully. "Let's just say that not everybody in this city loves Senator Squires. He's powerful, but he's not God."

"He's the closest thing to God you're going to find in Philadelphia."

"Even God has enemies."

This sounded serious. "Who would we be talking about? The Mayor's office? City Council? The Anti-Christ?"

He glanced around to make sure no one was listening. "I'm not naming any names. But like I said, there's people who'd like to see the Senator and his law firm eat a little dirt. There's others who want to protect them at all costs."

"And you're in the anti-Squires camp."

"I'm not saying that."

"Of course not."

"But I'll tell you this much," he confided. "The anti-Squires camp thinks somebody murdered Babylon and they want to find out why. They're looking for anything that could take him or his law firm down."

I brought the song I was playing to a somewhat discordant conclusion and squinted curiously into Bardahl's bloodshot eyes. "What does all this have to do with me?"

"I need that surveillance tape."

"What surveillance tape?"

"You know what surveillance tape. The one that shows who stole the files from the state inspection archive. And don't ask me what files."

"I've told you before"—I must have raised my voice because people were turning around and staring in my direction—"I don't have that surveillance tape. I never had it. And I don't know where it is." Bardahl had touched a nerve, and his gloating expression showed it. The whole disbarment nightmare seemed on the verge of engulfing me again. The anger, the fear, the sickening disillusionment that I thought I'd overcome—his leering grin brought it all back like a sudden, nasty hangover. And that coarse, insinuating voice conjured up hours of questioning in smelly, windowless rooms, with my so-called defense lawyer whining and manipulating the process for what I'd assumed was my benefit when in reality he'd put on this masterful performance for the protection of the firm and its clients—more specifically, a real estate developer named Tom Riordan, who'd actually stolen the files from the state inspection archives because they showed that one of his properties was an environmental disaster. Apparently there's a surveillance camera at the archives that must have photographed Riordan when he stole the files, but the tape disappeared right after the files. After Bardahl found the stolen files in my office, the cops had asked me over and over again, "Where's the surveillance tape?" And every time I'd told them I didn't know.

"I'm trying to help you, Cloud," Bardahl said, keeping his voice low. "I'm giving you a chance to clear your name."

"If I had that tape, don't you think I would have come up with it long ago?"

"Unless it shows you stealing the files."

"It doesn't. I know that because I didn't steal the files."

He knew that but he couldn't admit it, because he was the one who arrested me. And I couldn't admit that although I didn't steal the files from the state archive, I did sort of steal them from Riordan. "Or unless," he added, "what I've always thought, you were playing along with the firm, part of your deal with Babylon to take the fall so they could protect Riordan or Squires or whoever they were trying to protect—"

"I didn't have any deal with Babylon."

"—and now that Babylon's dead you don't really have a deal anymore, do you? So you can tell me where the tape is."

I leaned as close to Bardahl's face as I could without risking the loss of my lunch and shouted through my teeth, "I'm telling you, there wasn't any deal! Babylon screwed me, that's all. And if I had any idea where that tape was, I'd go get it myself!"

2.

Bardahl and I might have come to blows if Niko, the owner, who'd been anxiously watching from the kitchen door, hadn't swooped in to intervene. Niko and I don't see eye to eye on very much, since I'm six foot three and he's all of four ten and a half, not to mention the fact that he thinks I'm gay and might overpower him in the men's room late at night, but as long as he's standing up and I'm sitting at the piano we get along just fine.

"Everything all right here?"

"No problem, Niko. Greasy Sludge here was just leaving."

Bardahl grunted but showed no inclination to budge.

"Keep your mind on the piano playing," advised Niko nervously. He gestured toward my tiny audience. "You got customers."

It was true. Sometime after Madison's departure, three of the regulars had draped themselves around the piano bar like a dysfunctional Greek chorus, ignoring each other as they paid close attention to my encounter with Bardahl. One of them I recognized as Brian O'Dolan, a former Jesuit priest and philosophy professor who now sells newspapers in Thirtieth Street Station and passes his evenings arguing with the other patrons of the Pickwick Club about the decline of western civilization. The others were Jim Hively, an alcoholic lawyer who used to work at Rittenhouse, and a woman named Rhoda whom I know only as a slightly-built divorcee from Minnesota who drinks rye manhattans and requests Cole Porter tunes.

"In my opinion," said Brian O'Dolan, who had spread the tabloid *Philadelphia Daily News* across the lid of the piano and seemed to be reading it as he spoke, "this crime is symptomatic of our times. Neil Babylon was murdered by someone he knew and trusted, probably another lawyer at the same firm."

"Yeah, that's what they say," growled Jim Hively in his basso profundo voice. "I saw that in the paper. But it doesn't make any sense."

"How could it be otherwise?" retorted O'Dolan, emphatically thrusting a finger into the smoky air that surrounded him. "According to the paper, he attended a cocktail party in the firm's reception area, left abruptly after an argument with a female attorney, and apparently died in his office a short time later."

Brian O'Dolan quotes from the *Philadelphia Daily News* the way he once quoted from the gospels. He lives by himself in a seedy apartment hotel on North Broad Street, but in spite of his modest means he dines out seven nights a week, invariably appearing at the piano bar after dinner for a glass of burgundy wine. His story is actually quite tragic, as he's told me many times. In the 1980s he traveled the world as a noted lecturer on Heidegger, passing many idle weeks in Bavarian monasteries, Tuscan villas and Caribbean haciendas where his vow of poverty was never allowed to detract from the enjoyment of fine wines and gourmet cooking. But at the age of forty-five, within a span of two weeks he lost both his faith and his virginity, the latter to a beautiful graduate student in philosophy named Miranda Quill. He withdrew from the order to marry her, but a week before the wedding she eloped with a Sandinista commandante, leaving the baffled former priest behind with nothing to show for his years of self-denial but a taste for haute cuisine and certain rare vintages of Chardonnay.

He downed his wine, warming to the combat, and wagged his glass toward the waitress to summon another dram. "It's completely obvious, I would even say self-evident, that Babylon was done in by one of his legal colleagues."

Jim Hively opened his mouth to speak, and I braced myself for a sonorous but incoherent reply. He worked at Rittenhouse in the old days, long before I got there and presumably before his life and his career started going down the drain. Now he handles minor traffic cases and drinks himself silly every night. You would never know it, looking at his puny, rumpled exterior, but Hively has an incredible bass voice that starts about three octaves below middle C and resonates with the power of a pipe organ. Every once in a while when I'm half way through some sentimental ballad, I hear a deep growling sound like a freight train tunneling under my piano, and I realize it's Hively humming along with the tune. When he gets really drunk he may start to sing and then I have to segue to a faster song before he clears the room. Hively worked his way through law school doing radio commercials for the now-defunct John Wannamaker Department Store and if you hang around long enough he'll deliver an entire lingerie commercial for you as he sits at the bar, complete with sound effects, static and dramatic theme music played on the famous Wannamaker organ.

But this time it took Hively too long to activate his enormous vocal apparatus. Before he could emit more than an introductory gurgle he was cut off by Rhoda, the gal from Minnesota, who sang out her verdict with a devastating certainty that left both men speechless.

"It was the wife, you fools!" she announced. "Who else could have had as strong a motivation to kill him? It was the wife!"

Interesting, I thought. The woman's perspective. I was anxious to hear what Elena would say.

The opening chords of the next song took shape unconsciously on my fingertips. I think it was "Don't Blame Me."

Bardahl had listened to this conversation with a seeming lack of interest or attention, fending off attempts by the cocktail waitress to replace his Coors Light with another. "You know, Cloud," he grunted after Rhoda's outburst had stunned the men around the piano bar into a catatonic state, "things could get a lot better for you or they could get a lot worse." He hoisted himself off the barstool and started adjusting the belts and buckles on his trench coat as if he was preparing to parachute out of the bar. "I mean, what if it turns out you really did kill Babylon?"

"It won't, because I didn't."

"You have an alibi? You were sitting here playing the piano last night, is that it? Or were you home playing with yourself?"

"Monday's my night off."

"Let me guess. You spent a quiet evening alone, watching TV."

"Something like that."

"Then it's only a question of evidence."

"Isn't it always a question of evidence?"

He grabbed his beer bottle before the cocktail waitress could snatch it and dribbled the last few drops into his mouth. "A stray fingerprint here, a trace of DNA there. You'd be amazed at what the crime lab can come up with."

I wanted to shove the beer bottle down his throat. "Bardahl, if there's a lower form of life than you, I must have missed that chapter in my biology book."

"So I'm a cop. What else is new?"

"I'd say you're a plainclothes dick but I'm trying to be polite."

He lowered his voice to a menacing whisper. "I'm trying to help you, Cloud," he said. "I told you the Department isn't all one big happy family. There are those who love Lou Squires and those who hate him. But you know what? There's one thing the two factions have in common."

"What's that?"

"You. Both of them would flush you down the toilet if it suits their purpose."

"I get it," I said. "The age old struggle between evil and evil."

He started toward the door. "You got it."

"There's only one thing I don't get," I called after him. "Which side are you on?"

Philadelphia in January is a better time than most for a murder. It had been raining for days, with the temperatures hovering just above the freezing point and the tops of the tallest buildings shrouded in fog. The central core of the city—what the natives call "Center City"—is totally flat and about six inches above sea level, and in the winter months when there's no horizon you sometimes feel that the narrow streets are below ground, like wagon ruts worn into the uniformly low rooftops that stretch for miles in every direction. They said a cold snap was on its way, with an Arctic storm to follow in another week. At that moment I would have welcomed any change. I spend half my life in this dingy tavern, inhaling other people's disappointments, and when I leave I want the world outside to be bright, optimistic, sharp in its distinctions. Even an Arctic chill would be an improvement over this lingering malaise of fog and rain. And today something important had happened. But when I left the Pickwick that night—my work day ends at midnight—there was no sign that the heavens had taken notice of Neil Babylon's departure. It will clear eventually, I told myself, and Neil Babylon won't be here to enjoy it. That should have given me some satisfaction, but it didn't. It only made the drizzle seem more pointless and depressing.

3.

"What I don't understand is exactly what Bardahl wants you to do."

Elena peered at me over a steaming cup of coffee with her dark, penetrating eyes as if I were an overconfident witness at a murder trial. We sat at her mother's kitchen table, where we have lunch together almost every day while the court takes its noon recess.

"You remember that surveillance tape from the DEP archives that the cops were always asking me about?" I said. "He wants it."

"Why?"

"I wish I knew."

I don't know when I had ever been happier to see Elena. After work the night before, I'd stopped at Little Pete's 24-hour diner across from the Warwick for coffee and an order of bacon and eggs. Home was about six blocks away in the Coolidge House at 16th and Spruce (they call it a "House" because it's twenty stories of apartments built over a parking garage), but I knew that when I got to my apartment I'd have only the usual four walls to talk to, and in my current state of mind I wasn't sure I could trust them. I walked around Rittenhouse Square a couple of times, which is probably a crazy thing to do at one o'clock in the morning, but my mind was racing like an Italian greyhound and I couldn't stop. I caught a few hours sleep, punctuated by nightmare visions of Neil Babylon's corpulent hulk sprawled on the floor of his office and Bardahl's gargantuan biomass splayed over the end of my piano bar. I don't know which image was more horrifying. In my dreams the two seemed to meld together into one overpowering image of corruption. When I finally woke up it was after eleven and I violated Rule No. 1 of our mock-illicit relationship and called Elena in her chambers.

Elena Fiore is a judge of the Court of Common Pleas of Philadelphia and one of the rising stars of the local judiciary. She's also my best friend and I've been in love with her for years, since long before she was a judge. We have never slept together but we treat our friendship as if it were an extramarital affair, keeping it secret from our friends, surreptitiously arranging to spend our afternoons together, pretending not to know each other when we pass on the street. I admit it's an unusual relationship. Elena is brainy and beautiful and I would gladly turn our fantasy into reality if there were any way to do it without destroying her life. But the fact is that she can't afford to be associated with me in any way. Not only is she a judge, she's married (unhappily but faithfully) to one of the most prominent lawyers in Philadelphia (a complete jackass, by the way) and they have two beautiful daughters who are the joy of her existence. I'm no hero, but in my lucid moments I know I can't ask her to abandon everything she has made of her life and take her chances with me.

That afternoon, as we sipped coffee in her mother's dimly-lit apartment, I could see that Elena was troubled by Neil Babylon's sudden death and what I'd told her about Bardahl's visit to the Pickwick Club. She seemed edgy and out of sorts, almost inquisitorial. I didn't know it, but we were about to have our first fight.

"Did Bardahl really say there isn't going to be an autopsy?" she asked.

"That's right," I said. "It seems that Senator Squires has a friend at the Medical Examiner's office."

"Yes. That would be the Medical Examiner himself. The Senator helped him get his job."

"The Senator helps everybody get their job." It was Elena's mother, Theresa, who stood by the table with the coffee pot in one hand and one of her ubiquitous Marlboros in the other. Theresa is a wiry refugee from South Philadelphia who has bathed her vocal cords in cigarette smoke for so many years that everything she says comes out in a conspiratorial stage whisper. She bent toward me and jerked a thumb toward her daughter. "He helped her get her job! And you know what? He—"

"Mom," Elena interrupted—though she couldn't disagree, since we all knew that she owes her judgeship to her husband's political connections with the Senator. "We're trying to talk."

"The Senator's a great man," I told Theresa.

"You better believe it!"

"My hunch," Elena said, ignoring her mother, "is that they've already done the autopsy."

"And now they're covering up the results?"

"Not necessarily. Just keeping them quiet until they have a suspect."

"That shouldn't take long," I said. "There are dozens of people who had perfectly good reasons for killing Babylon."

"Yes," she nodded. "And who are they? Partners at the firm, wealthy clients, politicians."

"Exactly."

"And then of course there's you."

I didn't like the sound of that. "You don't really think they'd try to pin this on me, do you?"

"They did something like that once before," Elena replied. "And so far"—she raised her eyebrows with the slightest hint of reproach—"they seem to have gotten away with it."

We both lapsed into a glum silence.

"More coffee?" Theresa stood by the stove checking on the three or four kettles of pasta that seemed to simmer there at all hours of the day and night. She lives by herself and she only weighs about a hundred pounds, so I've never understood what she does with all that pasta. Does she feed the homeless (doubtful), or use it in some ancient Sicilian ceremony intended to put a curse on her enemies (more likely)? Or could it all be consumed by those frail aunts and uncles and occasional white-haired cousins from South Philadelphia who appear unexpectedly from time to time and sit in a row on the sofa watching TV and arguing with each other far into the night? Whatever the purpose of that pasta, she simmers her sauces tirelessly, smoking like Mt. Etna all the while. And as a result the kitchen has a certain unique atmosphere, like a combination steambath and pizzeria that never empties its ashtrays.

"Sure, I'll have a little more coffee," I told her.

"Don't look so happy," she said as she poured it. "Wait till you find out what prison food is like."

"Mom, for God's sake! Pete isn't going to prison!"

Theresa lowered her eyes slyly and leaned toward me in her conspiratorial way. "You killed Babylon, didn't you?"

"No. Of course not!"

She looked disappointed. "Why not? After what that bastard did to you?"

"It's just not my style."

"Then somebody else killed him," she reasoned.

"Maybe it was his wife," I suggested, turning to Elena. I wondered if she shared Rhoda's views on marriage. "Neil was quite the womanizer, you know."

"I've met his wife," Elena said. "Yvette."

"By the way, he never womanized you, did he?"

"He tried to, but I was already a woman at the time."

"I'd like to see him try to womanize me," growled Theresa. She turned to her daughter. "You weren't there, were you?"

"There? Where?"

"At the cocktail party." Theresa picked up a copy of the *Inquirer* from the counter and started reading. "It says here Babylon got into an argument with a woman at the party and she poisoned him."

"Let me see that." Theresa handed me the paper and I scanned down to the part about the cocktail party. "It doesn't say she poisoned him," I objected.

"You've got to read between the lines."

"In fact," said Elena, reading over my shoulder, "it says she didn't poison him."

"You believe that?"

I read the relevant passage out loud: "`Mr. Babylon attended a cocktail party honoring a retiring partner Monday night and died soon afterwards in his private office suite. Police are investigating reports that an argument took place between Mr. Babylon and a woman who attended the party. Arthur Valunos, the firm's new Managing Partner, discounted rumors about the reported argument and any suggestion that Mr. Babylon might have been poisoned.'"

"Naturally they would say that," Theresa argued.

"Mom," Elena said, "please let me talk to Peter about this. It's pretty important and I have to get back to court."

I took a sip of my coffee and waited as Theresa retreated into the living room to watch "Days of Our Lives." Her apartment is identical to mine but it's furnished like a mortuary, with purple wallpaper, dark florid rugs and enough overstuffed chairs and sofas to conceal a corpse, which was probably their original purpose. The shades are always drawn, the lights always dimmed, and of course Theresa never talks above a whisper. The result is an air of menace reinforced by the portentous gurgling of soap operas twenty-four hours a day.

"Well," I said, "if they do try to pin this on me, I hope your mother isn't on the jury."

"If they try to pin it on you, it won't matter who's on the jury The evidence will be overwhelming, you can be sure of that."

I was starting to feel a little sick.

"Your best strategy," Elena continued, "is to start fighting back now and put them at risk."

"What do you mean?"

"You don't want to make it too easy for them. They'll be looking for an expendable suspect, somebody easy they can blame in case the real killer is somebody they have to protect." She looked at me knowingly—and again, I thought, a little reproachfully. "Just like the last time around."

Just like the last time around. The last time around was the disbarment nightmare, and Elena was right. There was a disturbing resemblance between then and now, and Elena knew all about it. She'd been with me when I retrieved the boxes from Riordan's storage shed and that made her the only person whose testimony could have cleared me of the charges that brought me down. In those carefree days, when Elena and I were both practicing law, we used to drive around together in my black Expedition (long since repossessed), thinking we were invulnerable behind its tinted glass. I was still married to Denise, of course, but in my innocence I didn't think that made any difference. One evening, following one of Elena's famous hunches, we drove up to the sprawling wasteland of Northeast Philadelphia and sneaked into Riordan's storage shed like Lois and Clark and rummaged around until we found what we were looking for. Two boxes of asbestos inspection records that were unaccountably missing from the Department of Environmental Protection archives up on Route 1. They were the records of asbestos inspections conducted by the DEP about ten years earlier at the old Summermyers Foundry down by the riverfront, which Riordan was trying to get out of bankruptcy so he could develop it into a casino. Why did I take them? It was for Riordan's protection, really—to keep

him out of jail—and my own. I would have been in big trouble
if it came out that I'd been representing a client who stole and
concealed government records to advance his case. (Hell, I
could even have been disbarred!) The big mistake was letting
Elena get involved. Like Lois and Clark, we must have thought
at least one of us was invulnerable because we dragged those
files out of Riordan's shed and into the back of my Expedition
and hauled them up to my office at the firm. And when
Bardahl appeared with his search warrant and I was thrown
into the clutches of the legal system, Elena was the one person
who could have saved me. She could have testified that I took
the boxes from Riordan, not from the DEP, and she
desperately wanted to come forward even if it meant blowing
up her whole life. But I was absolute in my insistence that she
stay out of it and I kept it that way. There was no other choice.
The fix was on and she would only have been dragged down
with me to no purpose.

"Do you know where the surveillance tape is?" she asked
me.

"I told Bardahl I didn't, but that was a lie. In fact I have a
pretty good idea what happened to it."

"You do? Where is it?"

"When Riordan and Babylon realized that the tape existed,
they would have needed some serious political clout to get it
away from the state."

"Lou Squires?"

"He's the only one at Rittenhouse who could get it."

Elena smiled. "Lou has always been strong on constituent
services."

"And then Lou would have given it to Babylon, and Babylon would have called up Riordan and said, 'Tom, that matter we discussed has been taken care of.' And that would have been that."

She looked puzzled. "So then who ended up with the tape?"

"Babylon," I answered. "He was the world's leading pack rat. He kept every draft of every document he ever worked on, as if he were Richard Nixon preserving his papers for a tax deduction."

"Nixon kept his tapes," said Theresa, who had sidled back into the kitchen looking for a cigarette. "The idiot! He should have torched them."

"Babylon had the same mentality," I nodded. "He always liked to have something he could hold over his clients. It was a kind of blackmail. He not only knew about the skeletons in their closets—he actually kept some of them in his files. It kept the clients coming back year after year—and they always paid their bills."

We carried our dirty dishes over to the sink and rinsed them off without saying anything. Then Elena washed her hands and started getting ready to return to court. "So if Babylon kept the tape," she asked softly, "where would it be now?"

"If I were going to look for it," I said, "I'd start right in his office."

"Then the tape should be fairly easy to find."

"It would be, if I were going to look for it."

"You mean you're not going to look for it?"

"No, I'm not. That's another thing I lied to Bardahl about."

"Why not?"

"Because I don't want to get any more involved in this mess than I have to."

Elena stalked off in search of her raincoat, which Theresa had draped over the closet door. Then she sallied back into the kitchen looking for her umbrella. I could tell she was getting annoyed. "Pete," she said when she found the umbrella, which Theresa had hidden under the sink, "if that tape still exists it shows who really stole the files. This is your chance to clear your name."

Where had I heard that before? "That's exactly what Bardahl said."

"Maybe it's not such a bad idea. Maybe you could get your life back."

I shrugged. "Maybe I don't want it back."

She wrestled her way into the raincoat and wrapped the belt around her waist as if she were trying to strangle someone. "You'd rather sit in your depressed little corner, playing show tunes for drunks? Is that what you want to do with your life?"

At that moment anything seemed preferable to sitting locked in the sights of her unblinking black eyes. "Objection," I grimaced. "Badgering the witness."

"Sustained," she said, her voice softening. She allowed herself a little smile. "The question is withdrawn."

I stood up and took a step toward her. "There's a difference, you know, between depression and acceptance."

"Pete—"

"I've learned to accept my situation in life." I turned to Theresa, who seemed to be enjoying this as much as one of her soap operas. "It's a kind of Zen. Some people meditate for years to reach my mental state."

"My nephew Eddie used to meditate," Theresa agreed. "You remember Eddie?"

"Yes," Elena conceded, annoyed at the diversion.

"He was a follower of one of those Indian gurus. He used to say, 'If you meditate long enough, you enter the state of Nevada.'"

"'Nirvana,' I think he meant."

"Wherever it was, when he finally got there he lost his shirt at the craps table."

Elena opened the door and turned back to face me. "Pete, you were a great lawyer. I know that because I worked with you. You fought hard for your clients and what you believed in. You were on the right side in most of your cases, and you loved every minute of it. And now you pretend to believe that all lawyers are sleaze buckets so you don't have to think about what you've lost."

"I'm not pretending."

She shook her head. "Please, don't tell me you've just accepted your fate."

"Elena—"

"And don't tell me you're not bitter."

She turned and walked out without saying goodbye, letting the door slam behind her.

"I'm not bitter," I said. But Elena was on her way down the hall, and the only one who heard my protest, chuckling cynically as she gagged on her latest Marlboro, was Theresa.

☐

4.

Theresa may not be the ideal chaperone for Elena and me. True, she lives in the apartment next to mine—or perhaps I should say I live in the apartment next to hers, since I only live there because Elena came to my rescue after my wife threw me out. But she has little use for Elena's husband—his name is Geoff Goodwin—whom she always refers to as "Mighty Mouse." He's a Main Line WASP who shoots in the low 70s and keeps his body temperature in the same range. At least once a day Theresa whispers something in her hoarse, conspiratorial way suggesting that I ought to have sex with Elena and do away with her husband. "Don't worry about Mighty Mouse," she says. "Maybe he'll just disappear, the way my ex-husband did—under an exit ramp on the Schuylkill Expressway!"

On that particular afternoon my thoughts were far away from the cuckoldry and mayhem that Theresa imagined for her son-in-law. After Elena's angry exit, I collapsed on one of the overstuffed chairs in the mortuary that Theresa calls her living room and tried to understand the emotional turn my conversation with Elena had taken. Beneath all the questioning and arguing, there was something important that both of us knew but neither was saying. We both knew that with Neil Babylon's death the landscape had changed forever. My deal with Babylon—which until now had seemed the only hope of undoing my disbarment—had died when the big man breathed his last

I should explain that I had lied to Bardahl when I told him I didn't have a deal with the firm. Neil Babylon, for all his faults, was not a complete wretch. We had spent ten years in what had been a friendly working relationship. And so when the crisis came I had no reason to expect that he would throw me to the dogs. I went directly to Neil and told him that I'd found the inspection files in Riordan's storage shed and intended to turn them over to the court. Alone in his private office, Babylon was surprisingly reasonable, understanding and—I would say fatherly, only my own father would probably have beaten me to a pulp in the same situation. "Why are you doing this?" he asked me. "Your career is just taking off."

I would not participate in a cover-up, I explained: with the files in my possession, I had no choice but to turn them over to the court if Riordan refused to do so. He asked me to think hard about my decision and talk to him again the next day. Of course I knew the files would disappear if I left them in my office overnight, but before I could remove them Bardahl arrived with his search warrant. I was whisked away to the precinct station, and before I knew what was happening, one of the firm's lawyers showed up to defend me—the unctuous W. Clement Brightbill, a partner specializing in white-collar crime who instructed me not to answer any questions on grounds of possible self-incrimination. In this way the firm prevented me from telling the truth to the police—I never told them where I'd found the files, and thus I was able to avoid saying anything that could have dragged Elena into the case. And before long I was being offered a deal I couldn't refuse: the investigation and all criminal charges would be dropped if I consented to voluntary disbarment.

Naturally I was incensed at this proposal, but again Babylon took me aside for some more fatherly advice. "Peter," he said, "this is a bad situation, but it could be a lot worse. I think you know what I mean." He pursed his lips and raised his eyebrows in a pantomime of lechery, and I realized that he'd found out about Elena.

"It's not like that," I protested.

"Still," he agreed after a pause, "it would be a shame for two careers to be ruined, wouldn't it?"

I was speechless with rage.

"I think you've mentioned that you were interested in taking a sabbatical," he went on. "Well, think of this as a sabbatical."

"A sabbatical?"

"I give you my word that after a couple of years, when Judge Karney and the D.A.'s office have calmed down, we'll be able to get you your ticket back. Is it a deal?"

Babylon's proposal was a masterstroke. It not only bought my silence and cooperation: it was the only thing that prevented Elena from throwing her life away and coming forward to defend me. I never told her about Babylon's threat to implicate her. Knowing Elena, she might have taken that as a challenge and sabotaged the deal to protect her honor. And so for two years my life had been wrapped in a painful irony: I would have spurned Babylon's offer and fought the charges but for his threat to implicate Elena, which she knew nothing about; and she agreed not to come forward and implicate herself only because I accepted that offer, for which, evidently, she viewed me as a coward.

Now all that was history. Babylon's promise, if it ever meant anything, had died with him. That was why Elena had been so eager to learn if I was going to search for the surveillance tape—it was now the only evidence, other than her own testimony, that could clear my name.

A few minutes after Elena walked out someone tapped on the door, and Theresa, who had spent the intervening time reconstructing the elaborate system of deadbolts, chains and braces that guarded her entrance, peered through the peephole and then spent an equal amount of time dismantling the fortifications. When the door opened again Elena blew back inside, and   without saying anything to her mother she whisked into the living room where I was sitting.

"I got out to the parking garage," she said, "and realized how ridiculous this is. We both know what I'm thinking about."

"I guess we do."

"Before you made your deal with Babylon, I had the power to extricate you from that whole situation."

"Yes, and I wouldn't let you.

"It wasn't a question of what you would or wouldn't let me do. You know me better than that. I would have gone to the police and told my story if you hadn't made your deal and convinced me that Babylon would set everything straight after a couple of years."

"That was the deal."

"And now he's dead, and the deal's off. So your two-year sabbatical has just become a permanent punishment for something you didn't do."

"And as I was trying to tell you, it doesn't really matter anymore."

"Well, it matters to me."

"Elena, please—"

"I know what I have to do. What I should have done two years ago."

"Please don't."

"Right now I have to get back to court. Bye now. I'll talk to you later."

The door slammed again, a little more gently this time, and I buried my face in my hands. "I don't believe this," I muttered. "She's going to wreck her life."

Theresa stood before me shrouded in smoke like a genie who had just emerged from a bottle. "Not if you find that tape first and clear your name."

"You heard her. She's going to do whatever she thinks is right. It doesn't matter what I do."

"That's crap. She wouldn't admit it, because she wants you to decide for yourself. But she's telling you to find that tape."

I picked my way through the funereal gloom back into the kitchen, where I poured myself another cup of coffee and sat down. For a few minutes I concentrated on stirring my coffee—I always drink it black with a teaspoon of sugar—and peering out the window, where the fog and drizzle of the night before had given way to a steady downpour. The sky was hardly lighter than it had been when I left work at midnight. In this muffled world the trucks and taxicabs contended slowly, their headlights twinkling in the rain, and on the sidewalk umbrellas bobbed like corks being carried away on a stream.

"Listen to me," Theresa said. "Find the tape, and before this is over you'll have Elena wrapped around your little finger."

"What do you mean?"

"I know my daughter. I heard what she was saying before. She's trying to tell you something. Do I have to draw you a picture?"

I looked up (or I should say sideways, since Theresa and I are at the same eye level when she stands beside me at the table) and tried to imagine the picture she was offering to draw. Her black eyes danced with the same glistening energy as the umbrellas on the sidewalk.

"Elena has high standards," she said. "Did she ever tell you why she wanted to be a lawyer? It was because of her Uncle Carlo, my brother. He was a man. He stood up to the union bosses and ended up dead."

"My standards are a little lower than that."

"He believed in justice and people respected him. Don't you get it? That's why all her life Elena wanted to be a judge. Because justice is what she respects. That's what she wants to see in a man. God knows she doesn't see it in Mighty Mouse, but she wants to see it in you."

"Mighty Mouse? What are you talking about?"

"I guess you do want me to draw you a picture. OK, here's the picture: You'll never get Elena into the sack if you don't stand up for your rights."

I stood up, but not for my rights. It was time to go. I headed for the door.

"And besides"—she followed me gesturing like a loan shark with her smoldering cigarette—"you find that surveillance tape, and you can show the world that Riordan stole the files and the firm helped him cover it up."

"Goodbye," I said, opening the door. "Thanks for the lunch."

"Maybe you'll even discover why they had to whack Babylon." A sly Sicilian shimmer had crept into her eyes. "What could be a sweeter revenge?"

5.

Back in my apartment, alone with the usual four walls.

For lack of a better idea, I swiveled in my lounge chair and studied them. They're decorated inexpensively with large photographic posters of some of my favorite musicians. On the wall by the bedroom, Miles Davis and Cannonball Adderley, New York, 1958. On the west wall, between my apartment and Theresa's, Charles Mingus at the Newport Jazz Festival, 1959. On the wall leading to the kitchen, Jimmy Rowles and Ray Brown, Los Angeles, 1955. And over the couch, Frank Sinatra in a rakish fedora and skinny green suit, circa 1960. To look at my apartment, you'd think the Eisenhower era was the high water mark of western civilization. My only regret, I mused, was that I was born too late.

I leaned too far back and the lounge chair almost dropped me on my head. No, I reminded myself, that was not my only regret. One of my other regrets was that I had experienced Elena's anger for the first time and allowed myself to be manipulated by her and her mother into embarking on a course of action which, if successful, would put an end to my cozy but unproductive lifestyle, and if unsuccessful—I didn't even want to think about that possibility. And all in the name of justice, which was something Elena, as a judge, naturally thought about all the time, but which I had lost my affection for after being ground to a pulp in its pitiless machinery. Theresa's notion of justice was strictly South Philly: breaking some guy's kneecaps in the parking lot of the Melrose Diner because he insulted your sister. Elena's was the Ivy League version: a class action on behalf of the children of guys who'd been crippled in the parking lot of the Melrose Diner. And what was mine? It was trial by ordeal, rooted where I grew up in southwestern Pennsylvania. In our Greene County coal mining town near the West Virginia line we fought to prove our worth, so we had to fight fair. We played football and baseball and basketball, of course, but there were never enough kids to play those sports the way we needed to play them—as the ultimate test of our place in the universe. For that we turned to scholastic wrestling, which in that part of the world plays the same role in the average person's life as the scholastic philosophy of the middle ages played in the life of a monk. Wrestling was the activity that united all of the town's contending factions—rich and poor, Catholic and Protestant, black and white—and provided the answer to all difficult questions. What is justice? That one is simple. Justice, to a wrestler, means inflicting every conceivable type of torture on another person in your own weight class under the watchful eye of a referee—and winning.

Justice? Justice is what I would have liked to do to my older brothers if I could have scaled them down to my own size. There were two of them, Steve and Mike, and from them I learned when to fight (only when you can win) and more importantly, when to give up (the rest of the time). My mother taught me a few things too, by never interfering when my brothers beat me up. She knew they wouldn't really hurt me and she wanted me to understand that too. That was how people said 'I love you' in our family—by not breaking your neck when they had you in a stranglehold. Except for my Dad—who worked as a stonemason and expressed his love every night, in response to our behavior at the dinner table, by issuing the most bloodcurdling threats any boy had ever imagined, and then, before he could carry them out, slipping away to the American Legion hall to get patriotically drunk

And so I learned love and justice at the same time, and I wrestled almost before I could walk. By the time I was in high school I would win the state championship and still have enough time and energy left over to learn how to play the piano and graduate at the top of my (admittedly small) class. I always wanted to go to law school. I imagined that the legal system was the level playing field we'd heard vague rumors about in our crooked, craggy town. Litigation was like wrestling, I imagined—intense competition under consistent rules and a neutral referee. And if your case was better, you'd win, and that would be justice.

It was Neil Babylon who set me straight, the very first week I started practicing law. He and Art Valunos took a few of us new associates out to lunch at the Union League. "I enjoy sports as much as anyone," Babylon said as we sipped our snapper soup. "And of course practicing law can be a little like a sport or a game. Some lawyers look at it that way, don't they, Art?"

Valunos leered at the new associates as if he knew we were about to lose our virginity.

"It's competitive, and there are rules that everyone's supposed to follow," Babylon went on. "And of course at the Rittenhouse firm, we play by the rules. But you know what? It's really not that much like a sport if you know what you're doing. First of all, you don't have to pick on someone your own size. The other guy doesn't get handicapping points because he's a moron, or because his client can't afford as much discovery as yours can."

Babylon and Valunos shared a laugh. "And second of all," said Babylon, still laughing, "the rules—if you're in court in Philadelphia—are whatever we say they are."

"The judges make the rules," one of the associates objected.

"And we make the judges," Babylon cut him off, a little less jovially. "Don't ever forget that."

I glanced up at Frank Sinatra in his rakish green fedora—you can't appreciate how much innocence has been lost until you realize that as late as 1960 a man like Frank Sinatra felt no embarrassment parading around in a fedora—and remembered what I was supposed to be doing. Figuring out a way to protect Elena from her own high principles—that was my goal, wasn't it? Absolutely, until Theresa, like some imp of the unconscious, had suggested darker motives that I couldn't entirely disavow. Was I bent on revenge against the firm? That seemed an unworthy motive in a man who preached the Zen of acceptance—but in the cold light of day I had to admit that thoughts of revenge were never far from my mind. And what about the outrageous suggestion that my true goal was to lure Elena into my bed? I turned from Sinatra to glimpse Charles Mingus huddled lovingly over his string bass and realized that this too could be a possibility.

It was almost four o'clock and the sky seemed to be clearing. As Elena had said, I knew what I had to do. I called the answering machine in her chambers and left a message that she would understand: "No need to go ape. I've decided to look for the missing link." And then I went back to staring at those four walls until I came up with a plan.

At 4:30 I put on a pair of dress jeans, a yellow shirt and a plaid necktie, and selected an ill-matching tweed jacket. Though my business would take me to the Rittenhouse law firm, I took care not to look much like a lawyer. There was one bit of housekeeping I needed to attend to before I left. I picked up the phone and dialed the Pickwick Club, hoping that Niko wouldn't be there to answer.

"Pickwick." It was Niko.

"Niko. This is Peter. I'm going to be late tonight."

"No, no, no, no!" he sputtered. "You can't be late. You be here at seven o'clock sharp or you're fired!"

"Sorry, Niko. Family emergency. You'll have to play some records. No one will notice."

You could play the piano at the Pickwick Club all your life without anyone noticing. But how was I going to get into Rittenhouse without being seen? The firm occupies six upper stories in the Third Millennium Center, one of the city's largest office towers. And at the front desk on the forty-third floor sits a receptionist named Ingrid who is under strict orders to call the security guards and have me shot on sight if I ever set foot in the building again. Fortunately I knew that would not be necessary. I had a plan.

The lawyers in any firm circulate around the outer windows like moths trying to escape into the light, leaving an enormous core area in the middle of each floor that is taken up by file rooms, freight elevators, power transformers, telephone relays and other mysteries that are largely beyond the ken of the attorneys. At the very center of all this lies the mail room, which in many ways is the firm's nerve center. Here the mail, faxes and Federal Express packages are sorted, bundled and routed; from here the messengers depart for the courthouse at thirty minute intervals; and here—or more often in an adjoining windowless room—can also be found the computer servers that connect the attorneys to each other and the world of the internet. For anyone trying to penetrate the firm's institutional shell, the mail room is its most vulnerable point. And the freight elevator is the secret passage that can take you there without Ingrid being any the wiser.

I walked the six blocks to the Third Millennium Center, hugging my jacket around my neck against the biting wind that had blown in behind the wet weather of the past few days. The sidewalks were filling up with the first wave of rush hour desperation. I had to thread my way through the onrush of office workers being whisked toward me by the wind, keeping my eyes cast down in case I met someone I knew. In the side street behind the Third Millennium Center I shuffled down a curving ramp into the dim netherworld of the parking garage, past the first entrance and on down to the lower level. I dodged past the turnstile and continued down the truck ramp to the lowest circle, the one reserved for delivery trucks and freight haulers. I knew I would be safe here, even from the surveillance cameras that prowled the parking garage. I climbed onto the loading dock and rang the 43rd floor for the freight elevator. An incomprehensible voice squawked through a tinny speaker, demanding to know who I was and what I wanted. I squawked back even more incomprehensibly in a pseudo-Chinese accent, and within a minute the doors to the freight elevator opened and I was elevated through the center of the building to the Rittenhouse mail room in complete comfort and privacy. Luckily when the door opened I was greeted by one of the few friends I had left at the firm..

"Hey, man! How ya' doing?"

It was Lockjaw, the mail room boss, a huge and kindly Bahamian who owes his nickname to an enormous jutting jaw that makes him look as if he could literally bite the head off anyone who makes too many complaints. Not that anyone would ever complain about the mail room guys. Most of them are former post office employees, and everybody knows what that means. You mention that a delivery was a little late, maybe express a little dissatisfaction with your appeal being filed in the wrong courthouse—and the next thing you know, half a dozen mail room guys are going postal in the reception area, dropping clients like flies with AK47s. That's the worry, anyway. I never credited it myself. But that afternoon as I glanced around the mail room it seemed like too many people were trying to work in too small a space, and they all looked a little crazed.

Except Lockjaw, who was his usual mellow self. I counted him as one of my dearest friends, because he never changed the way he treated me even when I was being booted out the door.

"I'm doing O.K., Lockjaw," I told him. "How are you?"

"Fine, just fine. Now what are you doing here? Not here to get me in trouble, are you?"

"How could I get you into any more trouble than you're already in, what with senior partners getting murdered in the office and all?"

His sunny smile disappeared and his voice dropped to a whisper. The joking and jostling in the office seemed to halt suddenly as all ears tuned in to our conversation. "What you talking about—murdered? Mr. Babylon wasn't murdered. I'm told he died of a heart attack. Isn't that so, Ernie?"

I glanced around to find a young man with a white face and a shock of orange hair, an assortment of earrings in each ear and a wide-eyed stare that made me remember why I avoid the post office on hot summer days.

"That's what they told us," he agreed.

"This is Ernie," said Lockjaw.

"Nice to meet you, Ernie" I said, though I had my doubts. As it happened Ernie and Lockjaw and I started talking about the Sixers and then about the Flyers and after a while Lockjaw had to step away to take a phone call and I realized that Ernie was the only friend I had in that place. He had enough wires and hooks threaded through his ears and eyebrows to stock a small bait and tackle shop, but I found that if I looked him straight in the eyes I could overcome the urge to run the other way at least half the time. Although he wasn't the kind of friend you would want to be standing next to during an electrical storm, before long I was able to ask him for a very big favor. I couldn't admit that I was there to search Babylon's office for an incriminating surveillance tape, but I needed to find a way to get out of the mail room without arousing suspicion. So I told him I needed to get inside to talk to some of the attorneys. "About the murder," I confided.

"No problem," he whispered, knowingly. "No problem. Who do you want to talk to?"

He handed me the interoffice phone and I buzzed my old pal Patsy Jessup, a junior partner who specialized in divorces (her own), bankruptcies (her clients', after they get her bills) and firm scuttlebutt (mostly about the sordid sex lives of the senior partners). She was eager to see me in her office, which was on the same floor as the mail room, but how was I going to get over there without being recognized and unceremoniously tossed out the door? Ernie, surprisingly enough, had a brilliant idea and was kind enough to help me carry it out. He handed me a couple of large but empty Federal Express boxes, which I hoisted onto my shoulders. He picked up a couple of boxes himself and I followed him out of the mail room and down the long corridor where the attorneys' offices began. It was a great trick, and I came to the conclusion that Ernie was all right after all.

"Hey, where you guys going?" Lockjaw called after us.

"I've got to talk to Patsy, and this is the only way I can get in," I said.

Lockjaw laughed. "It's a perfect disguise," he said. "You could walk around here all day carrying a box, and nobody would ever look at your face."

The disguise worked brilliantly. To reach Patsy's office we had to pass Art Valunos himself, who stood outside his corner office giving instructions to a secretary. Valunos, who had been the number two partner when I was there, had succeeded to top dog upon Babylon's demise. He stood five feet six inches tall and had dark, sunken eyes beneath a brooding Nixonian brow. I had dubbed him The Lesser Evil and he must have heard about it. Even before the disbarment incident he'd been trying to get rid of me, and afterwards he'd personally warned me never to set foot in the office again. But that afternoon I walked right past him carrying a box and I might as well have been invisible.

"If any more reporters call, tell them I'm in a meeting," he was saying to the secretary. "The only person I want to talk to is Oscar Feierabend from Third Millennium. If he calls, try to find me."

I slipped into Patsy's office and nodded appreciatively to Ernie, who winked and continued down the hall with his empty box. Patsy sat at her desk clipping her fingernails and brushing the nail clippings into the desk drawer. A copy of the *Inquirer* lay open in front of her.

"Hey, Patsy," I said, closing the door.

"Well, if it isn't." She swept the last of her nail clippings into the drawer and slammed it shut. "One partner bites the dust, and another comes back from the dead."

"Just visiting," I said, taking a seat in front of her desk. "How have you been?"

"Peachy."

"So what do you think about all this?" I waved my hand toward the newspaper.

"Well, you know how much I loved Neil Babylon." Patsy is not an attractive person—scrawny, ill-groomed, her face discolored by a quarter century of cigarette smoke—but she's as smart and as deadly as one of those heat-seeking missiles that can find an enemy plane and blow it out of the sky. "Quite frankly," she said, "the son of a bitch was always hitting on me and I'm glad he's dead because maybe now he'll stop." Patsy has a rich fantasy life and has been reprimanded by the courts more than once for her uncontrollable mouth. She never listens to anything anybody says, but somehow she always seems to know everything sooner than anyone else.

"I guess that makes you the number one suspect," I said.

"Yeah, but I didn't do it, to my everlasting regret. What about you? I've heard you did it."

"I've heard that nobody did it."

"That's the party line," she agreed. She leaned forward with a suddenly excited conspiratorial air. "Do you realize that Art Valunos called a meeting of the Executive Committee while Babylon's body was still cooling down on the floor, even before they called the police?"

Patsy's temperature always rose when she talked about Valunos, who had once tried to oust her from the partnership after she insulted one of his clients. She'd threatened a sexual harassment case and he backed down, but after that the two of them were like pit bulls that had to be kept in separate pens. "Fran came running to Art when she found the body, and he ran up and checked to see if Babylon was really dead," she continued. "And then he told Fran not to call the police, that he would do it. And then he got the Executive Committee together for over an hour to figure out how to spin the story while Babylon rotted on the floor. Jesus, you should have seen how bloated and purple he looked by the time they finally lugged his guts out of here!"

"So what do you think really happened?"

"Quite frankly, I think it was the Lesser Evil."

"Valunos?"

"Why not? Babylon wasn't bringing in the big clients the way he used to, but he still made extravagant demands on the firm. Chauffeur driven limousines, club memberships, lunch every day at the Four Seasons. Threatening to leave and take his clients with him unless they raised his draw. Let's face it, he was costing a lot more than he was worth."

"Nothing new about that."

She lowered her voice and wagged her head excitedly as her stringy hair flew out in all directions. "No, except you may remember that $10,000,000 note that all the partners had to sign the last time Babylon tried to bail out and the banks called their loans. It's coming due in a month."

"And?"

"And the firm can't pay it. It has to be renegotiated, which couldn't be done as long as Babylon was in a position to take a large chunk of the business somewhere else."

I thought Patsy would leap across the desk when she made this revelation. It was obviously something she was not supposed to say, especially to me, but the temptation to slander Valunos had overcome her.

I played the devil's advocate. "Why Valunos, then? It could have been any one of the partners."

There was a tap on the door, and it pushed open. An elaborately coiffed but slightly balding head, which fortunately I did not recognize, protruded inside. "Here's one of them now," Patsy said.

The owner of the head smiled diffidently. "One of what?" he asked.

"One of the suspects," she said, and his smile disappeared.

☐

6.

The man slipped inside and shut the door behind him. "Patsy, this isn't a joke! The police are taking the partners one by one into a conference room and giving them the third degree." He noticed me, since I wasn't carrying a box, and extended his hand. "Rick Taconelli," he said.

Before I could answer, Patsy jumped in. "This is Howard Ferguson, from Microsoft," she said. "They're considering hiring me as their general counsel."

Taconelli showed no sign of skepticism at this outrageous lie, but no interest in it either. He was the self-absorbed, narcissistic type, a criminal defense lawyer as I later learned. He was wearing an $800 Italian suit and a pair of cordovan leather Cole Haan loafers. "Wait till you hear this," he said. "They're going ahead with the wedding on Saturday."

"You're making that up!"

"I kid you not." Taconelli was the type who could say "I kid you not" with a straight face.

"Quite frankly," said Patsy, "it's just what you would expect of Yvette. She's never been one to miss a party. And why let all that food from the viewing go to waste? They're probably using the same caterers for both affairs."

"And you know," Taconelli sniffed, "the little princess sort of has to get married, doesn't she? Where would she find anyone else who would marry her now?"

Patsy glared at Taconelli as if to warn him not to go further with that line of innuendo. "She wasn't really his daughter, so I guess she can do whatever she wants."

I gathered from the subsequent discussion that Babylon's stepdaughter Alyssa, who had been working at the firm as a paralegal since her graduation from Wellesley, was scheduled to be married on Saturday in an extravaganza that had already attracted guests from all over the world. His wife Yvette, out of regard for the guests and possibly not to sacrifice her standing with the caterers, had decided not to postpone the affair. The band was booked and paid for, the shrimp was ordered, and many of the guests were already en route to Philadelphia for what had now become a surprise double bill.

"Memorial service on Thursday, wedding on Saturday," as Patsy summed it up. "What are they going to have for those people to do on Friday? A bus trip to Atlantic City?"

"I've got to run," said Taconelli. "Just wanted to give you the latest tidbit." He waved a limp wrist in my direction. "Nice meeting you, Howard."

"Good to meet you." I turned back to Patsy, who was leaning back with her feet on the desk. I tried not to look at her legs, which were badly in need of a shave.

"Were you at the cocktail party?" I asked her.

"Is the Pope Catholic? Of course I was at the cocktail party."

"What happened?"

"It was a retirement party for Ken Gillingham. After thirty-five years, all he rated was cheese and crackers on a Monday night. One plate of cold cuts. No shrimp, no salmon.

Valunos didn't show up, even though Ken worked for him all those years."

"Babylon was there, obviously. Did he give the Bittersweet Occasion speech?"

She snorted. "Was there ever a time when a partner left when he didn't give the Bittersweet Occasion speech?"

"He didn't give it for me. I didn't even get cheese and crackers."

"Left voluntarily, I should have said. Not disbarred, for Christ's sake!"

I could picture the scene at the cocktail party, since it was a replay of dozens I had attended while at the firm. Such parties take place in the darkly paneled foyer of the law library. Lockjaw wheels in a portable bar and the receptionists lay out other food and drinks on folding tables. The lawyers start drifting in at about 5:30, led by the die-hard drinkers like Patsy. Neil Babylon would typically arrive at about six o'clock. After another half hour of frenetic drinking and chatter, one of Neil's underlings would chime on a wine glass and the room would fall silent. All eyes, naturally, would turn to Neil, who would be standing surrounded by sycophants near the bar. Turning on his famous charm, he would make a lot of windy pronouncements about himself, the firm and the departing Ken Gillingham, who, five minutes earlier, he had probably been trying to screw out of his last paycheck.

"'This is a bittersweet occasion,'" Patsy mimicked, affecting Babylon's pompous, low-pitched voice. "'Sweet for Ken, who for many years has looked forward to the day when he could devote himself full time to gardening—which should not be difficult because Ken himself is practically a vegetable—and to his many other activities, such as struggling to keep from drooling during meetings. But for the firm, although we share in Ken's joy and wish him the greatest of happiness and success in his new endeavors, it's a day of reflection, a day when we must ask ourselves, How are we going to get along without Ken Gillingham? The firm will go on—this is too great an institution to be dependent on any one man—but we know it will be difficult without this man who has selflessly devoted himself to the firm since the early days of the Coolidge administration...'"

I might have continued where Patsy left off, but by this time we were both laughing too hard to go on. Our laughter continued in fits and starts, punctuated with a few inappropriate jokes, until Patsy's secretary, a buxom African-American wearing a Sixers sweatshirt and a pair of leopard skin tights, suddenly came through the door with a file in her hand. She eyed me suspiciously and handed the file to Patsy with a brief explanation.

"This time it really was a bittersweet occasion," I said after the secretary had left. "Especially for Neil."

"Bitter for Neil, but for the firm..." Patsy finished the sentence with a vague sweep of her hand, as if she couldn't quite bring herself to finish the sentence.

"Was he acting strangely, or doing anything unusual?"

She shrugged. "Quite frankly, I didn't notice anything at the time, except for the little scene with Connie Liebman."

"Connie! Was she the woman he had the argument with?"

She nodded disparagingly. "That poor innocent little creature! Yes, it was Connie all right. But Neil had it coming. I would have done the same thing if he was hitting on me. Which he's done plenty of times, by the way."

Connie is a mid-level associate in the real estate department and she's the kind of woman Patsy Jessup hates—single and attractive, with a kind heart, a warm smile and no tolerance for office intrigue. "What did she do?"

"Nothing. She just shrieked and pushed him away. Almost slapped his face. He had his hands all over her."

"Wasn't that a little unusual, even for Neil?"

"He was a pig right up to the bitter end."

Patsy stood up and stretched her long arms toward the ceiling. She's never been one to stay very long in the same place. "I've got to get out of here," she said.

"Do you think he was murdered?" I asked her.

"Well, there are plenty of people who had good reason to kill him. Apart from you and me, of course. His wife—she hated his guts. Valunos, and practically everybody else who ever worked here. Even Lockjaw."

"Lockjaw?"

"A couple months ago Neil was overheard making a racial slur about some of the guys in the mail room. It caused quite a scandal around here for a while. Lockjaw was mad enough to kill. And you know he was tending the bar that night."

Patsy had to leave to pick up her juvenile delinquent son at his sharpshooting lesson. She was hoping he would grow up to join the Special Forces if he wasn't already serving a life term before he was old enough to enlist. But before she left she sat back down and swiveled her chair around to face the computer that stood on the credenza behind her desk. "Let's see what time the funeral is tomorrow," she said, clicking madly from one web site to another.

"You mean that's on the web?"

"Everything's on the web."

Personally, I don't own a computer and I've never learned how to use one, so I was doubly impressed to watch Patsy whipping through the internet in search of the funeral listings. "Your computer system seems to be a lot more advanced than when I was here."

"State of the art. You know that kid Ernie from the mail room who brought you in here? He's our computer guru. He showed me how to do all this stuff."

"The attorney who was here before—what's his name? Rick? He must be new."

"Yeah, but he's not exactly state of the art. He came over from Morgan Lewis about a year ago, supposedly with a nice white collar crime practice. He keeps his collar white enough but the practice hasn't materialized—turns out most of his clients are in jail, thanks to his incompetence—and I think he spends more of his time gossiping with the secretaries than doing any work. Quite frankly, if his IQ ever hits 100 he ought to sell." She stopped talking for a moment while she concentrated on her web searching. "Jesus Christ! Will you look at this? There's already a Neil Babylon Murder Home Page!"

There was indeed. It summarized everything I knew about Babylon's death and then some. There was even a list of

"Possible Suspects," which I found some comfort in being omitted from. Obviously whoever had created the web site was misinformed when it came to suspects. But they listed the time and place of the funeral—Thursday morning at ten o'clock—and they had links to all the obituaries and news stories that had been published so far. Somehow they had obtained color photographs of Babylon, his wife and several of the firm's partners, including Art Valunos, Patsy, Rick Taconelli and the retiring Ken Gillingham, as well as a number of people I didn't know. Patsy and Rick were both listed as Possible Suspects and Patsy was furious.

"If I find out who put this website up I'm going to sue them for libel!" she roared. "'Possible suspects!' What the hell does that mean? That you're not a suspect yet because there's no reason to suspect you, but it's possible you might become a suspect in the future?"

"You said you were glad he's dead."

"I take that back." She clicked furiously with her mouse and shut down the computer. "I didn't go near him that night. And right now I've got to pick up my juvenile delinquent."

"Listen," she said as she put on her coat, "I had my differences with Neil. He was a sexist, racist, homophobic, autocratic, selfish, money-grubbing, flatulent bag of crap. But I wouldn't have killed him even if I got the chance, and you know why? The Valunos regime is going to be much, much worse."

☐

7.

When Patsy turned out the lights and skittered out the door—
"I gotta run. See ya'"—I hoisted the Federal Express box onto
my shoulder and carried it down the hall to Senator Squires's
office, lowering my eyes and blocking my face when I passed
someone I knew. Since the Senator rarely if ever sets foot in
his office, I figured this was the safest place to hang out for a
few hours until all the attorneys had gone home, and while I
was waiting I could begin my search for the crucial surveillance
tape. Not that I really expected to find the tape in the
Senator's office. Assuming he had obtained it from the state,
he would have passed it on to Babylon at the first opportunity.
But since I was going to be spending some time there—and as
luck would have it, I had failed to bring along anything to
read—I had little choice but to violate his reasonable
expectations of privacy and search the place from floor to
ceiling.

Lou Squires is listed as one of the firm's attorneys, and you
often see references in the press to Rittenhouse as "his" law
firm, but the truth of the matter is that practicing law is not
one of his interests. His relationship with the firm is a simple
one. There are many people out there who, for reasons of
their own, want to make generous gifts to the Senator, which
as a conscientious public servant he could not accept. That
would be bribery, especially since all those generous people

have dealings with the state government or some board or authority that the Senator controls. So instead they hire his law firm to work on some expensive and sometimes totally unnecessary project. Other attorneys from the firm spend countless hours drafting documents and attending meetings, charge for their time at an exorbitant hourly rate and then send the client an outrageous bill, which the client pays enthusiastically, knowing that the grateful Senator will receive the lion's share of the proceeds. By the way, as Art Valunos has explained many times, this is all perfectly legal.

His office, I soon discovered, was a sort of Potemkin village, set up to resemble what his law office would look like if he actually practiced law. There were the pictures of his loving wife and devoted children; there were his diplomas, his framed views of Boat House Row—why does every successful lawyer in Philadelphia feel obliged to display framed views of Boat House Row?—and the innumerable signed photographs of the Senator with President Reagan, the Senator with President Clinton, the Senator with Luciano Pavarotti, the Senator with the Virgin Mary (I assumed that the little bald fellow sitting on her lap was the Senator, since he was in all the other pictures). And on the shelves, law books—or at least the spines of law books, since on closer inspection I discovered that one shelf concealed a well-stocked liquor cabinet. Well, maybe the Senator did spend some time in his office after all.

I made myself comfortable in his desk chair and began a leisurely inspection of the desk drawers and their contents. I did not find the surveillance tape or anything the least bit interesting or incriminating, other than about seventy-five unpaid parking tickets dating back to 1992. The file cabinet behind the desk was locked, but the key, naturally, was in the desk drawer. There was nothing much in the file cabinet, though in one of the files I found some ledger sheets with some rather large numbers on them that seemed to relate to the allocation of firm profits and liabilities. There was also a stack of interesting but incomprehensible papers in the "To be Filed" folder, which seemed to be notes taken at an Executive Committee meeting a few weeks before. This was intriguing because of a scribble that appeared to allude to Elena's husband—"Talk to Geoff G" was how I read it, though I might have been mistaken and in any case I had no idea why Geoff Goodwin, who practiced at a different firm, would be relevant to a Rittenhouse Executive Committee meeting. As I've mentioned, the law books behind the desk were partly fake, with enough booze stashed behind them to keep even a Senator busy on a cold winter evening. After I finished snooping through the Senator's papers I helped myself to a shot of Jack Daniels and settled in for the long wait.

My thoughts drifted back to my days at the firm. Those were happy days, by and large, especially in the early years before disillusionment started setting in. It was a new and exciting world, light years away from Greene County and almost as far from the Philadelphia Public Defender's office where I'd worked for two years after finishing law school. Our clients included some of the richest and most powerful families in the region, the kind of people who could be seen on the society page smiling comfortably in their dinner jackets as they planned gala fundraisers for the Philadelphia Orchestra or

Children's Hospital—and I found, much to my surprise, that I liked them and they liked me. Then there were the Tom Riordan types, high society wannabes who were still in the process of stealing their fortunes, and the politicos like Senator Squires, who spent their lives stealing somebody else's fortune. That was where the disillusionment started, even before the disbarment fiasco. In general I got along well with the other attorneys at the firm. There were a few stuffed shirts and a few hysterics among them, but for the most part they were a humorous, enjoyable group. I never cared for Art Valunos, but to give the devil his due—as I was grudgingly willing to do after a few shots of Jack Daniels—the man has his good points. He's the dedicated father of four, happily married to the same woman—Babylon couldn't have imagined that—for over thirty years, and an active supporter of numerous worthy causes, some of which don't even bring in any business. His clients are fiercely loyal to him, and he to them, which could never be said for Neil Babylon. Babylon was a hired gun, a knight errant who galloped from one battle to another. There were exceptions—Tom Riordan, to my regret, was one of them—but in general Neil took his clients where he found them, and usually dropped them there when the case was over. Valunos loves the firm as an institution and will do everything in his power to protect it, while Babylon cared only about the people who surrounded and supported him. In the end, of course, he had thrown me to the dogs, so as a father figure he left something to be desired. But as I sat there that night, thinking about him lying dead in his office, I felt strangely accepting of Babylon and all he had done. I won't say I had tears in my eyes, but to my surprise—perhaps encouraged by another dollop of Tennessee sour mash whisky—I drank a solitary toast to Neil Babylon and silently mourned his passing. Even in death, I thought, the man was larger than life—and probably still the best lawyer in Philadelphia.

I spent the next hour sobering up and thinking about Senator Squires. The first thing I'd asked Elena that morning, before we got into our little tiff over the surveillance tape, was whether she knew anything about the anti-Squires faction that Bardahl seemed to be working for. It's common knowledge that the Mayor despises the Senator, and there are others, such as his arch-rival Senator Vince Fumo, who might have been trying to undermine him. But the most likely suspect was our recently-elected State Attorney General, who campaigned on a platform of cleaning up corruption in the award of state contracts in Philadelphia. Elena had heard a tantalizing rumor about a secret grand jury investigation. It was possible, in her view, that the Attorney General had made some inroads in the Philadelphia Police Department. Normally the cops loved Lou Squires because he backed their union in its battles with the Mayor, but in the face of an aggressive investigation there would always be a few defectors, marginal types like Bardahl whose only hope of advancement is to play the quisling. And maybe there were others, higher in the power structure, who saw the investigation as a threat, or more likely, as an opportunity. Whoever they were, they seemed intent on exploiting the Senator's ties with the struggling Rittenhouse firm to bring him down. I doubted if they would succeed.

The door flew open and I almost leaped out of my chair as the cleaning lady waddled in to empty the waste paper basket. Why was she doing that, I wondered, when she must have known there's never anything in it? I was tempted to call her down for startling me like that but instead I ignored her, as I knew the Senator would have done, pretending that I belonged there sipping whisky behind that big desk. Maybe she thought I was the Senator himself. In any case it made no difference: she peered into the waste basket, satisfied herself that it was empty, and closed the door behind her as she left without acknowledging my existence. After this encounter I found myself getting nervous and antsy. I stopped drinking, and by nine o'clock I was crawling out of my skin and so famished that I decided to take my chances leaving the room at a time when some of the lawyers might still be around.

Just as I cracked the door open I heard voices in the hallway. One of them was the unmistakable murmur of Art Valunos, who sounded conspiratorial even when he was ordering lunch at the Union League. I peeked down the hall and caught a sight that stopped me in my tracks: Valunos and Senator Squires walking towards me, engrossed in an animated conversation. I backed up and let the door ease shut in front of my face. If they opened it I was a dead man. What on earth was the Senator doing at the office? I glanced around the room for an escape route or a hiding place and saw nothing but four walls and a sealed window that looked out forty-three floors above the street.

Sometimes the best hiding place is right out in the open. I had nothing more to lose, so I decided to take a chance. The one thing that would spook Valunos, I guessed, was another dead body. So I quickly became one, lying face down on the floor in a contorted position with my feet towards the door and my face jammed unrecognizably against the desk pedestal. Another perfectly healthy man drops dead. And not a moment too soon, because suddenly the door clicked open and the voices burst inside the room.

"What the hell is this?"

"Oh, my God!"

"Who is it?"

"Don't touch anything!"

Both of them sounded scared out of their wits. Neither had the decency to reach down and see if I was really dead. The Senator sounded more angry than anything else. "Two bodies in one day! What the hell is going on around here?"

Valunos started murmuring again. "Don't touch anything, Lou! We'll get it out of here. Nobody needs to know."

"You're goddam right nobody needs to know! Right in my office. Christ Almighty!"

"Come on, Lou! Nobody needs to know about this. Let's go down to my office. I'll call somebody I know—I have an acquaintance—who takes care of this sort of thing."

"No cops."

"No cops. I promise."

The door slammed and their voices faded quickly down the hall.

8.

One of the advantages of being dead is that people think you'll stay put. So I had what seemed like an eternity to think about what I would do next. Obviously, the first order of business was to avoid Valunos's "acquaintance" who would be showing up to dispose of my body, but even allowing for speedy service and off-peak travel this would have to take at least as long as Domino's Pizza. I figured I had thirty minutes to accomplish what I had come for.

Brushing myself off, I eased the door open again and peeked through the doorway. Not a soul in sight. Muffled voices coming from Valunos's office around the corner. I padded softly toward Babylon's office, which was on the opposite corner of the building. It was probably locked, I realized. Babylon was only partner in the firm who routinely locked the door to his office, even during business hours. He had a buzzer on his desk that opened it like the outside door to an apartment house, and even his secretary didn't have a key. And as I came around the corner within sight of the office I realized that it was also blocked with yellow police tape. But the odd thing was that although the police tape had not been cut, the door stood ajar and there was a light on inside.

I stuck my head inside and saw the gray uniformed back of a maintenance man who seemed to be searching the office. He turned to face me and I could feel the pit of my stomach dropping down to the forty-second floor. It was McVeigh, the sicko stalker I had thrown out of the Pickwick Club just the night before.

Momentary paralysis gripped us both. I didn't know if he recognized me, and for all I knew he was Babylon's killer. I felt my throat swelling shut and remembered my necktie, which gave me a status that he couldn't claim. I looked at him sternly. "Can I help you?"

"Just checking out the heating ducts," he said, eyeing me warily. "We had a report of smoke up here."

"A fire?"

"Nah. Probably just somebody smoking in their office. Maybe coming from a different floor."

"How did you get in here? This office was locked."

For an instant I was afraid I had gone too far. How did I know it was locked? His eyes flashed hostility, fear, the same cornered look I'd seen the night before. I could tell that he'd recognized me but was hoping I didn't recognize him. But then I knew that he knew, and we both knew we were playing a masquerade. He reached into his pocket.

"We have a master key," he said, his hand jingling up with a crowded key ring. "For any of these offices that are kept locked. But I don't see anything here. You smell any smoke?"

"No. I don't smell anything."

"False alarm." Staring at me boldly now, almost smirking. "OK? Have a good night."

He picked up his toolbox and I watched him down the hall and out of sight. What was he doing there? He was at once too polite and too impudent to be a real maintenance man.

He'd left readily enough when I arrived, as if he'd already found what he was looking for.

I shut the door and searched the office thoroughly, trying not to leave any fingerprints. The desk, the credenza, the bookcases with Babylon's proud collection of books about Winston Churchill—few of which he had ever opened, let alone read—and even the liquor cabinet, which was much better stocked than the Senator's. Like the Senator, he had the same pretentious array of signed photographs of himself with every president since McKinley and I looked behind each one for a wall safe. I was about to give up when I found an unlabeled videotape in a plastic bag stashed behind some books on a low shelf behind the desk.

There was a TV and VCR in the room, and I was so excited I almost turned it on to watch the tape right then and there. But I glanced at my watch and realized it was getting late. In a few minutes Art Valunos's acquaintance would be arriving to dispose of my body, and I wanted to make sure I was safely out of sight. I shoved the videotape under my jacket and headed for the elevator.

Only one elevator runs at that hour, from a small elevator lobby that is locked from inside the office lobby. Carelessly, as I stood waiting for the elevator I took the tape out from under my jacket and examined it. When the elevator arrived I came face to face with a short, serious-looking man in a knit shirt and a dark sports coat who nodded courteously as he stepped out. He had thinning dark hair, a high forehead and a pair of sunken eyes that reminded me of a raccoon's. He carried a small valise that might have contained tools or cleaning supplies.

"Art Valunos on this floor?" he asked me, glancing at the video cartridge I held in my hand.

"He sure is," I said, slipping into the elevator. "Just push that button and he'll buzz you right in."

At the guard desk downstairs I exchanged pleasantries with the guard as I signed out but was careful not to look him in the eyes. "Lazarus," I wrote as I imagined Valunos calling frantically down to the desk to ask if anyone had left the building. But a chill tingled through my veins when I deciphered the ignorant scrawl that had been left by the person who signed out just ahead of me.

"Your a dead man," it said.

Wednesday is a busy night at the Pickwick, and when I slipped in a little after ten o'clock it seemed noisier than usual. Luckily Niko was nowhere in sight, so I just took my place at the keyboard as if I'd been there all night. Before I started to play I stashed my stolen videotape inside the piano bench.

Brian O'Dolan, the former Jesuit, sat on his usual barstool carrying on a heated debate with Jim Hively and a man in a yellow bow tie about the futility of life. "Just look around you and what do you see?" he asked. "A lot of people seemingly enjoying themselves, seemingly content with their lot. But they're all going to die, you know, every last one of them. Maybe they'll die tomorrow, maybe years from now, but sooner or later they'll be dead. And that is no chance occurrence! No, sir! It's the law of the universe. So except for this"—he held up his glass of burgundy—"is there really any point in getting out of bed in the morning?"

I had winced when he said some of us would be dead by tomorrow and now I caught my breath when I realized he was staring right at me.

"Say, Pete," he said. "Why so late tonight?"

"Family emergency."

"No connection with, you know"—he winked theatrically—"the Babylon matter."

"Why would I have any connection with that?"

"That policeman was here earlier tonight," O'Dolan said. "The one who was here last night. Asking for you."

"Policeman? What did he look like?"

"You know. Balding, a little on the stout side."

I had to laugh in spite of myself. Saying Bardahl was a little on the stout side was like saying Gandhi was a wee bit thin. "What did you tell him?"

"Well," said O'Dolan. "Forgive me if I stepped out of bounds, but I had a hunch you might not want him pestering you. So I told him you didn't play here anymore."

"Good work."

"I might even have said something about a certain restaurant out in Malvern that would take him at least an hour to drive to, assuming no traffic or construction on the Schuylkill Expressway."

"That's an unrealistic assumption."

"Life is very short," he agreed, returning to his original theme. "But the Schuylkill Expressway can take forever."

For me it was this night that seemed to be taking forever. By eleven o'clock O'Dolan had convinced Hively, as if he needed convincing, that life was not worth living, and Hively slouched out dejectedly, no doubt looking for a good place to hang himself. The man in the bow tie also seemed to fade away in despair. But O'Dolan himself, once he had demonstrated the futility of life to the others, did not seem especially troubled by it. He cheerfully polished off one last glass of wine, paid his bar tab and whistled his way out the door after leaving a generous tip in the brandy snifter on top of the piano. I felt better about my life when I saw that. If a man is a good tipper, you can put up with almost any amount of existential despair.

At midnight I signed off as usual with "One For My Baby" and hurried home with the stolen surveillance tape. As I walked down Locust Street toward my building I felt like Dr. Richard Kimble when he found that picture of the one-armed man. What I held in my hand was the smoking gun that could prove my innocence and send my false accusers to jail! Elena would be proud of me—maybe even wrapped around my little finger, as Theresa predicted, though I tried not to dwell on that image—and she wouldn't have to sacrifice her own happiness for my vindication. I had waited so long for this moment that I didn't want my delicious anticipation to end. I wanted to draw it out for as long as I possibly could. So when I arrived back in my apartment I didn't pop the tape right into the VCR as you might imagine. I changed into more comfortable clothes, listened to my phone messages, made myself a cup of coffee. And finally, when everything was just right, I arranged a comfortable chair in front of the TV and plugged in the tape.

I can't tell you when sex has been a bigger disappointment. Yes, sex. That's what was on the tape, and it wasn't the type of sex I care to watch even in the privacy of my home. One of the participants was Neil Babylon himself, all two hundred and eighty pounds of him. His partner was a blonde middle aged woman I had never seen before—it was not his wife—who looked like she'd had a lot of liposuction but still needed more. Presumably the film had been recorded for documentary purposes only, perhaps as a warning to people in Third World countries not to immigrate to the United States. Not a pretty sight by any stretch of the imagination. And for me, it was the latest in a series of bitter disappointments. Was this wretched home movie what I had risked my life for, feigning death before the most powerful man in Philadelphia, staring down a murderous skinhead, exchanging pleasantries with a mafia undertaker who even now was probably on his way over to dispose of my body? Was this all I would be able to show Elena for my superhuman efforts? The answer was yes, and I felt like crying.

I didn't cry, but I did manage to put away half a bottle of tequila before I went to bed, and I left an incoherent message on Elena's office voice mail, hoping pitifully that I would see her at her mother's the next afternoon.

9.

As it turned out, I saw Elena well before our usual noon rendezvous. At 7:30—a scant three hours after I had fallen asleep—her mother started banging on my door with a frying pan. I had turned off the telephone, as I always do when I want to sleep in the morning, but there was no resisting the force of Hurricane Theresa.

"C'mon!" she shouted. "Wake up! You're gonna be late!"

Late for what? I never go anywhere in the morning. Then suddenly I realized my mistake. In my drunken disappointment of the night before I had completely forgotten that Thursday was the day of Neil Babylon's funeral.

I pulled on my pants and staggered next door to Theresa's apartment, where I found Elena seated at the kitchen table, wearing a dark suit and a bright, almost mischievous expression. "Well," she said. "You're looking cheerful. What do you say we take in a funeral this morning?"

"Will it be mine? Because if it isn't, I'm going back to bed."

"Have a cup of coffee," ordered Theresa, still brandishing her frying pan.

"Whatever you say."

"Well," Elena asked, a little hesitantly, "did you get a chance to look for the missing link?"

I gave her hand a little squeeze, just to show that I had no hard feelings from the day before, and sat down at the table. "Thereby hangs a tale."

And as Theresa served our coffee as I related my previous night's adventures. Elena and her mother seemed suitably impressed by my resourcefulness in getting into the firm and roaming the halls under cover of a Federal Express box. But to my dyspeptic annoyance, they both laughed uproariously when I described myself stretched out like a corpse on the floor of the Senator's office while he and Art Valunos argued about how to dispose of my body. "It reminds me of my cousin Sal," said Theresa. "Only he wasn't just pretending."

Elena's amusement subsided when I described my encounter with McVeigh. And she groaned in disappointment when I got to the end of the story and revealed that the tape I'd found in Babylon's office was just a homemade porno flick of the big man and one of his over-age bimbos.

"I'd like to see that," said Theresa.

"Oh, no you wouldn't."

"Pete," Elena said, "I'm sorry. I wanted you to look for the tape but I don't want you to get killed doing it."

"I haven't given up yet."

"Maybe you should. It's too dangerous."

"Will you promise me you'll give up the idea of telling the cops about where we found it?"

She looked away without answering. "Where else were you planning to look?"

"I'm thinking of tracking down my friend McVeigh."

"McVeigh? Is that his real name?"

"No, I just made that up. I have no idea what his real name is. He signed out 'Your a dead man,' so all in all I'd prefer to keep calling him McVeigh."

Elena shook her head quizzically. "What does he have to do with this?"

"I don't know. But it's possible I got to Babylon's office just a little too late."

Theresa lifted our coffee mugs so she could clean under them, muttering something about the damage we were doing to the formica tabletop.

"So you think McVeigh found the real surveillance tape?" Elena asked.

"It's possible. Maybe that's why he was smirking as he went out the door. Or maybe he was looking for the porno tape and found the surveillance tape by mistake. In that case he might have been just as disappointed as I was when he got home."

"But doesn't the fact that he signed out 'Your a dead man' indicate that he didn't find what he was looking for?"

"Not necessarily. Don't forget he wanted to kill me the other night at the Pickwick when I chased him away from Madison."

"Madison?"

"The Asian go-go dancer. Remember?"

"How could I have forgotten?"

I stood up and carried our empty mugs over to the sink. "I thought about this last night," I said, pacing around in the tiny kitchen. "When it comes to McVeigh there are several possibilities: Either he was looking for the porno tape and didn't find it, because I scared him off, or he was looking for the surveillance tape and found it, because it wasn't there when I looked for it—assuming it was there in the first place. Or maybe he was there to plant the porno tape so it would be found during the murder investigation."

Elena smiled. "Or maybe the reason he was there had nothing to do with either the porno tape or the surveillance tape."

"Maybe he was looking for other evidence about the murder."

"Or covering it up."

"You don't know much about this guy, do you?" asked Theresa.

"No, we don't," I conceded. "But right now he's my only chance for finding the surveillance tape and somehow I need to track him down."

"Are you sure you really want to do this?" Elena asked.

"Absolutely."

"I don't want you risking your life for me."

"At this point it has nothing to do with you."

She knew I was lying, but she played along. "OK," she said. "I know how you can find McVeigh."

"How?"

"He's interested in Madison, isn't he?"

"Yes, I guess you could call it that."

"And Madison owes you a favor for chasing him away the other night."

"True, though I'm not sure she sees it that way."

"So if he's still after her, you ought to be able to find him. Just keep your eye on her and sooner or later he'll turn up."

I could hardly believe what she was suggesting. "Use Madison as bait? The guy's a psychopath! What kind of judge are you?"

"A pragmatic one. Think of it as stalking the stalker. Chances are he's going to walk into your trap and get what he deserves."

Elena glanced at her watch and stood up to leave. "I have to go," she said. "The funeral's at ten o'clock. Are you going?"

"I wouldn't miss it for the world."

"I'll probably see you there. I'm going with my husband. He was great friends with Neil Babylon, you know. At least until recently."

"What happened recently?"

"I don't know, but I'm sure it had something to do with money or politics. Geoff won't talk to me about it."

I remembered the surprising page of notes I'd found in the Senator's office. "What has he been saying since Babylon died? Anything juicy?"

She hesitated, looking away.

"I'm sorry," I said. "I shouldn't ask you about your pillow talk with Geoff."

"That's not it," she said, blushing. "It's just that Geoff doesn't tell me much. I hardly see him, and when I do see him..." Her voice trailed off.

"I found something interesting last night in the Senator's files," I said. "It was financial stuff about the firm, some handwritten notes about an Executive Committee meeting, and for some reason the Senator—or whoever took the notes—had written 'Talk to Geoff G' across the bottom of the page."

Elena's jaw dropped halfway to her knees. "What was it about?"

"I couldn't tell."

She bit her lower lip as if she was trying to keep herself from doing something she knew she shouldn't do. "If you're going back up there—"

"I'm not."

"I know, but if you do for any reason—do you think you could get me a copy of that—what is it, just a single page?"

"Yeah, just one sheet out of a legal pad."

"I'd love to see that." She turned to leave. "Oh, one more thing. Can I take that videotape along with me? I want to watch it tonight and see if I recognize the bimbo. And besides"—she glanced at Theresa, who stood at the stove stirring tomato sauce with a long wooden spoon in an almost erotic fashion—"I want to make sure it doesn't fall into the wrong hands."

10.

The funeral was at a well-known funeral home in North Philadelphia. I put on a dark suit and drove up there in the battered 1995 Toyota Corolla which was the only item from our marital estate Denise had allowed me to keep, parking on a side street a few minutes after ten. The weather had turned frigid but it was still gray and nasty, and as I drove up North Broad through one of the bleakest neighborhoods in the city I was trapped behind a garbage truck that was spewing out scraps of paper and small plastic bags like leaflets being dropped on some recently conquered population. What few people there were in that devastated area paid no attention—they had been conquered too long before. Around the funeral home the neighborhood was much better, almost suburban. No abandoned crack houses, no homeless guys sleeping in refrigerator boxes, no liquor bottles strewn on the sidewalk. But in the gray wind there was still an echo of desolation, and as I walked from my car I felt as cold as the bare, twisted treetops that shuddered over my head. All in all a perfect day for a funeral.

It was a mostly secular affair, more like a testimonial dinner than any funeral I 'd ever attended, but there was a rabbi who said some suitably inspiring words about Babylon's love for his family and his service to the community. If the rabbi believed in a heavenly afterlife, he carefully avoided any suggestion that

Babylon might be going there. Art Valunos, in his eulogy, was less circumspect. He paid a glowing tribute to Babylon's years as the firm's managing partner and concluded with a little joke. "I don't know where Neil Babylon is today," he said. "But I'm sure of one thing—wherever he is, pretty soon he'll be running the place." No one in the audience knew whether to laugh or cry, so they just coughed and cleared their throats and shifted in their seats.

"If it's Hell," Patsy Jessup whispered in my ear, "at least he'll have had plenty of experience." I had slipped into the seat beside Patsy in the back row, confident that I wouldn't attract too much attention sitting next to someone that no one else wanted to look at. It was an inspired choice, because even the solemnity of the occasion didn't stop her from providing a juicy commentary on each of the assembled mourners. Valunos had stationed himself in the front row with the family— Babylon's current wife Yvette and her three children, including the eldest daughter Alyssa who was to be married on Saturday ("Quite frankly," said Patsy, "I'd be surprised if Yvette didn't have this room booked months ago"). The beautiful Alyssa sat between her teenage sister ("The Britney Spears clone next to Alyssa goes by Jennifer or Lolita, I can't remember which"), and my friend Connie Liebman, the Rittenhouse attorney who'd been the object of Babylon's last known attempt at womanizing ("Statistically, at her age she has a better chance of being murdered by a serial killer than finding a husband"). In the second row sat his most recent ex-wife, whose name I think was Beth, and their respective children, and this pattern was repeated for the next three or four rows back ("As the rabbi said," Patsy observed, "the man was dedicated to his family"). I caught a glimpse of Elena and her husband Geoff in the third row (fortunately without commentary by Patsy). Senator Squires also sat with his wife in the third row—the wife looked vaguely familiar, undoubtedly she was an attorney I had run into at some bar function—and behind them sat most of the firm's other partners, including Rick Taconelli ("I hope I didn't give you the wrong impression about Rick," said Patsy— "He has moments of adequacy") and the recently-retired Ken Gillingham ("If you look closely, you can see the moss growing on his north side"). In the next several rows, junior attorneys huddled attentively, as if awaiting instructions. And as the rows receded, the firm's social hierarchy bottomed out. First came the paralegals, then the secretaries, then the receptionists and the file clerks. And in the very back, along with Patsy and myself, lurked the primal forces of the mail room: Lockjaw, Ernie and assorted renegades from the U.S. Postal Service.

Apart from people who worked at the firm, everybody who was anybody was there that day. The judges, the politicos, the business leaders, the rainmakers from the big firms. There were even a few clients, most noticeably Tom Riordan who sat on the aisle with one of the female partners. And with all due respect to Art Valunos—which is admittedly a very low threshold—none of us were wondering where Neil Babylon had gone. He was there too, surrounded by flowers, inside a small brass canister that looked like a garden ornament.

"Wait till you hear this," whispered Patsy. "Remember I told you about that $10,000,000 bank loan that was falling due in March? Well, it just so happened that the firm had a life insurance policy on the Big Kahuna for exactly that amount."

"You're making this up."

"I am absolutely telling you the truth. The bank—it was Third Millennium—insisted that we have key man coverage for the top five rainmakers. And now—alakazam!—the loan can be paid off and the firm will be more solvent than it's ever been. Why do you think Oscar Feierabend is looking so happy?"

She gestured towards a portly, silver-haired gentleman who sat across the aisle from Valunos wearing a beatific smile. "He's the president of Third Millennium and when he thinks of Neil Babylon he thinks of a bad loan that's about to be paid off." She cackled noiselessly. "There's only one thing he ought to be worrying about."

"What's that?"

"Well, you know, if it turns out that one of the partners killed Babylon, it would be like a husband murdering his wife. The firm wouldn't be able to collect on the insurance."

The service ended with a brief non-theological prayer about pro bono work—to tell the truth, it sounded more like a fund raising appeal than a prayer—and the family members filed out ahead of everyone else. The bleached-blonde Yvette Babylon wore a stricken look and daubed her eyes with a handkerchief as she passed, but (as Patsy observed) there were no tear-streaks in her makeup. Alyssa seemed more genuinely affected than her mother, even though Babylon was only her stepfather. She was a striking young woman, tall and athletically built, with a classic high-cheekboned beauty that reminded me of Sophia Loren. This is what Yvette must have looked like, I realized, before she started bleaching her hair and spending too much time at the tanning salon. Babylon's grown children from various prior marriages, who filed out next with the various ex-wives who were their mothers, were a much less attractive bunch, probably because they looked like their father. Not to say that they were all jowly and bald, but even the ones who weren't jowly and bald—for instance, some of the daughters—looked like they would end up that way.

One thing came across loud and clear: the Babylons had plenty of money. The clothing and jewelry they were wearing, even in mourning, left no doubt about that. The lawyers and judges and clients in the room probably didn't even notice. But the secretaries and the file clerks and especially the mail room guys, who were standing right in front of me, seemed awestruck by the display. If they had still worked for the Post Office, they would probably have headed up to the roof with their assault rifles.

The Senator didn't follow the family procession but stood near the front, shaking hands solemnly with various well-wishers and political cronies. As always, he was impressive in his very lack of impressiveness. Apart from a rather florid complexion beneath his neat graying hair, there is nothing about the man that attracts attention, nothing that would make you think he was more powerful or important than a hundred other men in the room. Soft-spoken, seemingly modest, he draws people into his orbit and makes them strain to hear him, makes them pay court to him and his power. Art Valunos, by contrast, never stops trying to be impressive, and he never succeeds. I could see him circulating nervously, a minor satellite caught in the aura of power that the Senator gathered about him. He greeted people a little too warmly, shook their hands a little too graspingly, turned away from them a little too abruptly. Too obvious that he was there to work the room, even at his partner's funeral. But of course Valunos must have decided that Babylon's funeral was precisely the time and place where it would be essential to establish his authority.

And there by his side was Rick Taconelli, somewhat surprisingly since Rick was such a new addition to the firm. I saw Valunos introduce Rick to Elena's husband Geoff, who in turn introduced Elena. She of course needed no introduction, being a judge, but Geoff is vain enough to fancy himself more important than she is and he always goes out of his way to introduce her to people she already knows. I tried not to watch. As always when I see them together in public I found myself seething with jealousy. How could she spend her life with this pompous ass? Just look at him: he wiggles his forefinger when he talks, he wears his hair in a pompadour like an aging country music singer, he looks like he has twice as many teeth as his mouth can accommodate—what is it about this clown that a woman like Elena would want to spend her life with? Instead of me, for God's sake! I felt like leaping over the seats, knocking out all those superfluous teeth, and carrying Elena away to an island paradise.

Fortunately Tom Riordan caught my eye and stepped towards me wearing the patented friendly smile of a real estate developer. It was the first time I'd seen him in the two years since I was railroaded out of the firm on his behalf. He looked as tall and confident and ambitious as he always had—and to me, who knew him a little too well, every bit as shameless. Either he didn't know what had happened to me or he was too good a salesman to let it show. "Pete!" he said brightly. "Good to see you! How have you been?"

"Not bad, Tom. How are you?"

"I'm great," he said. "Hey, that was a shame you got tangled up in all that bankruptcy business. You know, I never did get control of that property. But then casino gambling hasn't gone anywhere around here anyway, so I'm just as glad it turned out the way it did."

"Yeah. So am I, Tom."

"Shame about Neil, isn't it?" He was still smiling.

"It's a tragedy."

"Say, I've got to get going." Still smiling. "Great to see you again!"

And that was that. My whole life had gone down the drain because of this man, and I don't think he even knew I didn't work at the firm anymore. I was starting to feel a little sick. First watching Valunos glad-handing the funeral guests, then Elena arm in arm with her pathetic husband, and now myself being scraped off the floor by the man who had squashed me like a bug—it was almost more than I could bear. For a long, desperate moment I imagined Theresa's croaky voice urging me on to a bloody revenge: 'Find Babylon's killer,' it intoned, 'and blow that law firm wide open, even if it lands you inside a jail cell or an exit ramp! And wherever you go, take Tom Riordan down with you!' I wasn't quite ready to go on a murderous rampage, but under Theresa's tutelage I was beginning to appreciate revenge as one of life's guiding principles. As the firm and its minions filed past me I amused myself by imagining the war of vendetta I would wage against them the next time they dared to cross me or stand in my way.

For the moment I had some less dramatic business to attend to. What Patsy had told me about the $10,000,000 life insurance policy reminded me of the handwritten notes I'd seen in the Senator's office, which Elena had asked me to retrieve. Sitting with the mail room guys triggered an inspiration for a safe and painless way to obtain it.

Lockjaw and Ernie were still standing in front of me. I tapped Ernie on the shoulder, stifling the urge to look away as he turned his facial hardware toward me. "Ernie," I said, "are you going back to the office?"

"Uh...." He glanced at Lockjaw to see if it was all right to talk to me.

"I'll give you a call," I said. "I want to ask you to help me with something."

"I dunno."

I tried the same approach that had worked the night before. "It's about the murder investigation."

Lockjaw flashed me a look and turned sideways, so that no one would know he was talking to me. "Now don't you be dragging Ernie into any of your crazy schemes!" he whispered. "I heard about what happened last night with another dead body on the floor. And in the Senator's office! Now they're trying to find out how you got in."

"How do they know it was me?"

"They don't, but I do. Who else would do such a crazy thing?"

"You want to help me find out who killed Babylon, don't you?"

"Nobody killed Babylon, Pete. He just up and died. That's what life is like. Can't you accept that?"

"No, I can't accept it, not in this case. There's something going on here, I feel it. I need your help."

"Let it alone."

Suddenly Patsy nudged me with her elbow. "Don't look now," she said, "but either you are being singled out for unwanted attention or the Lesser Evil is making a pass at me." I looked up in time to see Art Valunos, who was still standing near the front of the room, staring in our direction as spoke with another man, who was pointing at me over the crowd. The other man was his serious-looking acquaintance from the night before, the undertaker who'd been summoned to dispose of my body. He stared at me with his cavernous eyes and nodded his head as he pointed, as if to say, "That's the wise guy I saw by the elevators."

"Do you know that guy with Valunos?" asked Patsy.

"We've met."

"Well, I have to tell you," she said, starting in on one of her diatribes—

But I was already heading for the exit. Something told me that unless I was careful, before too long I might get a chance to practice my impersonation of a dead man under real life conditions. The vendetta would have to wait.

11.

I looked over my shoulder more than once as I headed back to my car, but there was no sign of the friendly undertaker. And when I cruised down North Broad Street towards home, there were no wise guys trying to turn my Toyota Corolla into a hearse. Not that I expected old Raccoon-eyes to pursue me in so crude a fashion. No drive-by shootings, no hit and runs, no muscle-bound goons working me over in a dark alley. No, this was undoubtedly a man of subtlety and discretion who would wait for the right moment and then dispose of my body without leaving a trace. I was afraid to go home, but what choice did I have? I wasn't sure whether Valunos or anybody else at the firm even knew where I lived, but they did know where I worked. And I knew that if I wasn't at the Pickwick Club by seven o'clock that evening, I'd have to add Niko to the list of people who were trying to kill me.

I took a nap and when I woke up I was still dog tired. Stumbling from the couch into the shower, I tried to get a handle on all the things I had to accomplish. My priorities came right out of the House That Jack Built—to enlist Madison to help look for McVeigh to track down the surveillance tape to clear my name to keep Elena from spilling her guts to the cops—and if that wasn't enough I somehow had to retrieve those handwritten notes I'd found in the Senator's office. That was actually my highest priority since it seemed so important to Elena. I clearly remembered finding the notes in the Senator's file cabinet in the folder marked "To be Filed." They seemed to be his notes of a recent meeting of the firm's Executive Committee—there were some names and numbers on the page that didn't mean anything to me when I saw them, but I had a pretty good idea whom "Geoff G" referred to—and after hearing Patsy's story about the $10,000,000 loan and the $10,000,000 life insurance policy, I couldn't help but wonder if those notes would shed some light on Neil Babylon's demise. But how was I going to get hold of that file? With Valunos on the warpath and the undertaker in hot pursuit, I couldn't very well go back and start nosing around in the Senator's office. At the funeral, sitting behind Lockjaw and Ernie, it struck me that I could hire Ernie to make a copy of the file. I knew it wouldn't be hard to convince him to work for me. He'd already shown his willingness to bend the rules, and now that trout season was coming he would probably need a little extra cash to have all those fishhooks removed from his eyebrows.

The more I thought about this idea, the more I liked it. To accomplish everything I wanted to accomplish, I would need an assistant, and even more than that—I would need a mole. I needed someone who could operate inside the firm, making copies of documents and getting me in and out without being arrested. True, Ernie looked like something out of Ripley's Believe It Or Not and he was definitely a little understocked in the cognition department. But who else could I turn to? This was not rocket science, or even Popular Mechanics. And I had the feeling that with Ernie the price would be right.

Photocopying is usually a dime a page, so I figured I could get him to do the work I needed done for about ten bucks. That was my first major miscalculation.

"Ernie," I said when I reached him on the phone, "I appreciated you helping me out yesterday. Getting me in to see Patsy and all."

"No problem, man."

"I guess you heard what happened last night."

"Yeah, sort of. Lockjaw told me Valunos was pissed."

"Well," I said, "don't worry. They won't find out who let me in, at least not from me."

"We figured that."

"Ernie, I didn't want to talk about this at the funeral, but I was wondering if you'd like to earn a little extra cash."

"I don't know," he said. "Depends."

"I just need a copy of something. A piece of paper I found in Senator Squires's office."

He lowered his voice to a whisper. "You're crazy, man. I could lose my job."

"You won't lose your job," I assured him, "because they'll never find out. All you have to do is make a copy of this one item and put it in an envelope and leave it for me with the guard downstairs. Nobody will ever know."

"How much?"

I was feeling generous. "Ten bucks."

He wasted no time thinking it over. "Twenty-five."

"Come on, Ernie!" I said. "All you have to do is—"

"Actually, I'm thinking in terms of fifty."

"For fifty dollars I could get it copied on parchment by Benedictine monks!"

"It's fifty or nothing. And you better tell me what it is I'm supposed to copy, because I can't hang on this phone much longer."

I was seething but I knew I had no choice. "All right, I'll pay you fifty," I agreed. And then I had a sudden impulse that turned out to be another big mistake. "But for fifty I want it hand delivered."

"Okay, where do you live?"

I hesitated. "That's all right. On second thought I'll pick it up."

"No, I can't leave it hanging around here. Where do you want me to bring it?"

In a moment of weakness I told him I worked at the Pickwick Club and he insisted on bringing the package over that night so he could collect his fifty dollars. Of course at that time I couldn't foresee who would be sitting around the bar when he arrived.

After we hung up I opened a can of Dinty Moore beef stew—one of my favorite dishes, and one of the best features of being single—and bolted it down with a bottle of Yuengling lager. Then I pulled on one of my dark navy turtlenecks—the kind I wear when I play at the Pickwick—and headed up the street. It was still early, but I had an errand to run on my way to work.

ZuLu's is a smoky, seedy joint with a circular bar in the middle and a small stage for the dancers in the middle of the bar. Depressed-looking men from all walks of life sat around the bar sipping Budweisers from the bottle while semi-naked women pirouetted on the stage or worked their way around the bar shaking them down for tips. It wasn't hard to blend in with the crowd. I ordered a Bud and carefully surveyed each of the dancers, concluding that Madison was not among them. And neither was there any sign of McVeigh, though I noticed a few guys with their tongues hanging out who looked like they might have been friends of his. I picked up my beer and stepped toward the back of the room, where a group of off-duty dancers sat in a booth smoking cigarettes under a hand-made sign that said RESERVED FOR GO GO DANCERS. A frizzy-haired blonde glanced toward me and I smiled but she looked the other way, probably on the authority of another sign over the booth that said NO, I'M NOT INTERESTED IN HEARING YOUR LIFE STORY. A little impolite, I thought, but how could I blame her? I wasn't even interested in hearing my life story. Anyway, Madison was nowhere to be seen.

I took a seat at the bar and before long a willowy young thing clad only in G-string and pasties was cozying up to me like a cat on a cold night. "Hi!" she purred. "I'm Amber."

"Hi, Amber," I said. "I really enjoyed your dancing."

That was a lie, of course, since I'd only arrived about two minutes before. But it earned me a big smile. "Oh, thank you!"

"Very professional. You must have studied dancing in school."

"You know," she confessed, "I never did!"

"That's amazing," I said. "By the way, do you know a dancer named Madison?"

Her smile vanished. "Why is she so popular all of a sudden?"

"I don't know. Is she? Has somebody else been looking for her?"

"Yeah. About an hour ago there was another guy asking for her. What's she got that I don't?"

"What did this guy look like?"

"I don't remember."

I pulled a five dollar bill out of my pocket, and she snatched it and tucked it into her G-string before I could blink. "Sort of a skinhead type?"

"Yeah, that describes him. He a friend of yours?"

"Just an acquaintance. So is Madison going to be here tonight?"

"That's what your skinhead friend wanted to know. Only we're not allowed to give out that information." She eyed me up and down. "Too many weirdoes."

I slipped her another five. "Couldn't you make an exception for me?"

"You look more like the rule than the exception," she said, sidling away with my ten bucks. "But if you leave your number with the bartender maybe Madison'll call you the next time she comes in."

It was good advice, though not worth ten dollars. In fact it was what I was going to do anyway. I wrote a little note to Madison on one of my cards—"Come and see me at the Pickwick. Urgent"—and left it with the bartender. Then I finished my beer and headed down the street toward the Pickwick Club. My visit to ZuLu's had made me feel fortunate that I worked where I did. But ZuLu's did have its strong points. For example, I thought of the sign over the dancers' booth and considered whether to put something similar over the piano bar in the Pickwick—NO, I'M NOT INTERESTED IN HEARING YOUR LIFE STORY—or maybe a whole series of signs that could change depending on the situation. NO, I'M NOT INTERESTED IN HEARING YOUR VIEWS ON HEIDEGGER. NO, I'M NOT INTERESTED IN HEARING THE WANAMAKERS LINGERIE COMMERCIAL FROM THE EARLY SEVENTIES. NO, I'M NOT INTERESTED IN LOOKING FOR ANY SURVEILLANCE TAPES. That last sign was the most important. If I'd had that one over the piano on Tuesday night maybe I'd be able to walk down the street without looking over my shoulder every ten steps. I decided to ask Niko if he had a piece of cardboard and a magic marker.

But when I stepped inside the club I knew it was too late. There loomed Bardahl on one of the barstools beside the piano, leaning on his gargantuan elbows as he spread the *Daily News* across the lid. He pretended to ignore me as I sat down and started to play. "Well," he finally said to no one in particular. "It says here the police have completed their investigation of Neil Babylon's death. The Medical Examiner concluded that he died of natural causes and the case has been officially closed."

Fortunately, Brian O'Dolan had already taken up his customary post at the end of the bar next to Jim Hively and Rhoda the bird woman. Since Bardahl had introduced one of his favorite topics—death—he leapt into the conversation without missing miss a beat. "Everyone dies of natural causes," O'Dolan pointed out. "Even murder victims. For example, isn't it natural to die if you're poisoned with arsenic, or strangled, or shot in the head?"

"Or stabbed through the heart," added Rhoda bitterly, as if from personal experience.

"Of course it is," O'Dolan answered himself. "And therefore, the idea that the police closed their investigation based on such a conclusion is absurd."

"Ridiculous," Hively agreed.

"The police never investigate the real crimes," declared Rhoda.

Bardahl tried to ignore the regulars, but as I had learned long before, it was a losing battle. Sitting across from him at the piano bar, they naturally assumed he was there to get drunk and listen to their maunderings. For my part, I wished I could escape from the whole lot of them. How can a piano player be expected to do his job with all these jackasses yammering at him as if he were just another drunk hanging out at the bar? I closed my eyes and concentrated on the music I was playing (the bird woman had requested "Miss Otis Regrets," a Cole

Porter tune about a debutante who murders her lover after surprising him with another woman), drawing out the harmonies as I improvised new melodic variations, modulating into remote keys, even sliding into a medley of similar songs. Anything I could think of to claim a little mental space for myself in this madhouse.

But when I opened my eyes I had two new complications to deal with. Seated next to the bird woman—and directly across from Bardahl—was my friend the undertaker, wearing the same neatly buttoned knit shirt and dark sports coat I had seen him in the night before. And lurking uncomfortably by my side was the gangly figure of Ernie from the mail room. In his hand he held an envelope, which he seemed eager to shove in front of my face.

"Ernie!" I said, desperate to make this delivery look like a routine transaction. "How you doing? Got a letter for me?"

"Yeah," he said. "I found what you wanted. And something—"

"Hey, thanks a million!" I exclaimed, snatching the envelope from his hand. "It's been such a long time since I've heard from my Mom!"

"No, man, this isn't—"

"She's been sick, you know. But she promised to send me her recipe for chicken tamale pie, and I'll bet anything that's what's in this envelope."

A light bulb seemed to go off over Ernie's head. But even with all his exterior wiring, I couldn't be sure that it was brighter than 40 watts. "Yeah," he said, "but—"

"I think I'll just fold it up and stick it in here"—shoving it into the inside breast pocket of my jacket—"so it doesn't get lost."

I brought my wallet out with the same motion and quickly found a fifty dollar bill which I slipped into his hand.

"I wanted to tell you," he said, a little slowly, as if he was trying to be clever and it took extra voltage, "there's more. And like, fifty, man, fifty isn't—"

The bastard wanted to haggle. He knew I was desperate to get him out of there and he wanted to haggle in front of a cop and a Mafia undertaker. I felt like grabbing his nose ring and plugging it into a wall socket.

"Sixty," I said. "That's what she was on her last birthday. You'd never know it, would you?"

"No, man. I think she's a lot older than that. I think she's about a hundred."

"My Mom? How could you say that about my Mom?" I slipped my hand around his wrist and pulled him down towards me. "You can't tell me my Mom looks a day over sixty!"

Luckily we were now within whispering range. "Listen, you idiot," I said, "you take that fifty and get out of here, and if you're lucky and I don't break you in half I'll give you another ten tomorrow. Now get out of here!"

He pulled away, smirking, and took a step backwards. Then he gave me a little wave good-bye and disappeared.

When I looked up everyone at the piano bar was pretending not to have noticed my little encounter with Ernie. Bardahl and the undertaker were also pretending not to have noticed each other. Their faces bobbed and weaved around their drinks—Bardahl was sipping his usual Coors Light and the undertaker had ordered a martini—as each of them tried to focus his eyes somewhere other than directly across from where he sat.

"Any requests?" asked O'Dolan, as if he were hosting a private party.

Bardahl looked at me. "Yeah, I've got a request," he said. "Why not let the rest of us take a peek at that recipe you just had hand delivered? I'll bet your Mom makes the best chicken tamale pie this side of Tijuana."

"Mom's real sensitive about sharing her recipes," I said. "Unless you have a search warrant, of course."

"Come on, Cloud. I just want to copy down the recipe and take it home to my wife."

"You've got a wife?"

"I've got a wife if you've got a Mom."

The undertaker thought that was funny, though he didn't exactly laugh. He said "Heh, heh," like a character in a comic book.

"I meant a request for a song," O'Dolan said.

"Here's one," said the undertaker. His voice was thin and high-pitched, like a radio evangelist's. He looked at me. "How about 'I Remember You'?"

"He can play anything," said O'Dolan.

I played, but I felt a chill settling through me that I may never be able to forget. *I remember you.* He was eyeing me like a taxidermist at a petting zoo.

O'Dolan seemed determined to draw the shy newcomer out of his shell. "You know," he said, "he's not just an ordinary piano player."

The undertaker shrugged.

"He used to be a successful attorney."

"No shit."

"At the Rittenhouse firm. Where the managing partner was found dead the other day."

"Neil Babylon," added the bird woman.

Bardahl leaned forward and looked straight at the undertaker for the first time. "You've heard of Neil Babylon?"

"I read the papers," said the undertaker.

"All right, then," said O'Dolan, "if you read the papers you know the police have closed the case. They say Babylon died of natural causes, whatever that means. But we're not the police and we can continue our investigation for as long as we want. So let me ask you"—he was looking at the undertaker—"who do you think killed him?"

The undertaker shifted uncomfortably on his barstool, casting his raccoon eyes from side to side, and for a moment I thought he was going to walk out. Instead he held out his empty glass to signal the cocktail waitress for another martini. "I think it was somebody who knew him," he finally said in his high, dry voice. "Probably somebody who used to work at the firm."

"Interesting," said O'Dolan. "Why somebody who used to work there? Couldn't it have been somebody who still works there?"

"Whoever killed Babylon knew his way around the firm, right?"

Everyone nodded in agreement.

"But the people who still work there would've known they'd be the prime suspects, you know what I mean? So if they wanted to kill him, wouldn't they find a way to do it somewhere else?"

O'Dolan seemed convinced. "Instead of right in the middle of a firm reception."

"Exactly."

"It was the wife," said Rhoda, shaking her head. "You guys just don't get it, do you? It was the wife."

"The wife used to work there," Jim Hively observed, and there were nods of approval all around. This was starting to sound like a lynch mob.

I felt obliged to point out the basic flaw in the argument. "It hasn't been established that anybody killed Babylon."

They all ignored me—one of the hazards of playing the voice of reason to an audience of drunks—and went on with their investigation. "So," Bardahl said, with a sly glance in my direction, "it was somebody who used to work there but doesn't anymore. Maybe somebody who had a score to settle against Babylon."

"My idea exactly," said the undertaker.

"In other words," said Jim Hively, "one of the many people Babylon screwed during his long career as a son of a bitch."

Hively's face turned the color of a Harvard T-shirt. "Didn't you used to work there?" asked O'Dolan.

"That was a long time ago," Hively stammered. "Before they moved to the new building. I've never even been in that office."

"That rules you out," the undertaker assured him. "The person I'm talking about would have been up there more recently, so he'd know how to get in and out."

"Right," Hively agreed. "That's right."

"And after the murder," continued the undertaker, "what would he do next? Maybe he'd return to the scene of the crime, snoop around some of the partners' offices trying to dig up dirt so he could blackmail the firm in case they caught on to him. You know what I mean?"

"Yeah."

"He might do that."

"Right!"

"Now here's a funny thing," said the undertaker. "I happen to know there was a guy at the firm last night who was snooping around in one of the partners' offices and when he was about to get caught he laid down on the floor and played dead."

"Played dead?"

"Yeah. Just laid himself down on the floor and pretended he was dead. With his face down so nobody could recognize him, you know what I mean? And then he disappeared right before the undertaker arrived."

Bardahl squinted skeptically across the bar. "How do you know all this?"

"Cause I was the undertaker. And let me tell you something. As a rule, undertakers don't take kindly to that sort of crap. They don't like the dead people to get up and walk away before they get there. It's bad for business." He shook his head, apparently in sympathy for himself. "And it sort of makes your flesh crawl, you know what I mean? Especially when you realize you ran into the deceased in the elevator on the way into the building."

"Then you know who it was?" asked Hively.

"I do now." All his listeners leaned forward, and I stepped on the soft pedal hoping to hear what he would say. "But I'm keeping that information to myself."

There were groans of disappointment, but to my relief the undertaker refused to take his story any farther. "This would explain a rumor I heard today," said Bardahl. "They say there's a videotape floating around that could be embarrassing to Senator Squires."

The undertaker, who had enjoyed being in the spotlight, seemed suddenly taken aback. "What kind of videotape?" he demanded.

"I don't know," said Bardahl. "You know who was snooping around the office. Maybe you ought to ask him."

His face darkened, and for a second I thought he would leap over the piano and choke it out of me. But I was no less confused than he was. The only videotape I knew about—the one I had lifted from Babylon's office—would have been highly embarrassing to Babylon, but not to the Senator except in his capacity as a member of the human race. Was there another one I didn't know about? In any event the undertaker wasn't about to bring me into it. For some reason he didn't want the others to know that I was the corpse who had eluded him the night before. He ignored Bardahl and turned away from me, waving to the waitress for another martini.

Brian O'Dolan took this opportunity to give the conversation a philosophical turn. The undertaker's story had everything—death, an apparent resurrection, a whiff of political corruption—everything O'Dolan needed to build a meditation on the futility of life in a decadent age. "What could be more characteristic of our declining civilization," he began—but before you could say *Zeitgeist* his speech was derailed by the arrival of another surprise visitor.

It was the lovely Madison, responding to the note I'd left at ZuLu's. She was wearing her street clothes rather than professional attire and carrying a canvas tote bag, but she looked so sexy and beautiful that she drew at least a sidelong glance from every man in the Pickwick. Even the undertaker, cold fish though he was, couldn't take his eyes off her, and I doubt if he was sizing her up for a coffin. As for me, I thought back to the night McVeigh had followed her into the club. This time it was my turn for some theatrics.

When Madison glided up beside the piano, I stood up to embrace her with a long, passionate kiss. There was laughter and scattered applause from the crowd. Fortunately she played along, as I had played along with her on that other occasion, and I was able to whisper a few sweet nothings in her ear.

"Thanks for coming over," I said. "We can't talk, there are people at the bar listening to every word. But I need your help. Write down your phone number and leave it for me with the bartender at ZuLu's."

"What's going on?"

"I can't explain. Don't hang around here, just go back to ZuLu's and leave me your phone number. I'll call you later. After midnight."

"No problem."

She smiled sweetly and I kissed her again. I realized I wasn't just acting, and I hoped she wasn't either.

"Go on, now," I whispered, and she headed for the door.

When I turned around to sit back down at the piano I found my way blocked by Bardahl, who stood so close that I could count the razor nicks on his double chin. "What are you running here, Cloud? A drug operation or a call girl ring?"

"I'm just the piano player."

"First you get an envelope from the orange-haired freak, and I'm thinking drugs. Now you're whispering directions to this whore that you seem to be making out with every time I come in here. What the hell's going on?"

"I told you, I'm just the piano player."

"You heard that dirt bag," Bardahl said. "The firm is setting you up as the fall guy again, only this time it's the big one."

"I don't understand why they would want to do that. Aren't they claiming there wasn't any murder? How can they set me up for a crime that wasn't committed?"

"Stranger things have happened. All I know is, you better find out who the real killer is before it turns out to be you."

"I really don't want to stick my nose under that tent."

Bardahl laughed. "Your nose is already so far under the tent they're selling tickets to it."

He stood aside and I squeezed back onto the piano bench to resume the tune I'd interrupted. But when I peered over the piano bar I felt a little queasy. There sat Hively and O'Dolan and Rhoda the bird woman and a couple of other random barflies, and the undertaker's martini stood untouched on the bar. But the undertaker himself was nowhere to be seen. He must have followed Madison out the door.

12.

I fled the Pickwick at the stroke of midnight and headed around the block to ZuLu's. Same smoky atmosphere, same loud music, same paunchy, depressed clientele. Only at this late hour the floor had evidently been turned over to second-string talent. The young thing—she wasn't a day over forty—who was now wrapping herself around the dancing pole had a distinctly bovine appearance, with a large tattoo—or was it a brand?—on one of her pendulous breasts. Neither Madison nor Amber were anywhere in sight. Nor did I notice McVeigh or the undertaker, which was a shame. They had so much in common. If I introduced them, maybe I would get lucky and they would kill each other.

The bartender was a friendly but jaded type who readily handed me the note Madison had left with him. "You're not the skinhead so I can give this to you," he said.

"Was the skinhead in here tonight?"

"Didn't see him."

"What about another guy? About fifty, sort of fat, sunken eyes?"

"Yeah, right." He rolled his eyes around the bar.

I laughed. "What time did Madison leave?"

"Usual time."

At least that told me she had made it safely back to work without being intercepted by the undertaker or McVeigh. I decided to call her as soon as I got home.

As I walked the six blocks to my apartment I thought about what Bardahl had said about the undertaker's visit to the Pickwick. *The firm is setting you up as the fall guy again, only this time it's the big one. You better find out who the real killer is before it turns out to be you.* Of course I still didn't know if there had been a killer. That might have been no more than a preconception of the anti-Squires cabal that Bardahl seemed to be working for. But if the undertaker—undoubtedly with Valunos's encouragement—was setting me up to take the rap as the murderer, the firm must have had reason to believe that a murder had been committed, even if they were still denying it. Maybe Bardahl was right. Maybe I had stumbled far enough into this quagmire that the only way I could avoid being buried was to find the killer myself. That was a dangerous, possibly violent path I had been trying to avoid.

But when I opened the door to my apartment, I knew that the turning point had already been passed. The place had been ransacked from one end to the other, and everything I owned was strewn around like the debris from a train wreck. Every book had been thrown off its shelf, every piece of clothing ripped out of the closet. The drawers had been emptied, the shelves toppled, even the garbage was scattered all over the floor. My emotions quickly ran the gamut from fear—were they still in the apartment?—to anger, to bewilderment. Was it robbery, or revenge, or some kind of warning? Or had they been searching for something?

It didn't take long to figure it out. The only things missing, so far as I could tell in that chaotic mess, were my videotapes. I only had a few—a double-cassette edition of "Braveheart" (one of my prized possessions), the documentary records of my kids' birthday parties, and a couple of shows I had taped off PBS. And every tape I had in the apartment was gone. So it was pretty clear what had happened. When the undertaker suddenly left the Pickwick, he wasn't going after Madison. He had heard what Bardahl said about some video that was embarrassing to the Senator and decided that I had snatched it from the Senator's office the night before. Knowing that I had to play until midnight, he dispatched a couple of his goons to the Coolidge House to ransack my apartment, which would have the added benefit of teaching me a much-needed lesson about the proper behavior of corpses.

But fortunately for me, and unfortunately for the undertaker, the only unusual video I had was the porno tape I'd found in Babylon's office. That one implicated Babylon, not the Senator, and in any event it could not have been found in my apartment. I had given it to Elena that morning.

There was a good chance the search party would return after they tired of watching birthday parties and nature documentaries. I knew I'd better get out of that shambles I called home before the next bomb went off. But where could I go at one o'clock in the morning?

A reasonably attractive man in the prime of life should never be at a loss for a place to spend the night. There is a warm bed waiting for him somewhere. I gave the matter some thought and decided against calling Madison. After all, we had only just met, and I didn't even know her real name. Her telephone number was literally the only thing I knew about her.

So I grabbed my toothbrush and a clean shirt, checked my answering machine—which also seemed to be malfunctioning—and headed down the hall to my old girlfriend Theresa's.

"Wake up, Sleeping Beauty!"

I pulled the pillow over my head, rolled over on the narrow couch and tried to go back to sleep. Sleeping Beauty! Was this a dream or a fairy tale? Be careful, I told myself. That was not the voice of a lovely princess. It was the raspy voice of an old crone, possibly a witch offering a poisoned apple.

"Come on, lardass! It's almost noon!"

The voice belonged to Theresa, and I was lying crumpled on her short and miserably uncomfortable couch. I peeked out from beneath the pillow and found her looming over me in a cloud of smoke. In one hand she held a broom and in the other—in lieu of a poisoned apple—the inevitable cigarette.

"I've got cleaning to do in here."

"Okay. I'll get up. Just give me a chance to put my pants on."

Theresa had been kind enough to open her door to me at one o'clock in the morning and offer a pillow and a blanket and a spot on the bed of nails she called her couch. That is, I could sleep on the couch as long as I didn't mind sharing it with a pair of sadistic cats who took turns digging their fangs into my bare toes throughout the night. I pulled on my trousers and limped to the kitchen table, where Theresa had already poured me a cup of hot coffee.

"Is Elena coming over?" I asked her.

"Yeah, she called. She's coming for lunch."

Theresa finished her cleaning in the living room—undoubtedly a delegation of cousins from South Philly would soon be arriving to argue over what soap operas to watch on TV—while I drank my coffee and tried to collect my thoughts. It was pretty clear that my visit to the Senator's office had touched a nerve. Valunos had dispatched the undertaker to put an end to my shenanigans, if not my life, and thanks to Bardahl the undertaker had concluded that I had something on the Senator that I was hiding in my apartment. Was it just a coincidence that Bardahl and the undertaker had shown up at the Pickwick at the same time? Why had Bardahl gone out of his way to plant the notion that I was harboring a videotape damaging to the Senator? And what was the smiling undertaker going to do next?

I found my jacket and the envelope Ernie had brought to the Pickwick the night before. Inside was the memo I'd seen in the Senator's office. It still seemed pretty cryptic:

EC - 1/8
OF extend loan
Bank fees guar $1M - 5 years
5 x .40 = 2M
TR -$1M max (no share)
Bank Comm. - mtg 2/15
Have to know by 2/1
TALK TO GEOFF G.

The EC was the Executive Committee, which must have met on January 8. Somebody named "OF"— and I didn't know of any partner with that name or initials—must have told them something about extending a bank loan, presumably the $10 million loan from Third Millennium that would come due on March 1. Or would have come due, if Neil Babylon hadn't been considerate enough to generate a timely payoff under the key-man life insurance policy. Who "TR" was, and the Bank Committee, and what they needed to know by February 1, I couldn't begin to guess. In any event my thoughts were interrupted by Theresa, who had stepped into the kitchen to attend to some marinara sauce that was simmering on the stove.

"Now," she said, "what did you say happened to your apartment?"

"It was ransacked."

"A break-in? What'd they take?"

"Nothing much. They were looking for something. Remember that videotape I gave Elena yesterday? I think that's what they were looking for."

"The porno tape? It must be pretty good."

"I'm not sure they were really looking for that. They might have been looking for another one."

"How many porno tapes do you have anyway?"

Before I could answer, I realized that Elena had let herself into the apartment. She must have been surprised to find me sitting there, unshaven and in my undershirt, deep in a discussion of pornography with her mother. "What's the matter?" she asked.

"He slept here," answered Theresa.

"He slept here?"

"On the couch. My apartment was ransacked."

"They were looking for porno tapes," Theresa explained.

"Oh, my God!" Elena's face wore a troubled look I had seen only once or twice before. She pulled her coat off and sat quickly down at the table as if she needed the support. "I think I know why."

"Why?"

"Didn't you get my message?"

"What message?"

She took a deep breath. "That tape you gave me—"

"The one with Babylon on it?"

"Yes. I watched it, and guess what?"

"It's an out-take from a snuff film."

"Worse," she said. "The woman he's having sex with is Lou Squires's wife."

I had to stand up. And then I had to sit down again. All the little pieces were falling into place, and for me it was a very dangerous place to be. I told Elena the whole story about what had happened the night before, and when I finished she looked more troubled than ever.

"I left you a voice mail message," she said. "Didn't you hear it?"

"No. I tried to listen but the machine was malfunctioning."

We locked eyes on the same alarming thought. Without saying a word, we ran over to my apartment and tried to listen to the message. But it was as we feared: the little cassette tape in the answering machine was gone.

"What did you say on the message?" I asked Elena.

"I'm trying to think. I think I said what I just told you. That I'd watched the tape and the woman having sex with Babylon was the Senator's wife. I know her."

"That's what I was afraid you were going to say." I allowed myself one last glance around the wreckage of my apartment. "Let's get the hell out of here."

Back at Theresa's kitchen table with the door bolted and a couple of fresh cups of coffee in front of us, we felt a little better, but not much.

"Well," I observed, "at least the ransacker knows why he didn't find what he came for. And he won't be able to find it unless he figures out who you are."

"That's a comforting thought."

"Do you think they'll recognize your voice?"

"A lot of people might recognize my voice. Half the attorneys in town—and half the criminals—have been in my courtroom. Sometimes I'm on TV."

"The first thing they'll do is play the tape for the Senator. Do you think he'll know you?"

She shook her head. "I doubt it, but—oh my God, what if they play it for Geoff?" Meaning her husband.

"Don't worry," counseled Theresa. "The only voice he ever hears is his own."

"And they might," Elena added. "Because he's a lot more involved with those people than I thought."

After the funeral Elena had persuaded Geoff to take her to lunch at the Four Seasons and before the entrees arrived she confronted him about his recent lies and evasions, forcing him to tell her about his connections with the Rittenhouse firm. Of course we knew he was friendly not only with Babylon but also with the Senator and Valunos and several of the other partners. But it turned out he knew quite a bit more than either of us had imagined—he even knew all about Tom Riordan. It seems he'd invested in one of Riordan's shady real estate deals and was none too happy with the results.

I handed her the Senator's cryptic notes of the Executive Committee meeting. "This is the item I told you about yesterday."

"How did you get this so fast? Did you go up there again?"

"I'll never tell."

She turned it over in her hands like a judge scrutinizing some new document that a unscrupulous attorney was trying to put into evidence. "'Talk to Geoff G,'" she read. "I wish I'd had this when I was cross-examining him."

"Can you figure it out?"

"It fits in with some of the stuff Geoff told me," she said. "The bank loan would be the $10 million loan from Third Millennium. 'OF' is Oscar Feierabend—the president of Third Millennium. Geoff told me there was a power struggle going on between Babylon and Valunos over whether the firm would keep representing Tom Riordan against Third Millennium."

"Was Riordan suing Third Millennium?"

"Indirectly. Riordan owns a minority stock interest in Harrison State Bank and he's been trying to get control of the rest."

I couldn't help but marvel at the grandeur of Tom Riordan's greedy ambitions. "That's a pretty big bank," I said.

"It's the second largest state-chartered bank in Pennsylvania, according to Geoff. And Third Millennium is also trying to get control of it. The other stockholders of Harrison want to go with Third Millennium but Riordan—represented by Babylon—has been blocking the deal and litigating with the other shareholders over it."

I was beginning to see how everything fit together. "So Feierabend offered to extend the loan if Babylon would drop the case."

"It's a little worse than that," Elena explained. "Third Millennium needs a favorable ruling by the State Banking Commission before they can take over Harrison. Feierabend offered to extend the loan for another five years if the Senator would make sure the State Banking Commission approved the merger."

"In other words, if the Senator would arrange politically what Babylon was trying to prevent through litigation."

"Exactly." Elena tilted her head ever so slightly and treated me to that ironic smile that the trial attorneys who practice before her dread more than the plague. "Now that doesn't sound like a conflict of interest, does it?"

"Not at the Rittenhouse firm," I laughed. "I remember they had a saying: 'There's no such thing as a conflict of interest between two paying clients.' But still it's hard to believe that Babylon would have gone along with it."

"He didn't. According to Geoff, he was bitterly opposed, and that was what led to the most recent feud between him and Valunos. Valunos supported the Feierabend proposal."

"Which could only mean one thing." I said. "That the Senator wanted it to happen. Valunos always pushes the Senator's agenda."

I pulled my chair beside Elena's and we took another look at that handwritten memo. "All right," I said. "There was an Executive Committee meeting on January 8. Oscar Feierabend was present, or more likely Valunos presented his proposal. He offered to extend the loan, and look at this—'Bank fees guar $1M - 5 years.' He must have offered another quid pro quo: that the bank would bring a million dollars worth of legal business to the firm every year for the next five years. But then look at this calculation—'5 x .40 = 2M.' What do you suppose that means?"

Elena and I stared at the sheet in baffled silence until Theresa, who had been spraying the tabletop with some foul-smelling disinfectant, peered over my shoulder and quickly did the math. "Five times forty percent of a million is two million," she said.

"You're right!" I exclaimed. "But what does it mean?"

"How the hell would I know?"

We studied the memo again in light of Theresa's explanation. "I think I know," I said. "Forty percent is the Senator's share of the fees for business he brings to the firm. It must have been understood that if the Senator rendered the desired service with the State Banking Commission, Third Millennium would be regarded as his client and he would get forty percent of all the fees paid by the bank over the next five years."

"I told you the Senator is a great man," said Theresa.

"Two million dollars isn't bad for somebody who never sets foot in the office," Elena agreed.

"And look at this," I said. "The 'TR - $1M max (no share)' must refer to what they expected to collect from Riordan. A mere one million dollars—with no share for the Senator."

"Why no share for the Senator?"

"Riordan was Babylon's client. The Senator wouldn't have gotten any share of that business."

Elena was shaking her head. "What I'd like to know is why they were supposed to call Geoff. Do you think this is the Senator's handwriting?"

"It looks like the same person's as the rest of the page."

"Why would Lou Squires be calling Geoff about this?"

"Listen," said Theresa—she was still wielding her disinfectant-sprayer, so I paid close attention—"Cousin Mike is coming over in a few minutes to watch 'Days of Our Lives.' His TV set is broken. So you kids are going to have to keep it quiet for a little while." She gave me a bawdy wink. "You could use the bedroom if you want to."

Elena looked at her watch. "I've got to be going."

"No, wait," I pleaded. "I want to hear the rest of the story. How did it all turn out? Who won the power struggle?"

Theresa laughed out loud. "Who won the power struggle? Babylon just got poured into a little brass canister and you're asking who won the power struggle?"

Elena was laughing along with her mother. "I told you the Senator is a great man!"

I didn't want to believe that Senator Squires—arguably the most powerful man in Philadelphia, if not in Pennsylvania—had been involved in killing Babylon, because I knew too much and he knew that I knew it. If he was a murderer he would probably make me his next victim. "You think Squires killed Babylon?"

Theresa nodded sagely, as if the issue were settled beyond all reasonable doubt. And Elena seemed to agree with the verdict. "Why not?" she asked me. "Wasn't Babylon sleeping with his wife?"

13.

Elena headed back to court just as Cousin Mike arrived. I greeted Cousin Mike, a barrel-shaped old gentleman with a shock of white hair that stood straight up four inches over his forehead, and settled into one of Theresa's overstuffed armchairs to watch the day's installment of 'Days of Our Lives.' It seems that one man, who was sleeping with another man's wife, was planning to divorce his wife so he could marry the other man's wife, but in the meantime the first man's wife contracted terminal cancer and their daughter was kidnapped by terrorists, leading to a tearful reconciliation with the wife that was interrupted by the second man's arrival at the door with an assault rifle. None of it made a lot of sense, though admittedly I was not a regular viewer and I had other things on my mind. I was trying to decide whether the facts I had learned gave Senator Squires a plausible motive to murder Neil Babylon. You can never underestimate the motivating power of sex, but it motivates everyone in a different way. Some men would murder their wife's lover, others would take him out and buy him a beer. The Senator had been married at least once before and the woman I'd seen on that videotape wasn't exactly a trophy wife. My hunch was that if the Senator had anything to do with Babylon's death his motives were financial and political rather than personal or sexual. It was conceivable that the Senator would have joined forces with Valunos to eliminate Babylon if there was no other way to avoid a default on the Third Millennium bank debt. And now this new twist made that scenario seem more likely. With Babylon's demise, the Senator would not only avoid a default and the possible collapse of the firm, but he stood to put a couple of million dollars into his own pocket. We were talking real money here. If I was going to find out who killed Babylon—and overnight I had decided that I had no choice—then I would have to learn more about Valunos and the Senator. I was already in over my head. I was the man who knew too much, but in fact I didn't know nearly enough.

Cousin Mike had fallen asleep in front of the TV. "He does it every time," said Theresa, padding in from the kitchen. "Gotta watch his show but can't stay awake long enough to get through the first set of commercials. Then for the rest of the afternoon he'll be nagging me to tell him what he missed."

"You didn't even watch it."

"Nah, I just make something up. There's a whole different version of 'Days of Our Lives' that's never been shown on TV because I just made it up to humor Cousin Mike."

I excused myself to use the telephone in the bedroom, a dimly lighted room in which I had never been before. The decor was Baroque in style, heavily religious in theme and generally reminiscent of the Spanish Inquisition. This suited my mood. If Art Valunos had lived a few hundred years ago he would have been torturing heretics with hot irons instead of doling out research assignments to junior associates. The Lesser Evil, Patsy called him, and she was at least half right. Now I needed to know more about him and his partner in crime Senator Squires. There was a great deal of information available inside the firm, and I knew only one way to get at it. And it galled me to think how much it was going to cost me. I dialed Ernie.

"Ernie, listen, I need more information."

"I don't know, man. It's tough."

"I'll pay. We can agree in advance."

Silence.

"Here's what I need," I went on. "I need all of Valunos's time sheets and telephone logs for the last couple of months. And Senator Squires's, if they exist."

"Copies?"

"No. I want to see the originals. Tomorrow's Saturday. Can you be there? I'll come up the freight elevator around nine o'clock."

Silence again. I'm thinking: this kid should have been a negotiator for the Teamsters Union.

"I'll pay," I pleaded.

"How much?"

"Fifty bucks."

"How long you gonna be here?"

"I don't know. Three hours."

"A hundred dollars an hour."

"A hundred dollars an hour? Are you nuts?"

"That's cheap for a law firm."

I slammed the phone down so hard that one of Theresa's crucifixes crashed to the floor. A dour saint whose statue stood on the dresser watched with a disapproving eye as I hurried to hang it back on the wall.

"What's going on in there?" Theresa shouted.

"Nothing! I'm almost done!"

The crucifix wouldn't stay on its hook. "Is there a trick to this?" I asked the saint, but he wasn't any help. All I got was another look of world-weary resignation.

Theresa banged on the door, which I had inadvertently locked. "What are you doing in my bedroom?" she yelled. "Open up before I call Security!"

"Just a minute!" Now the crucifix was hanging at a forty-five degree angle.

"Open up!"

I appealed again to the saint. "Why do I have to live in a world full of lunatics?"

More silence. He was as bad as Ernie. Probably trying to negotiate for a higher fee.

14.

I had one more call to make, a call that I hoped wouldn't cost as dearly as the last one. It was to the beautiful Madison, whom I confess I had dreamed about the night before. In my dream she was a waitress on a cruise ship who turned into a mermaid when I kissed her and dove into the sea. I pursued her in a lifeboat and finally caught her on a hook with my fly rod, but a giant whale leaped up, swallowing her in one gulp, and pulled me down to the bottom as I tried to reel her in. Was this a Freudian fantasy or just a jumble of Walt Disney cartoons I had watched with my kids? It fairly dripped with guilt, but there was nothing Freudian or unconscious about it. My plan was to use Madison as bait for a psychopath, and I felt guilty about that. But I did it anyway.

After I had unlocked the door and satisfied Theresa that I was not using her bedroom to engage in any unnatural or blasphemous practices, I dialed the number Madison had left at the bar. I knew it was a long shot. Why would a woman in her position hand out her phone number to a man she hardly knew? But after a couple of rings I heard the soft, unmistakable voice of my favorite mermaid.

"It's Peter Cloud," I said. "The piano player from the Pickwick."

"Oh! I'm so glad you called. I thought you were going to call last night."

"Yeah, I got a little delayed. I'll tell you about it later."

"You said you needed my help."

"There's a favor I was going to ask you. But I don't want you to feel obligated."

"I owe you a lifetime of devotion."

That was more than I could take. "I don't want you to feel obligated."

"O.K. I just want to help you. Is that better?"

I explained to Madison that I had my own reasons for wanting to track down her skinhead admirer and suggested that the next time he showed up at ZuLu's, she might agree to meet him somewhere under my watchful eye.

"We could do that this afternoon," she said. "I have his phone number."

"You have his phone number?"

"His cell phone. He left it for me the other day."

She had to start work at seven. We arranged that she would call McVeigh and offer to meet him for a drink around five at Abernathy's, a venue I had selected after considering several alternatives. It was a cheerful, well-lighted place—the kind of bar a person like McVeigh would probably hate but where Madison would be safe. On a Friday afternoon it would be crowded with office workers knocking off early for a beer before starting their weekends. It stood on a corner where I could park inconspicuously and observe people coming and going, in the kind of neighborhood where I could follow McVeigh and keep him in sight when he left the bar. Madison had no trouble grasping the game plan.

"Tell him you can only have a couple of drinks and then you have to go to work," I said, "and you'd rather not have him following you in and out of ZuLu's."

"That's against the rules," she agreed. "I could get fired."

"You've got it."

At four o'clock our plan went into action. I arrived early in my 1995 Toyota Corolla, which has the advantage of looking like every other car on the road, and found a spot in the parking lot across the street that gave me a clear view of the entrance to Abernathy's. Madison went inside and waited in a booth for her "date." I had asked her to try and find out his name, where he was from, and where he worked, but not to seem too suspicious or inquisitive. She was not to give out any information about herself, except a few false factoids I made her commit to memory.

At 4:45 McVeigh walked around the corner with a proprietorial swagger and stepped into the bar. I watched until 6:05, at which time Madison and McVeigh emerged together. They said a few parting words and Madison headed towards ZuLu's, supposedly to do some shopping before her shift began at seven. McVeigh walked in the other direction, unfortunately down a one-way street that ran the wrong way. I bolted out of my parking space and through a red light and raced around the block. At the next light I saw no sign of McVeigh. Then I caught a glimpse of him slipping into a black pickup truck that was parked near a construction site. The pickup lurched into the traffic without signaling, and the chase was on.

Up Market Street to City Hall, around the loop to the Parkway, right on 16th and onto the Vine Street Expressway. I followed close behind, dodging buses and taxicabs and sailing through one red light after another. The expressway was crowded with rush hour traffic, which only got worse when we reached the Schuylkill Expressway. I breathed a sigh of relief, knowing that for the next half hour we would be all but immobilized. But my relief was premature. Following McVeigh, even in gridlocked rush hour traffic, was like chasing a stunt man in a Bruce Willis movie. He wove in and out and sped along the shoulder, honking and shaking his fist as he squeezed his pickup through openings that looked too narrow for a motorcycle. I stayed right behind him, keeping my sun visor down so he couldn't see my face in his rearview mirror. He must have suspected something, though, because when we finally swerved off the Expressway and headed north on Roosevelt Boulevard I saw the pickup slowing down to see if I would pass. Instead I dropped back and let another car get between us. He sped up again and we navigated up the crowded Boulevard into the heart of Northeast Philadelphia— a vast wilderness of two-story brick rowhouses, strip malls and fast food joints stretching as far as the eye can see. It's a city-within-a city, mostly white, populated by cops and construction workers and teachers and beauticians, where unfortunately pickup trucks are not an uncommon sight. In fact—as I realized when I saw McVeigh's pickup turning left and disappearing into the traffic on Bustleton Pike—if you were trying to conceal a pickup truck in Philadelphia you could hardly find a better place to do it than on Bustleton Pike at 6 o'clock on a Friday night. It was getting dark now, and the street was jammed with angry commuters trying to honk their way through the intersections in their pickup trucks and SUVs. I tried following McVeigh's tail lights but after about a mile I admitted to myself that I had lost him.

Just as I was about to turn around I realized why the area looked so familiar. Tom Riordan's office and construction headquarters, from which Elena and I had lifted the environmental inspection records that got me disbarred, could not have been more than a couple of blocks away. I pulled into a Big Boy and found a Customers Only parking space around back where the Big Boy couldn't gape at me with his fatuous grin. Then I walked about two blocks farther along Bustleton and turned into the side street that led to Riordan's.

I wish I could take credit for foreseeing what happened next. Not being a detective, I can't even say I had a hunch. But there it was, parked in front of Riordan's office: a black pickup truck that looked suspiciously like the one I'd been following. I examined it more closely than I had been able to during our breakneck chase. The bed was littered with beer cans and on the rear window of the cab there was a faded bumper sticker that said, "A dirty mind is a terrible thing to waste." So far so good—definitely McVeigh's style. But was it really the same truck? There was only one way to find out.

Riordan's site is a fenced lot full of trucks and construction equipment scattered between several pre-fab storage sheds and a large cinder-block garage and welding shop where they repair the trucks and other equipment. On the edge of this eyesore stands a different kind of eyesore, a shoddy three-story office building like the ones Riordan has built all over the Philadelphia area. This where Riordan's offices are located. I slipped through a door marked "Subcontractors Entrance" and found myself in a sort of waiting room where subcontractors submitting bids or trying to collect bills are forced to pass their time on hard plastic molded chairs. The receptionist had gone home and I don't know why the door was unlocked; perhaps there had been a bid deadline late that afternoon. I could hear voices within, so I quietly slipped toward them down a hall. After a moment I came close enough to recognize Riordan's voice and his brittle laugh echoing out of an open office. I listened carefully to the man he was talking to, who had a softer, lower pitched voice. Was it McVeigh? I struggled to remember what McVeigh's voice sounded like.

"Can I help you?" Another man had appeared in the corridor, an angular black man with a beer belly and a John Deere hat.

"Is there a men's room around?"

"Yeah, right around that corner."

"Thanks."

He must have thought I was a subcontractor waiting for my bid package to be reviewed. He walked off, but I stayed put, because to follow his directions to the men's room would have taken me past the open door to Riordan's office. Instead I turned around and went back the way I came. The man in the John Deere hat came back down the hall and saw me. "What the hell are you doing?"

I nodded in a friendly fashion. "See you later."

Once outside, I could hear the man shouting and other voices joining in. Before I could think about it I was racing back towards Bustleton with two swearing construction workers running after me. One of them was John Deere and the other was a husky white guy with a shaven head. As I turned the corner at Bustleton a backward glance confirmed that the hunch I didn't have had turned out to be correct. The white guy was definitely McVeigh, and he had something in his hand that looked a lot like a crow bar.

15.

Sometimes virtue is rewarded in this world. Sometimes if you live a clean life and go to the gym regularly and don't develop a beer belly that knocks against your knees when you run you might be able to say to yourself that your virtuous life is the reason you were able to escape from that pair of thugs who wanted to hammer you into the earth. You might be able to say that to yourself, for instance, in the men's room of the Big Boy where you stand virtuously balanced on top of the toilet in a stall that says "Out of Order" because it has not been flushed in two weeks, holding your breath to keep from vomiting and also, incidentally, in case the next fellow who walks in carries a crowbar with which he intends to knock your brains out. Brains, like a dirty mind, are a terrible thing to waste, and so in an excess of caution you might hold this position for an unbearable length of time, reflecting not on your virtue but on your stupidity for letting yourself be put in this position, and by the time you climb down and step warily across the crowded Big Boy dining room it's after eight o'clock and McVeigh and his sidekick are nowhere in sight, for which you are thankful, because you're late for work and if you don't show up you're going to lose your job. You casually slip out to your car and point it in the direction of the Pickwick Club. But the thrill of escape is tempered by the realization that McVeigh, if he sincerely wants to kill you, will know right where to look.

Driving into town, I thought about the importance of what I had discovered: McVeigh worked for Riordan. I still didn't know why that was important, but I knew that it was. Two nights before, while I was playing dead on the floor of the Senator's office and Valunos was desperately calling the undertaker, McVeigh was pretending to be a maintenance man in order to gain access to Neil Babylon's office. When I unexpectedly arrived, he left carrying a toolbox that probably concealed his purpose in being there. Was he there for the same reason I was, to find those surveillance tapes that incriminated Riordan in the theft of the environmental inspection records? Or was his purpose somehow connected with the porno tape I took home with me—either to find it or to plant it there? Whatever he'd been doing there was undoubtedly at Riordan's direction. The next morning on my visit to the Rittenhouse office, I decided, I would add Riordan to my list of research topics, along with Valunos and the Senator. Then with a sinking feeling I recalled my last conversation with Ernie and realized that time was running out on this investigation. I couldn't afford Rittenhouse rates much longer.

By the time I reached the Pickwick I found myself dreading the long night ahead. Niko intercepted me at the door and chewed me out in Greek all the way back to the kitchen, where I went to hang up my coat. Luckily I can never understand much of what he says.

"Go ahead and fire me," I suggested.

"I will not!"

"You ought to fire me. I'm always late. Sometimes I don't show up at all."

"I will not fire you! Go to hell!"

My opening song was "I Should Care." Who would be first to sit down at the piano bar, I wondered—a defrocked priest, a Mafia undertaker or a homicidal maniac? As it happened, none of the people who were currently trying to kill me were there, nor were any of the regulars—other than Jim Hively, who sagged like a forlorn hulk at the far end of the piano bar, so depressed and impassive that I had come to think of him as furniture. I peered through the gloom, expecting to see McVeigh creeping toward me with a crowbar, but what I saw was only Patsy Jessup and Rick Taconelli, both already drunk, swinging giddily onto barstools with drinks in their hands. In Patsy's case I knew it would be Scotch, which is what she drinks even during business hours. Rick struck me more as the DuBonnet type, perhaps with a pinch of Pepto Bismol. This would be interesting, I thought. At one time long ago, when Jim Hively worked at Rittenhouse, he had actually dated Patsy and ended up hating her with a passion usually reserved for supernatural evil. His descent into whatever state he was in now was attributed by some to that relationship. Had Patsy or Rick even noticed Hively sitting there? I couldn't be sure. Patsy was laughing and chattering, and Rick never seemed to notice anyone but himself.

"Well, this is a surprise," I said. "Did you just get here?"

"Came over from the cocktail party," Patsy nodded. "Oh, I know what you're thinking, Pete. Quite frankly I was a little shocked myself—and you know I don't shock all that easily—

that they were even having the regular Friday afternoon cocktail party so soon after our release from the Babylonian captivity. Especially since the big man bought the farm right after the last one—when was that, Monday night?—and it was probably something he ate or drank that killed him. But I'll tell you, they didn't make the same mistake twice. No, sir, this time they had the associates line up for drinks at five o'clock like tasters at some medieval feast just in case there was poison in any of the bottles. After all, it's cheaper to hire a new associate than to replace all those liquor bottles, isn't it, Rick?"

"Huh?" Rick didn't seem to be paying attention.

"Rick's on the Hiring Committee," Patsy explained. "Or is it the Refreshment Committee? At any rate none of us partners showed up until after 5:30 and you can be sure that before we took a sip we checked to see if all the associates still had a pulse, and quite frankly that's not a slam dunk even when they're sitting at their desks. The Executive Committee scheduled a meeting so they wouldn't get to the cocktail party until after six, and Valunos was walking around with a bottle of Poland Spring. They're all afraid they're going to be next. Or I should say, they're all acting like they're afraid they're going to be next."

"Meaning what?" asked Rick.

Patsy looked at Rick as if he belonged to one of the lower orders of invertebrates. "Meaning, for those of us who have trouble following the conversation, that the one who actually killed him isn't afraid of being next, because he isn't planning to poison himself."

"And who do you think that is?" I asked.

She took a gulp of her Scotch. "Let's put it this way. At the last Executive Committee meeting, I'm told, the subject of the overdue bank loan came up. There was a long discussion around the fact that they weren't going to be able to pay it back, and finally Valunos said, 'Somebody's going to have to die to pay off this debt.'"

"Who'd you hear that one from?"

"I can't tell you. A reliable source."

A couple of other people had sat down at the bar, but Patsy talked past them and blew cigarette smoke into their faces as if she didn't acknowledge their existence. Hively sat hunched over his drink like a bear in hibernation.

"Another thing I heard," she went on, "and this is from a *very* reliable source, a friend of mine who works in the Attorney General's office—is that there's evidence that Babylon was murdered by one of the partners. Naturally the Lesser Evil thinks it was me."

"The Attorney General's office? What do they have to do with it?'

"Only that, as I'm sure you know, they're investigating Lou Squires."

I kept my eyes on the keyboard, pretending to concentrate on the song I was playing, but my mind was spinning with the reverberations of what Patsy had just said. This confirmed Elena's hunch that Bardahl's sudden reappearance stemmed from the Attorney General's investigation of Senator Squires. The AG's office was casting Babylon's death as a murder in order to gain leverage over the firm—and specifying that he was murdered by a partner, which had enormous implications.

As Patsy had observed earlier, if a partner killed Babylon the life insurance would be void and the firm would probably go down the drain. Suddenly I understood my own role in this drama—I was the sacrificial lamb that Valunos and his partners would offer up in case they had to find a murderer.

"What have you heard?" she asked.

"Me? I haven't heard anything. Just a lot of speculation."

"Like what?"

"Oh, you know, like the rumor that Babylon was found wearing a pink party dress and they're checking the rest of the Executive Committee for DNA."

"That's not true," said Rick.

"No," Patsy laughed. "The party dress was blue."

"What I meant," said Rick, "was that I'd know if they were checking the Executive Committee for DNA. I'm on the Technology Committee."

"Then you must know about the web site," I said.

"The web site?"

"You know, the Neil Babylon Murder Home Page. Patsy showed it to me the other day."

"Oh, yes. As a matter of fact, I was asked to try and track that web site down."

"As a member of the Technology Committee?"

"No, as a member of the iBusiness Committee. According to the police, it's almost impossible to trace. And nobody knows where they're getting their information."

"Do they have me listed as a suspect yet?" I asked.

"Yes, as a matter of fact." He squinted at me suspiciously. "I noticed this morning that you'd been added to the list."

By this time I was well into my next song, which I think was "Bewitched, Bothered and Bewildered," and quite frankly I was hoping that Patsy and her goofy date would look for another bar to hang around in. She was now conspiring in confidential tones with Rick, who seemed just as uncomprehending as ever. At the end of the day, I mused, how this moron ever got hired by the Rittenhouse firm would turn out to be a bigger mystery than who murdered Neil Babylon. I noticed that Father Brian O'Dolan had appeared on the barstool next to Hively. He greeted me, as he did every night, by nodding and raising his wine glass with both hands as if it were time for Holy Communion. His consoling presence apparently emboldened Hively to crank up his incredible voice and aim it in the direction of Patsy and Rick.

I don't know if I've mentioned this or not, but Jim Hively, though perhaps not profound as a thinker, has an amazing *basso profundo* voice. It is so deep, I once heard him tell O'Dolan, that when he starred as Old Black Joe in a high school production of *Show Boat,* the music teacher had to transpose the entire score down an octave in order to fit "Old Man River" into Hively's vocal range. When he opens his mouth to speak, it's like watching a distant explosion—you start to feel the vibrations long before you hear any audible sound. And so Patsy, along with everyone else within a ten-foot radius, had already caught her breath and turned towards him expectantly before his first words resounded across the piano bar.

"Has it ever occurred to you," he rumbled, "that Babylon might not have been the one they were trying to kill?"

"I beg your pardon?"

He was looking straight at Patsy. "Has it ever occurred to you that maybe they were trying to kill someone else who was at that cocktail party—like you, for instance?"

She turned a sickening shade of gray. "Why would anybody want to kill me?"

Again the voice was slow in coming but devastating in its impact. "You want the long answer or the condensed six hour version?"

"Do I know you?"

Hively laughed. "Apparently not."

She turned quickly to Rick. "Let's get out of here." And they ran out without a backward glance.

I segued into "The Lady is a Tramp," and Brian O'Dolan raised his wine glass in a silent toast to nothing in particular. "If men are from Mars and women are from Venus," he asked rhetorically, "what planet is she from?"

"The dark side of Uranus," bellowed Hively, and the two of them laughed until they had to cling to each other to keep from falling off their barstools.

The only other visitor of note that night was my good buddy Bardahl, who was getting to be enough of a regular that Brian O'Dolan treated him to a lengthy disquisition on the importance of nightly enemas. At one point I thought I heard Bardahl tell O'Dolan to "stick it up your ass," but I wasn't sure if this was an insult or merely his contribution to the discussion. In any event, after that comment Bardahl moved his own massive backside to a barstool closer to my end of the piano and sat blowing cigarette smoke into my face until it was time for my break. "What do you say you buy me a drink?" he murmured. "Over at the bar."

"I didn't know a police officer was supposed to accept gratuities."

"It's not a gratuity if I earn it, right?"

We relocated to the main bar, where Doug the bartender poured us a couple of Sierra Nevadas. "You find that surveillance tape yet?" Bardahl asked me.

"No, and I've looked for it."

"Yeah," he grunted. "That was you playing dead on the Senator's floor. I figured that out. Did you get into Babylon's office?"

"I did. And the tape wasn't there."

"What's this about another tape, with the Senator in it? You find that one?"

"I didn't find anything."

For an interminable moment he stared at me as if he were taking a long, last look before putting a slug between my eyes. "You going to the wedding?" he finally asked.

"What wedding?"

"You know what wedding. It's tomorrow night and I need to know if you're going."

"Well, for some reason I didn't get an invitation."

"You don't need an invitation to play the piano at the cocktail reception. Just show up in your tux at five o'clock and start playing."

"Why would I want to do that?"

He showed me a fine set of pointy, yellowed teeth. "It's a good chance to meet the family. Who knows? Maybe they have what you're looking for."

It was an intriguing idea, and surprisingly clever for Bardahl. "How do I know they're even going to have a piano? And where is the wedding, anyway?"

"College of Physicians. Twenty-second and Sansom. They have a piano."

"Maybe somebody else is already supposed to play it."

"Take it from me, Cloud, there isn't any piano player. I thought of that. There's a string quartet and you won't have any trouble drowning them out. The maintenance man—his name is Lester—is going to make sure your piano is unlocked and ready to go."

It turned out that Bardahl wanted some specific information about what went on at Alyssa's wedding, and for some reason he thought I was the person to collect it. Among other things, he wanted to know who was there from the Rittenhouse firm and whether the widow danced with certain of the guests. "The only problem," I pointed out, "is that a lot of these people know me. They're going to know I wasn't invited."

"You could wear a disguise."

"Right."

"Anyhow, don't worry," he said. "Nobody's going to look at the piano player."

Before I went back for my last set I called my friend DeWayne Hastings, an aging hipster who looks like Thelonious Monk and plays the piano ten times better than I can, who sometimes fills in when I can't make it to work. Fortunately DeWayne was available the next night, which was the night of the wedding. I didn't bother to tell Niko. There would be plenty of time for that. At midnight I signed off as usual with "One For My Baby" and realized, as usual, that I was hungry. The kitchen was closed so I walked over to Little Pete's all night diner on 18th Street on the way home. "Home" in this case meant Theresa's couch, because my ransacked apartment was not where I wanted to be.

After some eggs with scrapple and about three cups of hot coffee I walked down 18th to Spruce Street and then down Spruce toward my building. The night was cold and the street had an abandoned look, with the wind whipping through the alleys and the traffic lights all blinking yellow as if time had come to a stop in some dark, alien future. I noticed a van parked by the curb around the corner on 16th Street with its parking lights on and its engine running, but thought nothing of it. Then about ten steps from my door I heard the van tap its horn and two burly young men with beards and pony tails appeared in front of me and blocked my way into the building. They didn't have crowbars but they did have two-by-fours, cut to a length of about three feet. Before I could react the larger of the two had swung around behind me and I was trapped against the wall. When they moved in and started swinging their two-by-fours I had to make an instant decision. I knew that sometimes it's better to move in than to duck away, even if it means that your opponent lands the first blow. So I lurched toward my attackers as they brought their clubs down on me, jumping up and twisting around so the blows intended for my head would land on my shoulder blades. Electrifying pain shot down my back but there was no time to assess the damage. Without stopping I wheeled around and tackled the smaller of the two men around the neck before he could wind up for another whack. I probably could have broken his neck but instead I shoved him toward the other one as he struggled to break free of the head lock. The other, larger man didn't have room to swing his two-by-four so he started punching me in the face with his fists. I tightened my head lock and slammed the little man against the brick wall, then hauled off against the big one with a wide swinging punch that caught him under the jaw. He staggered backwards and glanced toward the parked van, which again tapped its horn. Both of them ran back and climbed in the van and it sped away without my getting a look at the driver.

I stumbled to the elevators and made my way to Theresa's door. Fortunately she had waited up for me, and she didn't seem the least surprised to see blood pouring from the cuts on my face. She helped swab the blood away with paper towels that she brought in from the kitchen. She helped remove my jacket and shirt as I stretched out prone on the floor to ease my back, which was still throbbing from the two-by-fours.

"Do you have any ice?" I asked her.

"I've got something better." She went to the refrigerator to find some cold meat to lay over my bruises, returning with a package of Oscar Mayer baloney. "I can't afford steak," she explained. "And the Genoa salami is too expensive. So baloney is all you're going to get. But this is a good brand. Three sixty-nine a pound."

I fell asleep on the floor and dreamed of cold sluglike creatures slithering over my miserable back. When I woke up the next morning I was as stiff as the floor I was lying on, my face was swollen beyond recognition, and I smelled like a piece of overripe baloney.

Something told me it was time to move on.

16.

When Elena arrived at 8:00 o'clock I sat hunched over the kitchen table in my shorts trying to sip a cup of coffee without moving my back, my lips or my hands. She let out a little shriek—I must have looked like some street crazy who had wandered into her mother's apartment—but as soon as she realized who I was she ran over and threw her arms around me.

"You poor man! What happened to you?"

"Well, I guess you could say my plan to track down McVeigh was a smashing success."

"Did you find out who he is?"

"No, but I found out where he works, and guess who he works for? Tom Riordan."

"You're kidding!"

"Nope. And unfortunately they recognized me and that's why a pair of hardhat types were waiting outside with two-by-fours when I came home from work last night."

"Two-by-fours?"

"They got in a couple of whacks and then I sort of took control of the situation."

As we talked she examined my lacerations and gently ran her hands over the bruises on my back and shoulders. "What's this slimy stuff on your back? God, it stinks!"

"Oh, that's from the baloney."

"The baloney?"

"The Oscar Mayer baloney your Mom put on my back to keep the swelling down."

"Mom! For God's sake!"

"What can I say?" Theresa shrugged. "The Genoa salami costs six bucks a pound."

Elena led me into the bathroom and tenderly washed all my wounds with soap and warm water. I was touched by her solicitude and her reassurance that I was going to be all right. The thought crossed my mind that it would be worth getting pummeled every day if I could persuade this wonderful woman to leave her jackass of a husband and spend the rest of her life doting on me.

"The swelling will go down in a day or two," she said.

"The only thing I'm really concerned about is my hands. I have to play tonight."

"Can't you take a couple of days off?"

"I don't mean at the club. Believe it or not, I'm playing at Alyssa Babylon's wedding."

Elena laughed. "Don't tell me Yvette asked you to play!"

"Well, not exactly. It was Bardahl who asked me to play. I doubt if Yvette knows anything about it. So maybe what those thugs did to my face was the best thing that could have happened."

"I don't get it."

I tried to smile. "Now I don't have to worry about a disguise."

"Yeah," Theresa agreed. "You can go as Quasimodo after a bad night in the bell tower."

It was Saturday morning and Elena had to drive her kids to their music lessons so she could only stay a little while. After she'd finished nursing my wounds we drank a cup of coffee together and in spite of my pitiful condition I felt happier than I had felt in a long time. There was something in Elena's eyes and in her touch that was different, more tender and caring than she had allowed herself to be since the early days of our relationship, when we knew we were more than friends but we still didn't know where our friendship was heading. In those days there was an excitement and a tenderness that had been lost when she decided she couldn't leave Geoff and we tried to stifle our affection for each other. And today that tenderness seemed to be coming back. Was it just sympathy, aroused by my battered condition? Or worry about the two of us being drawn more deeply into the whole Babylon quagmire than we'd ever intended to be? There was plenty to worry about, especially when it came to that porno tape—Elena knew the Senator's power and had seen what he could do to his enemies—but there was something else, something else that was preying on her that I could see in her eyes and she wasn't telling me about.

"So how are the kids?" I asked.

"Oh, they're fine."

"And Geoff?"

"I guess he's OK. He's not around much."

"Is that a good thing or a bad thing?"

"Unfortunately it seems like a good thing. When he is around we don't seem to get along."

"Did you ask him about that piece of paper with his name on it?"

"No. And I'm not going to."

She smiled her tender smile and changed the subject. "Right now I just want to make sure you're going to be all right. One night they ransack your apartment, the next night they attack you when you're coming home from work." She reached out and touched my hand. "I'm worried about you."

"I'm not so sure those two events were connected, by the way. Last night it was Riordan and McVeigh, and the night before it was the smiling undertaker searching for the porno tape."

"Don't you think we ought to just send the porno tape back to the Senator?"

"Not until we have a clearer idea of what's going on."

Theresa snatched away our coffee cups like a waitress dissatisfied with her tip. "And not until I've had a chance to watch it."

I was so touched by Elena's newly caring attitude that I was reluctant to tell her what I planned to do next. I suspected—correctly, as it turned out—that she would be jealous if she knew. So I waited until she left and then I slipped into the bedroom and dialed Madison. It was only nine in the morning and Madison was undoubtedly still asleep, but I left a message on her answering machine. "Madison," I said, "this is Peter Cloud. Things are happening quickly and I have to take you up on your offer of lifelong devotion. I need a place to stay in a hurry. I'll call you again around noon."

On the way out I stopped at my apartment to pick up a few things I knew I would need—my razor and my toothbrush, my tux and a clean white shirt. I stuffed them in my gym bag and headed over to the Rittenhouse firm. Ernie was expecting me at nine o'clock, and at his hourly rate I didn't want to keep him waiting.

17.

"God, man, what happened to your face?"

Ernie's shock at my appearance seemed tinged with admiration, as if cuts and bruises were the next best thing to nose rings and tattoos.

"Do you like it?" I asked him.

"Sure, man. It looks cool."

He led me to a work area adjoining the mail room, in which stood his desk and a large table that was normally used for assembling photocopies. "Before we start," he said, "are you OK with the hourly rate?"

"No, I'm not OK with it."

"Well, it's not negotiable. The lawyers don't negotiate about their hourly rates and I don't negotiate about mine. And you have to pay it up front. I don't want to be hanging out if you get arrested or something."

As I peeled out the cash, he sat down at his computer and typed in a few commands. "Wait till you see this." On the screen was a jumble of numbers which, he said, was a log of all the telephone calls that had been made from the firm during the month of January. "This is what you wanted, isn't it? You wanted to know who Valunos called. Here it is."

"That's just a bunch of phone numbers," I said. "What good does it do me?"

"What do you need, then?"

"I need to know who he called. The names, like you might find on a time sheet. Some of the secretaries keep a handwritten log of all their bosses' phone calls."

"OK. I'll try to get that. What else do you need?"

I have to admit that Ernie was efficient. Within ten minutes he had brought in a cartload of files for my inspection. Valunos's files, the Senator's files, and most important, the files on Babylon's representation of Tom Riordan. No one had thought to seal Babylon's files, and if you knew how to read them they told the story of his professional life during the past couple of years. I focused on the bank takeover saga that had been related to Elena by her husband. Babylon was in almost daily contact with Riordan on this subject. The files contained voluminous correspondence, notes and court papers documenting the litigation between Riordan and Third Millennium, the disputes among the Rittenhouse partners, and Babylon's contentious relationship with Riordan. Riordan was furious about the firm's switching its representation to Third Millennium, to the point where he sent Babylon a letter threatening to sue him for malpractice. Babylon replied with a veiled threat to send the surveillance tapes back to the state. When Riordan stopped paying his bills, Babylon turned up the heat and reminded him of his "attorney's lien" on all of Riordan's files and "other documents including, but not limited to, audiovisual recordings."

"Ernie," I said, "I want you to go through all of Babylon's other files—and any other place he might have stored things—and see if you can find any videotapes. Can you do that this morning?"

"Sure. You want me to look through these here?"

"No, I'll go through these. You see if you can find any others."

The files Ernie had brought me didn't contain any videotapes, but they were a gold mine of information. They showed Babylon assisting Riordan with a wide variety of legal problems, sometimes by himself and sometimes through more junior attorneys. For example, Riordan employed a Pakistani engineer named Ali Ramdallah who had immigration problems which Babylon successfully addressed by calling in favors from a local Congressman. Then there was a construction superintendent named Norman Ezra Sproat who worked on one of Riordan's big projects. Sproat was accused of abusing his ex-girlfriend and Babylon had worked out a consensual restraining order so the man could avoid jail time and keep working. But the bulkiest and most recent files had to do with one of Riordan's real estate projects that had gone bad. It was a huge townhouse development in Bucks County called "The Mists of Inverness" in which Senator Squires, Art Valunos and a group of other Rittenhouse partners—along with several others whose names I recognized, including Elena's husband Geoff Goodwin—had invested as limited partners. The quarterly reports in the file revealed a distress situation. The units weren't selling, two of the subcontractors had filed for bankruptcy and the bank was threatening to call the limited partners' personal guarantees unless Riordan put up more collateral. The limited partners, who thought they had given personal guarantees limited to $100,000 each, were astonished to learn that the guarantees held by the bank were unlimited in amount. For this suspicious circumstance they blamed Geoff Goodwin, who had represented the limited partners at the closing. Valunos and his faction also blamed Babylon, who was not one of the limited partners and whom they suspected of being in cahoots with Riordan. And to make matters worse, the bank was Harrison State Bank, the very bank Riordan was trying to take over with Babylon's assistance and in which he already owned a large equity interest. In short, the Mists of Inverness concealed a treacherous bog, into which half the partners at Rittenhouse had been sucked during the weeks before Babylon's death.

One thing I will say in Babylon's defense. The files seemed to absolve him of the charge of conspiring with Riordan. Babylon was furious when he learned about the unlimited guarantees, even though he wasn't one of the investors. He and Riordan had a heated telephone exchange on the subject, which was recorded (like many of Babylon's conversations) and later transcribed for the file by Babylon's secretary. This conversation occurred just two weeks before his death and was triggered by a visit from the very same Norman Ezra Sproat who had benefited from the firm's efforts to keep him out of jail a few weeks earlier. The transcript makes it clear that Sproat had made physical threats against Babylon and been thrown out of the office. "Don't ever send that dirt bag to my office again," Babylon told Riordan. "If I see him again I'm going to call the cops."

Ernie walked in with more files. "Ernie," I said, "do you remember an incident about a month ago when Neil Babylon got into an argument with a guy who worked for Tom Riordan?"

Ernie nodded with a dim glow of recognition. "Yeah. I remember that. Mr. Babylon was yelling and swearing all the way down the hall. He said this dude was threatening him."

"Did you see the guy?"

"Yeah. He was sort of weird looking."

Coming from Ernie, I had no idea what that meant. It might have been intended as a compliment.

"How do you mean?"

"You know, sort of like a skinhead."

For the first time since I got dragged into this muddle I felt the galvanic thrill of being on to something. At last I had a name for "McVeigh"—he was Norman Ezra Sproat. I flipped back through the file, and there he was: Norman Ezra Sproat, born Stillwater, Oklahoma, March 6, 1973. And I had more than that: a connection with Babylon and a link to Riordan. "Ernie," I said excitedly, "this is important. Have you ever seen that guy again?"

Ernie laid his files on the table and rolled my question around in his mind (I thought I could hear something rattling, but it might just have been the air conditioner). "Yeah, I did," he finally said. "It was a couple of weeks later. I answered the phone and the guy on the other end said he was Tom Riordan. Who I knew was a client, so I was trying to be real polite. I remember that. He wanted to talk to Lockjaw."

"Lockjaw?"

"Yeah, I don't know why."

"Do the clients usually call and want to talk to Lockjaw?"

"No. It never happened before."

"So then what happened?"

"Nothing. Lockjaw wasn't here, so I just took a message. I don't know if Lockjaw ever called him back."

"What about Sproat?"

"Who?"

"The skinhead?"

"Yeah. Well, that night I had to leave early. In fact I think it was the night Mr. Babylon died. I usually help Lockjaw with the cocktail parties but that night I had to leave early, and right before I was leaving this skinhead dude came up on the freight elevator and asked for Lockjaw."

"Was it the same guy?"

"I think so. I mean, I didn't think much about it at the time, but I wondered a little bit because I remembered that Mr. Babylon practically chased him out of his office."

I was so excited that I could hardly look at the rest of the files. If I'd been an investigative reporter doing a story on the Senator and how he used the firm to profit on state contracts, I would have thought I'd died and gone to heaven. But given my present focus I didn't see anything that gave me the same electrical thrill as what I had learned about McVeigh. Ernie did bring in one file that I found particularly interesting— Valunos's telephone log, which is kept by his secretary. You have to understand that when a man like Art Valunos wants to call someone he doesn't just pick up the phone and dial the number. No, he is far too important for that. Instead, he calls his secretary on the intercom and tells her to dial the number, which he does not reveal to her even if he knows it by heart.

Then he sits and waits while she looks it up and dials it and assures him that the other party is on the line. Not the other party's receptionist or secretary, but the other party himself, who by being required to be on the line first is reminded of Valunos's importance. And Valunos's secretary, in order to remind herself of her own importance, keeps a record of every one of these calls. Ernie knew right where to find it.

I skimmed through the log for the weeks before Babylon's death and it wasn't long before I came across something interesting: A couple of calls from Valunos to the Albert Wrubel Agency, a name which rang a dim bell in my mind.

"The Albert Wrubel Agency," I said. "That's the firm's insurance agency, isn't it?"

"Yeah. I have files about them too." Ernie reached in his desk drawer and pulled out a couple of files.

"You just happen to have those files in your desk drawer?"

"It's one of the things they have me doing lately. Putting all the firm's insurance coverages into the computer system."

"Really? When did that project start?"

"Oh, it was like, about two weeks ago."

That was about right. The date of Valunos's call to the agency was a week before Babylon's death. It was also the day after the Executive Committee meeting at which Valunos—according to Patsy—had said somebody was going to have to die to pay off the bank loan. And around the same time they had assigned Ernie to put all the insurance coverages on the computer, suggesting that they didn't already have a very good system for keeping track of such things. Had Valunos called the agent to ask about life insurance coverage on the partners?

"Ernie," I said, "I've got another job for you."

He rolled his eyes. "Same hourly rate. Or it could be higher if the work involves special expertise."

"It'll only take a few minutes. On Monday morning I want you to call the Albert Wrubel Agency and try to find out what that conversation with Valunos on January 9 was all about."

"How am I gonna find that out?"

"You don't know?"

"No way, man."

"Good. That establishes that you don't have special expertise. Now I'll tell you exactly what to say."

I took a yellow legal pad and wrote out a script for Ernie to follow in his call to the Albert Wrubel Agency. We went over it several times until I felt sure that he understood what to say.

"Why am I asking all this?" he asked.

"This could be the smoking gun," I explained. "Valunos called the insurance agent the morning after he told the Executive Committee that somebody was going to have to die to pay off the bank loan."

Ernie stared back at me blankly. "Whatever you say, man."

I arranged for Ernie to make copies of the most interesting documents, including a selection of memos and spread sheets that could incriminate both the Senator and the firm, in case that ever became necessary. At noon I called Niko and gave him the news that I wouldn't be able to play at the Pickwick that night as a result of my hand injuries. He was furious, naturally—so furious that when I suggested he fire me, he refused. Luckily I had already arranged for DeWayne Hastings to cover for me that evening. Feeling a sudden need to visit the men's room, I sent Ernie down the hall to reconnoiter and he returned to say the coast was clear. But before I left I had another bright idea, the timing of which turned out to be serendipitous. "Ernie," I asked, "is there a way to get into the computer and retrieve old email messages that are still in the system?"

Ernie sat quietly for a moment, to give the impression that he was thinking. "You'd have to get into the server," he finally said. "And then I don't know. There could be passwords or something. I'd have to figure it out."

"But you could do it?"

"I could try." His eyes narrowed with that cunning look I'd come to dread. "It would be a lot of work."

"Look," I protested, "I'm already paying you an arm and a leg. There's only one of each left."

"That sounds like the right number," he smirked. "One arm and one leg. It's a deal."

"I'm not agreeing to anything until you figure out whether you can do it or not."

"Fair enough. Whose messages do you want to look at?"

"Babylon, Valunos, the Senator, Tom Riordan."

"All of them?"

"And one other person: Geoff Goodwin."

"Who's he? A client?"

"No, he's a lawyer at another firm. In bed with Babylon and Riordan on these real estate deals."

Ernie shook his head and laughed. "One arm and one leg isn't gonna be enough to pay for all this."

On my way to the men's room I decided to take a short detour past Babylon's office. The yellow police tape was gone and the door stood open. I poked my head inside and startled Fran Collins, Babylon's secretary, who was busy packing up the papers on his desk.

"Oh. Hi, Fran," I said nonchalantly.

"Hi, there," she said. "How are you?" She was feigning the same nonchalance, but her eyes told me she was terrified. The word had gone out from Valunos that I was a dangerous psychopath, not to be allowed in the office, and Fran must have been certain that before the afternoon was over I would be painting the walls with her blood. She has always been a dour, unhappy woman, but the thrill of terror seemed to be doing wonders for her personality. At the thought that she was humoring a psychopath, she was smiling and nodding like a politician.

"Terrible thing about Mr. Babylon," I said.

"Yes, it certainly was, " she said, smiling and nodding. "A terrible, terrible thing."

"I don't suppose they've made any progress in identifying the killer?"

"The killer? Was there a killer? I don't know." More smiling and nodding. "I understood he died of natural causes."

"Really? What causes?"

"I wouldn't know. In all the years I've been his secretary he's never missed a day of work."

"Fran," I said, moving towards her, "surely you knew all about his health problems? And all his medications?"

Suddenly the smiling and nodding stopped and the terror took control. "Please," she murmured. "Please don't hurt me. Please leave me alone."

I eyed her coldly. The minute I walked out she was going to call the cops. What could I do to buy a little time?

"Nobody's going to get hurt," I said. "Sit down. Please." I directed her to the sofa across from Babylon's desk. "Now I'm going to tell you what I want you to do. I want you to sit on that sofa and stay there for ten minutes. Do you understand? Stay there and watch that clock over there and whatever you do, don't stand up for ten minutes. Do you understand? Nobody's going to get hurt."

"I understand."

"Good. Stay there. I'll be right back."

I hurried around the corner and ducked into the men's room, where I had to make an urgent stop before I could even think about escaping. Inside one of the stalls a toilet was flushing, and before I could turn around the door opened and I came face to face with Art Valunos. Fortunately, I say "face to face" only in a general sense. Art is an important man, even when emerging from his daily dump—indeed, I was surprised that he hadn't devised a way to delegate that task to one of the associates—and so he didn't look me straight in the eyes. A quick glance was all he needed to determine that I was not anyone who really mattered. And in my Quasimodo disguise I couldn't complain if people turned away in horror—even Elena had done that. But oddly enough Valunos seemed to mistake me for one of the junior associates.

"Riley," he said as he stepped over to the sink, "I'm going to need that Michaelson memo first thing Monday morning." He was wearing a suit and tie, even on a Saturday morning.

"Sure thing," I agreed, heading for one of the urinals.

We then had one of those odd conversations which can only take place in a men's room, with neither of us looking at the other as we each went about our business.

"And be sure to emphasize the waiver theory," Valunos continued as he washed his hands. "That's where the client sees his strongest position."

"I'm not sure I agree with that," I said.

"What do you mean?"

I realized that as long as I stood at that urinal he wouldn't look at me and I could say anything I wanted. "Well, if you don't mind my saying so, I think the waiver theory is sort of idiotic."

The faucet was turned off with what sounded like undue force. "Idiotic?"

"Well, moronic might be a better choice of words." Poor Riley, whoever he was, was getting closer and closer to the end of his career every time I opened my mouth.

"It doesn't really matter what you think," Valunos said, turning towards an automatic shoe shining machine that stood next to the sink. "Michaelson is the client and the only thing that matters is what he thinks."

He turned on the shoe shining machine and started buffing his wing tips with a whining sound that echoed through the cavernous room. I had imagined that I could provoke him, but

I was wrong. The man is so supremely dismissive of his junior associates that nothing I could say would provoke him.

"Neil Babylon wouldn't have done that, would he?" I pursued. "He wouldn't have emphasized an idiotic legal theory just to please a client."

Valunos laughed. "Neil Babylon would have run down his grandmother just to please a client. Which is probably why he's dead."

"You think he was murdered?"

"I know he was murdered. And I know who killed him. It's just a matter of time before we put together enough evidence to prove it."

I flushed the urinal and stepped carefully around Valunos to wash my hands. He was still concentrating on polishing his shoes. "Who did it, then?" I asked.

His answer made me a little queasy. "An attorney who formerly worked at the firm. Or I should say, a former attorney."

"He's not an attorney any more?"

"No." He turned off the machine and stood inspecting his wing tips. "He got disbarred. A real psycho."

Just then Valunos looked in the mirror and caught my eye for the first time. I was standing behind him, drying my hands on a paper towel, and I could practically see the blood draining from his face as he realized who he'd been talking to. I widened my eyes into a psychotic stare.

"You!" he gasped without turning around.

"Yes," I said. "Me."

Valunos is not a large or muscular man. I'm a foot taller and I must outweigh him by seventy-five pounds, and at that moment I stood between him and the door. There was panic in his eyes, but although he was afraid to turn around his first instinct was to invoke his authority.

"As the managing partner of this firm," he said evenly, "I demand that you get out of my way. I'm going to call the police and have you charged with first degree murder."

I didn't budge. "What I'd like to know," I said, "is exactly how you did it. Did you use some kind of drug that gave him a heart attack? How did you get it into his drink?"

"You're crazy."

"Were you and the Senator working together on this project?"

"You're crazy. Now get out of my way!"

In desperation he picked up the shoe shining machine, turned around and ran at me with it, as if he could whirr me away like a speck on his shoes. I pushed him back and he attacked again and again like a jousting dwarf, until finally I knocked the machine out of his hands and let him skitter out the door.

In spite of Valunos's fervor there was nothing he could do to add to the danger I was in. Unless Fran Collins was still sitting on that couch, the police were already on their way.

18.

I ran back to the mail room to grab my gym bag and headed straight for the freight elevator. Ernie came tripping out of his cubicle with an armful of new files he wanted me to look at. "Hey, man, you leaving already?"

"Pretend you didn't see me," I advised him. "I'll call you later."

Out on the street there was no sign of the cops, so I strolled casually around the corner and headed down 16th Street. A couple of police cruisers sped past me just before I ducked down the stairs into the subway, where I waited for the short train ride up to 30th Street Station. Underground, I realized, was exactly where I wanted to be. The people down here were my kind of people. Teenagers with white sneakers and boom boxes, old ladies with shopping bags, bald men eating soft pretzels covered with mustard. And not a single one of them was trying to send me to jail or the morgue.

At 30th Street Station it was a different story. The place was crawling with cops and men in suits, and they all seemed to be looking right at me with evil in their eyes. I found a pay telephone and called Madison, and luckily she lived nearby. She gave me her address and I walked about ten blocks up the hill past Drexel University to a seedy neighborhood where some of the students live. Madison's apartment was in a five-story brick apartment building over a laundromat. I felt a thrill as I climbed the stairs, remembering the first time she appeared at the Pickwick Club and introduced herself with a passionate kiss that made my lips tingle just to think about it. Like a fairy tale princess, her image was so beautiful in my mind's eye that I had to pinch myself and ask myself what I was doing there. Was I really seeking sanctuary from my enemies, or did I have other motives? If a woman less glamorous and beautiful than Madison had sworn her lifelong obligation to me, would I still have found an urgent need to come to her for help?

But when I saw her I almost ran back down the stairs. She met me at the door wearing sweat pants, a baggy sweater and a pair of dark-rimmed glasses, with her long black hair pulled back carelessly into a pony tail. Somehow the woman of my dreams had been transformed from an exotic dancer into a computer nerd.

"I'm in my last year at Drexel," she explained. "Computer Science and Engineering. The dancing is strictly to pay the rent."

"How old are you?"

"Twenty-three."

She shared the apartment with another young woman who fortunately was away for the weekend. It was an ordinary, almost shabby apartment, with a living room full of computer equipment and two bedrooms and a small kitchen that looked over the street. The only sign that it was inhabited by a gogo dancer was the neat piles of one-dollar bills arranged on the kitchen table like Monopoly money. She must have been the only tenant who paid the rent in singles.

She offered me a Coke and we sat down at the kitchen table. "I hope you don't mind me just showing up like this," I said.

She smiled sweetly. "I hope I can help you."

"I appreciate it. Right about now I'm not getting much help from anybody else."

"Could you sort of tell me what's going on? I mean last night you wanted me to meet that weirdo in the bar..."

"I'm sorry. I never explained why we were doing that, did I?"

I decided that if I was going to ask Madison for help, she was entitled to know the whole story—or almost the whole story. I didn't tell her why I was looking for the surveillance tape or even exactly what I was looking for, most likely—as I realize now—because I wanted her to perceive me as glamorous and shrouded in mystery. I might even have implied that I was some sort of detective, whose work was so secret and important that I had to work in deep cover as a piano player at the Pickwick. Along the way I filled her in on Babylon's death and the bizarre twists and turns my life had taken ever since. I told her how I'd found McVeigh snooping in Babylon's office, how I played dead on Senator Squires's floor and how I'd had my apartment ransacked after a narrow escape from the Mafia undertaker. Admittedly I embellished the story a little to emphasize my own heroics, and my Quasimodo-like appearance, which I had almost managed to forget, must have seemed a little inconsistent with the image I was trying to project.

"Did that weirdo do this to you?" she asked.

"This?"

"You know. Your face."

"Oh, yeah," I admitted. "Indirectly. He sat in his van while a couple of his buddies came after me with two-by-fours." I described my pursuit of McVeigh after she left him in front of Abernathy's (omitting unnecessary details, such as the hour I sweated it out hiding in the toilet of the Big Boy). "So I found out that he works for Tom Riordan. How was your little rendezvous in the bar? Were you able to learn anything about him?"

"Not very much," she said. "His name's Norman, and he wants to go out with me. I thought he was sort of repulsive. That's about it."

"Norman!" I exclaimed. "That clinches it!"

"What do you mean?"

"His full name is Norman Ezra Sproat and he's a construction supervisor for Tom Riordan."

"And?"

I hesitated to go on, but I was so excited that I couldn't resist telling her more than she probably needed to know. "He was accused of abusing his ex-girlfriend and Neil Babylon kept him out of jail."

"Really?"

"And there's evidence that he was somehow involved in Babylon's murder."

"Oh, my God!" Poor Madison seemed ready to pass out.

"I knew I shouldn't have told you that," I said, squeezing her hand. "Listen, don't worry about Sproat. I'll keep him away from you. He won't be walking around much longer."

"What am I going to do if he comes to the club?"

"Call me and I'll come down and pick you up in a taxi."

She squeezed my hand back. "Promise you won't let him hurt me?"

"Absolutely."

I spoke with conviction, but in fact I was beginning to panic. What was I getting myself into? Moving in with a twenty-three year old stripper who was being stalked by a lunatic—was this a wise move? What was I going to tell Elena?

Madison smiled at me with a distinctly female sparkle in her eyes, and my panic increased. I bolted down my Coke and stood up as if to leave. Luckily it was three o'clock, almost time to go to the wedding. "I've got to change," I said. "I'm playing at Alyssa Babylon's wedding."

I found my gym bag and stepped into Madison's bedroom to put on my tux, which was wrinkled beyond all recognition. Madison laughed when I walked back into the living room, and I laughed too when she marched me in front of a full length mirror. She spread a towel over the kitchen table and heated up a steam iron, and I went back into the bedroom to undress, handing her one piece at a time from behind the bedroom door. When I finally emerged in my freshly pressed tux we both laughed again at the idea that left to my own devices I would have gone to the wedding without ironing the tux.

"What would you do without me?" Madison asked.

"I guess I'd just go around looking like a clown."

"Well, you don't look like a clown now," she said. "You look very handsome."

It was time for me to leave. "When will you be back?" she asked.

"I don't know. Probably not until about eight o'clock."

"I have to go to work at seven."

"I probably won't be back by then."

She handed me a key to the apartment. "If you want to stay here tonight, that's fine," she said. "You can sleep in my bed."

My jaw must have dropped about a foot.

"Oh, don't worry! I'll sleep in Gretchen's room. She's in Cincinnati."

19.

The College of Physicians seems an unlikely venue for a fashionable wedding. Located on 22nd Street just south of Market, in a neighborhood that has seen better days, it occupies a block of darkly aging buildings that remind you of movies in which Boris Karloff might have been filmed wearing a white lab coat. It's not really a college but a medical society, and it houses one of the oddest of Philadelphia's many attractions, a museum of medical curiosities called the Mutter Museum. If the Mutter Museum were visited by everyone contemplating a stay in the hospital, our health insurance rates could be cut in half. Probably the most celebrated exhibit is a specimen jar in which is preserved, for the benefit of future generations, a cancerous tumor removed from the jaw of President Grover Cleveland. Another intriguing exhibit is the remains of a woman whose corpse, having been buried in alkaline soil somewhere in Philadelphia, gradually turned into soap. She is now resting comfortably in a glass display case, rescued from her grave by Dr. Joseph Leidy back in the pre-HMO era when doctors took a more personal interest in their patients. Dr. Leidy donated many other medical curiosities, too numerous and often too disgusting to mention, but to me the most interesting exhibit has always been the collection of human skulls, which fills an entire wall. These skulls were collected by Professor Josef Hyrtl of Vienna in the late nineteenth century, mostly from suicides and executed criminals who were denied burial in consecrated ground. What makes the exhibit so striking is the uniqueness of each of the skulls and the detailed biographical information about their former owners. "Simon Juhren, age 19. Suicide - Hanged himself because of an unhappy love affair." Alas! poor Simon!—I didn't know him and frankly I'm glad I didn't. But now I know his name and his dates and why he committed suicide and I know that's his skull pinned to the wall like a butterfly.

All in all, as I said, an unlikely venue for a fashionable wedding. But Neil Babylon was Chairman of the Board of Trustees of the College of Physicians, and the College has been trying to beef up its revenues by renting out the foyer and an upstairs hall for functions other than necrophiliacs' conventions. And in all fairness, the facilities for wedding receptions and the like are separate from the museum. The foyer is wide and handsome, with a grand staircase leading up to the banquet hall on the second floor. Except by special arrangement, the museum is kept closed when weddings are going on.

I made a point to arrive early so I could seek out the maintenance man, as recommended by my good friend Bardahl. He was an elderly African-American gentleman by the name of Lester and he must have been well coached by Bardahl, because he knew exactly what I was going to do. He showed me the piano and the location of all the exits. And he winked at me with a conspiratorial air when I asked him to open the museum and usher me inside if he heard the music stop and saw me making a hurried exit. He thought I was an undercover cop.

There was still no one there from the wedding party, but I knew they would be arriving soon after the ceremony. Lester opened the museum and I waited inside, passing the time by studying a collection of lobotomy tools. I should have had a lobotomy, I realized, the minute I graduated from law school. Then I would have been able to stick with the program. By now, instead of being a disbarred piano player running from the cops, the Mafia and the ghost of Timothy McVeigh, a deadbeat dad being sued for non-support of my deadbeat kids by my deadbeat ex-wife, I'd be a partner in a major firm, a player, a force to be reckoned with in the legal world, a homeowner, a husband, a devoted father. If only I'd been able to stick with the program! One little snip of the frontal lobes and I would have been a guest at this wedding instead of a gate crasher hiding out in this chamber of horrors waiting for the ax to fall like poor Fritz over there. Oh, well, I thought. The road not taken.

At five o'clock I emerged from the museum and closed the door behind me. At the entrance to the reception hall I found my way blocked by a tuxedoed young man with a red carnation in his lapel who seemed to be either a waiter or a member of the wedding party. "I'm the piano player," I said. "Where's the cocktail party?"

"Oh. It's in here. I guess... There's the piano over there."

Waiters and waitresses scurried about laying out platters of hors d'oevres on a long table in the center of the spacious foyer. In the far corner was the handsome baby grand Lester had shown me, not far from the spot where the members of a string quartet stood unpacking their instruments. I stepped decisively over to the piano, sat down and started to play before anyone had a chance to object.

Behind me I could sense the members of the string quartet milling around impatiently, then more irately as time went on. Wedding guests were filtering into the room and the noise level was rising. I was hardly into the second chorus of "Fools Rush In" when a tall, middle-aged blonde hurried up to the piano with a martini in one hand and a cigarette in the other.

It was Yvette Babylon. I would have recognized her leathery face and sculptured mop of frizzy hair anywhere outside of a poodle-grooming salon. Her widow's weeds consisted of a crimson silk gown with deep décolletage and a pair of diamond earrings that drooped almost to her knees. Her face was flushed and her eyes blazed with the tell-tale signs of too many martinis too early in the day.

"Excuse me," she said, a little too loudly. "I don't remember hiring you to play at this reception."

I nodded amiably without interrupting the song. "Mrs. Babylon? Nice to meet you. It was Mr. Babylon who hired me. Said he thought it would be a nice surprise."

She looked a little sick. "There's been a misunderstanding. We have a string quartet that's all ready to begin."

"But your husband specifically told me I was supposed to play between five and six."

"It must have been a mistake. Please just finish this song and leave."

I raised my voice. "Now? I was supposed to play for an hour and—"

"Just finish the song you're playing and leave."

"I'm supposed to get $150 for this gig. I asked your husband for half in advance and I didn't get it, and he promised I'd get my money..."

Her face was frozen in a leathery panic. "You'll get your money! Now please, stop playing and come with me!"

I improvised an abrupt final cadence and followed her out of the room, complaining irately as I went. "I don't appreciate being jacked around like this, Mrs. Babylon. Where's your husband?"

Lester stood fiddling with the museum door as we emerged from the reception hall. With a quick nod he unlocked the door and swung it open, and Yvette saw the opening and ducked inside.

She took a few steps forward and turned around to face me, taking up a position between Grover Cleveland's tumor and the woman who had turned into soap. "My husband is dead," she said, steadying herself against one of the glass display cases.

"I'm sorry."

She examined me carefully. "You already knew that, didn't you?"

"I'm still sorry."

"What are you doing here? Who are you?"

"My name is Peter Cloud. I used to work with your husband at Rittenhouse."

"Aren't you the one who got disbarred? Oh, my God!" She stepped back in fright and almost knocked over the world's largest fecal impaction. In an instant it had all become clear: I was the maniac who killed her husband and now I was going to kill her.

She tried to shove past me out of the museum but I blocked her way. "Don't get the wrong idea," I said. "I need to talk to you. I had an understanding with your husband that he would get me reinstated, and there's a videotape—"

"Get out of my way!"

"Listen to me. I think your husband was murdered."

She was shaking. "You killed him."

"No. Not me."

"Let go of me."

I did as she asked. "Please listen to me. There's some kind of cover-up going on. I'm here in conjunction with the police."

That was at least a half-truth. Since I was running from the police, my location, wherever I happened to be, was necessarily in conjunction with them. And it was the monstrous Bardahl—half cop, half beast—who had invited me to this wedding.

"What do you want?" she demanded. "Can't we talk on Monday. I'm in the middle of my daughter's wedding."

"It can't wait," I said. "Things are moving too quickly." So quickly that by Monday she'd know enough not to talk to me.

"I've already been questioned by the police," she said. "Over and over again. Let me give you a quick summary. Did my husband have any enemies? Yes, he had nothing but enemies, including myself. Was there anyone who would have benefited from his death? Yes, the entire human race. Did he have health problems? Yes, too numerous to mention."

"Was he taking any medications?"

"How did I know that would be the next question?" She smiled knowingly and gave me the name of a prescription drug that has been popularized on TV by a certain unsuccessful Republican presidential candidate who apparently suffers from erectile dysfunction as well as a tendency to speak of himself in the third person.

"Fifteen tablets a month," she added. "Did he need them? You bet. Have I been getting any? No way. Then who's been enjoying the benefit, if you want to call it that? I wish I knew, so I could warn her to get a VD test. Now is there anything else you needed to ask me?"

"Mom?"

It was Alyssa, the blushing bride, framed against the wall of skulls in all her high-cheekboned splendor. And blushing she was, having just listened to her mother's bitter denunciation of her sex life or lack thereof. Beside her stood her younger sister Jennifer, stunning in her bridesmaid's dress, and my friend Connie Liebman—ironically the last woman Babylon is known to have hit on before he died.

"I know everything about my late husband, including all about his love affairs. Don't I, Alyssa?"

Alyssa blushed again, then turned away rather than to look at me. "Stop it, Mom." She took her mother's arm and tried to lead her away. "Come on. It's time to take some more pictures."

"Even his affairs from the distant past," Yvette went on. "And just between you and me, those are the ones you should be investigating."

"What do you mean?"

"My husband's life was like this museum," she said. "Full of skeletons and rotten secrets that should have stayed buried. So go on and investigate if you want to."

She started to walk away with Alyssa and Jennifer.

"Can't you just give me—"

"But do me a favor," she interrupted. "Investigate on your own time. Not in the middle of my daughter's wedding."

"I just wanted to ask you—"

"I'm asking you to leave. Do I have to call the security guards and have you thrown out of here?"

"Yvette," said Connie Liebman. "You and Alyssa better go wherever they're taking the pictures. I want to stay and talk to Peter if you don't mind."

Yvette seemed offended. "Suit yourself."

"You don't mind if he stays a while longer, then? As my guest?"

"Whatever." Alyssa took her mother's arm and led her back to the reception.

I had a nice chat with Connie, who was always one of my favorite people at the firm. She must be over thirty by now, still single, a little overweight but quite pretty and altogether a very nice person. She and I enjoyed a few morbid jokes at the expense of the museum specimens but when we came to the display of lobotomy tools we decided to rejoin the human race, if that's the right description for the crowd at the reception. It was mostly lawyers and their spouses chattering madly at each other in tuxedos and evening gowns, and when I saw someone with an especially fine set of teeth or unusually prominent cheekbones I couldn't help pointing out to Connie that he or she would make a fine addition to Professor Hyrtl's skull collection. There were even a couple of women there who looked like they might have already turned into soap.

"What were you saying to Yvette that got her so upset?" Connie asked me after we had safely navigated our way to the bar and inched away with a couple glasses of white wine.

"I told her I think Neil was murdered."

"You do?"

"Yeah, but I don't think that's why she got so upset."

"No," Connie laughed. "According to Alyssa, Yvette would have liked to kill him herself."

I didn't laugh, and Connie's face fell. "Not that she did, of course."

"No, of course not. But she did have the motive."

Connie answered with a blank but slightly apprehensive look.

"All the love affairs," I explained. "That's what she kept dwelling on."

"Did she mention any in particular?"

"No. Maybe Alyssa would know."

"I wouldn't ask her if I were you."

"Why not?"

"This is her wedding, for God's sake!"

Just then Yvette lurched into view, arm in arm with a younger man whom I recognized, to my amazement, as Rick

Taconelli. She was leading Rick forward to introduce him to another couple, and she did this with a little more enthusiasm than might have been considered acceptable in a widow of five days. Rick looked embarrassed, and fortunately neither he nor Yvette glanced in my direction. I turned around to face the other way. "Were Yvette and Neil about to get divorced?" I asked Connie.

"I don't think so," she answered in a low voice. "Not from what Alyssa's told me. For all his conspicuous consumption— which was mostly funded by the firm—Neil didn't really own much. He'd been taken to the cleaners by his first three wives and Yvette knew there wasn't anything left for her if they got divorced."

"It seemed like there was some tension between Alyssa and her mother on the subject of Neil's love affairs."

Connie grimaced. "There's a lot of tension between them on a lot of subjects."

"I wonder what Alyssa could tell me that Yvette wouldn't."

"Pete," said Connie sternly, "at this point you're here as my guest. Yvette wanted to throw you out, remember? And I'm telling you, leave Alyssa alone. This is her wedding. End of story."

"She's probably leaving on her honeymoon tomorrow."

"Yep. At the crack of dawn."

As she said this, Connie was almost knocked over by an elderly gentlemen and his wife who were stumbling their way through the crowd. I recognized the man at once as Ken Gillingham, one of the most senior of partners in the Rittenhouse firm and one of my favorite lawyers. I recalled that it was Ken Gillingham's long-delayed retirement which had been the occasion for the cocktail reception at which Neil Babylon made his last public appearance.

So far my Quasimodo disguise had worked like a charm— none of the Rittenhouse people I'd spotted in the crowd seemed to recognize me—but when Ken Gillingham stepped on my toes and peered up at me through his Mr. Magoo glasses he knew exactly who he was looking at. "Why, Ruth, it's Pete Cloud!" He held out his hand. "How are you, Pete! So good to see you! And here's Connie Liebman too!"

Ken is a classic gentleman of the old school— Germantown Friends, Princeton, Penn Law School—and a top-notch corporate lawyer just a quarter of a century past his prime. His wife Ruth is a charming lady, accomplished in her own right as a musician and philanthropist. Unlike so many of my supposed friends at Rittenhouse who pretended not to know me after my disgrace—and for all I knew everybody in the room saw through the Quasimodo act and knew exactly who I was—Ken had been too much the gentleman to turn on a friend. He told me the latest about his son, who is a musicologist, and we had a brief conversation about fly fishing, which we had occasionally pursued together in my early years at the firm. Connie chatted with Ruth for a while and disappeared into the crowd—to my annoyance since she was practically an eyewitness to Babylon's death and I wanted to get her account of the fatal cocktail party. But I felt I couldn't just walk away from Ken and Ruth Gillingham, the perfect gentleman and his lady, leaving them to stumble around the reception while I went in search of Connie. So I decided I would catch up with Connie later, and brought the conversation around to Neil Babylon and his untimely demise.

"Oh, wasn't that terrible!" said Ken. "I never thought I would outlive Neil. Such a vital force!"

"And perfectly healthy," added Ruth. "Or so they say."

"Well, he couldn't have been too healthy," I said. "Unless you think there was foul play."

"Or some kind of accident," added Ruth.

"Good point, both good points," acknowledged Ken. "I don't know, but I don't believe there was any foul play. Not right in our offices, for heaven's sake!"

"You know," I said, "I was talking to Yvette Babylon earlier this evening, and she said something that got me thinking. Every family has its secrets. I wonder if there is something in Neil's past that could explain this."

"In his past? Such as what?"

"Such as a love affair or some such thing."

Ken glanced at his wife apologetically and lowered his voice. "Well, you know, Pete, I've never been one to tell tales out of school. But in Neil's case you don't have to go too deep into the past to find such things, if that is what you're looking for."

"Maybe only a couple of weeks," Ruth added.

"Not that I would know any of the details, of course."

"Of course not," I agreed. "But there was one rumor I kept hearing when I worked at the firm, about something that happened a long time ago. Something about a secretary who actually became pregnant, and Neil had to buy her a car and send her to school and pay child support and so forth."

Ken chuckled. "Yes, that was a long time ago. Probably twenty, twenty-five years. You know, Neil and I shared that secretary."

Ruth, who up to this point had been content to make kindly additions to her husband's comments, suddenly leaped into the conversation with her eyes blazing. "You what?"

"We shared her." As soon as Ken said it he blushed like a teenager under his blotchy old skin. "Not that way! No, don't be silly! I mean, she typed and took shorthand for both of us."

"Typing and shorthand, was it?"

"Now what was her name?"

"You don't even remember her name?"

"Let me see. Names are something I have a bit of trouble with lately. Was it Maureen? Or Eileen? No—Irene. That's it. Her name was Irene. Irene Fluegfelter."

"Where was she from?" I asked.

"Yes," demanded Ruth. "Where was she from?"

"Oh, I don't know. I don't know if I ever knew that. She was only my secretary."

I was just about to say good night to the gentle couple, who might have been on the brink of their first quarrel, when I felt an urgent tap on my right shoulder. It was Connie.

"Don't turn around," she whispered in my ear. "There are cops streaming in from every direction, and I think they're looking for you."

"Thanks," I whispered back. "I'll call you."

I bid the Gillinghams a gracious but hurried farewell and scanned the room for an escape route. Over in a far corner behind the bar I spied the welcome sight of Lester, who raised his hand to beckon me towards him. Ducking my way through the crowd, I reached the bar unmolested and took one glance over my shoulder to see if the police were close on my trail. They were. A detective in a suit and hat stood at the entrance to the reception hall pointing directly toward me while a number of similarly-clad city employees worked their way urgently through the crowd. When I reached Lester he stepped aside, revealing a narrow door, and gave me three words of advice: "Hang a right."

"Thanks, Lester. Thanks for everything."

Outside, I found myself in an alley that was crawling with cops. Lester had given me sage advice, for to my left was a police cruiser in full battle alert, blocking the alley with all its lights flashing and radios blaring. I ran to the right, where the passage out to the street seemed clear.

"Hey!" called a rough voice behind me. "Stop! Philadelphia Police!" I could hear the stamp of a small army closing in behind me.

Just before I reached the street a dark Crown Victoria lurched into my path and blocked the alley. As I tried to slip around it, one of the doors flew open and a rough hand reached out and grabbed my arm and tried to pull me into the car. "Get in!" a voice commanded.

I was in luck. It was Bardahl.

20.

"Once again I saved your ass," Bardahl boasted when we were cruising safely on the Schuylkill Expressway. I say "safely" only in relation to my pursuers, who according to Bardahl's police radio had given up the chase. There was nothing safe about weaving through the Schuylkill traffic at eighty miles an hour with Bardahl at the wheel. Every time he spoke he turned his enormous head all the way around to face me, as if he couldn't bear to carry on a conversation without complete eye contact.

I groped in the darkness trying to find the end of my seat belt. "Once again you set me up to walk into a trap."

"You loved every minute of it," he laughed. "What'd you find out? Did the bride wear black?"

"No, the bride wore a lovely white chiffon dress trimmed with lace. You can read about it on the society page."

Bardahl swerved off the Expressway at Montgomery and headed back into Center City on West River Drive at the same suicidal speed. "And the grieving widow? Who was she dancing with?"

"You know damn well I wasn't there long enough to see any dancing. I didn't even get dinner."

We skidded to a stop at the light by the Girard Avenue turnoff. "Listen, Cloud," Bardahl said, "I didn't set you up to walk into a trap. How could I know that you were going to go berserk this morning and attack Art Valunos with a shoe polisher?"

"I didn't attack Valunos. He attacked me."

"Whatever. The point is, he called the cops and now he's accusing you of murdering Babylon, so can you blame my buddies for trying to pick you up? I ought to haul your ass in myself."

"Why don't you?"

We blasted away from the light and Bardahl took his time before responding. I looked past his walrus profile toward the river, praying that he wouldn't think of an answer until we were stopped at the next light. But my prayers were ignored. He turned to face me just as we bolted around a curve and through the narrow underpass by the Art Museum. "Maybe I'm still hoping you'll be able to find that surveillance tape."

"Why are you so interested in finding it?"

"Who says I'm interested? Who says we're even having this conversation?"

"Then you might as well just take me to the station, because I'm not spending another minute looking for that tape."

He pulled the car over into an empty parking space along the Parkway. "If I knew I would tell you," he said unconvincingly. "But anything I say would just be speculation, because I don't really know anything. I'm just a lowly shmuck like you who doesn't really know why he does anything."

That one hit a little too close to home, but I let it pass. "All right, then," I said. "Speculate."

"If I was going to speculate, I'd say it could have to do with your favorite Senator."

"How so?"

"That tape was originally in the custody of a state official, right? Maybe that state official turned it over to the Senator for improper reasons, and now—for reasons of his own connected with a certain investigation—maybe he's willing to testify to that fact, but only if the tape can be found. Because—and again I'm just speculating—maybe because the prosecutors have concluded that his testimony without the actual tape wouldn't be enough to prove anything except that the state official should have kept his mouth shut."

I sat pondering what Bardahl had said while he took a short break to light a cigarette and have a coughing fit. "Are they investigating Riordan?" I asked him.

"How would I know?"

"The Senator's purpose in getting the tape was to protect Riordan. So Riordan must be part of this hypothetical investigation too. Some of his real estate deals could keep the. Attorney General's office busy for a long time."

"Hey," Bardahl said, still coughing. "You can speculate too. I'm impressed. But who said anything about the Attorney General?" He launched back into the traffic and headed back toward the Schuylkill.

"I did. The AG's office is investigating Squires, and you're investigating Squires, so I figure there must be a connection. But what I don't understand is what's the connection between the surveillance tape and Babylon's death?"

"Maybe there isn't any."

"You mean maybe looking for the tape and looking for the murderer are two unrelated activities?"

"Anything's possible."

"Or are they related just because they would both discredit the Senator?"

"That I wouldn't even speculate on." And he meant it, because he stopped talking and didn't even turn his head to face me as he drove.

"You can drop me off at 30th Street Station," I said.

At the train station he pulled into a shadowy alcove and waited until I was almost out of the car before he said anything. "One word of advice," he grunted, leaning towards me. "Now that you're a suspect—I mean a real suspect, not like you were couple of days ago—you better try and find out who killed Babylon, because if there's an investigation going on, the one thing the Senator and his friends don't need is a murder angle pointing at them. Maybe that's why they're pointing in your direction."

"Thanks," I said, slamming the door. "You're a true friend."

Inside the station I pretended to wait for various trains until I could be sure that no one was following me. I was tempted to take the train down to Penn Center and walk over to join Madison at ZuLu's, but that, I quickly realized, was a dumb idea. There was a good chance I'd be arrested, beaten up or embalmed if I set foot in that neighborhood. Better to follow my original plan. So around nine o'clock I grabbed a burger at McDonalds and walked the ten blocks up to Madison's apartment. She'd given me a key, so it was simple enough to let myself in, though I felt a little uncomfortable being there by myself. I hardly knew the girl, and yet here I was, letting myself in and out of her apartment, helping myself to a few goodies I found in her refrigerator, sitting on her couch flipping through the magazines on her coffee table. It gave me an illicit thrill, I realized, even though the magazines were mostly about computers. After all, she was a stripper, and I was sitting in her apartment waiting for her to come home. But remember, I told myself, the only reason I took Madison up on her offer of lifelong devotion was in order to have a place to stay where no one would find me. I would not take advantage of her. I was not that kind of person. But what if she wanted to express her lifelong devotion in some other way? My God, I realized, I'm going nuts sitting here in this apartment. It's not just Madison, it's being a fugitive for the first time in my life. This is not a pleasant experience. It makes you feel paranoid and impatient, fearful and foolhardy, desperate and discreet all at the same time. You're afraid to move, yet compulsively restless, driven to keep moving. I had to go out.

It was only ten o'clock. Madison wouldn't be home for a couple of hours. I walked over toward the Penn campus, where college students in pairs or groups of three or four roamed the streets talking to each other on cell phones. The University has its own police force, so I knew I would be safe as long as I didn't do or say anything that wasn't politically correct. But even that was a serious risk in my present state of mind. Seeing all those hip, beautiful kids having the time of their lives made me feel like a loser, a fugitive not only from the police but from life itself. Is this how my story was supposed to end, I wondered—skulking around like some character in a Dostoevsky novel, obsessing about the death of a man I would have murdered myself if I thought I could get away with it, hopelessly in love with a woman who held herself beyond my reach? Or was there still plenty of time for a turn in my luck? On my deathbed—assuming I would have a deathbed, which seemed increasingly unlikely—would I look back on all this and smile?

A pair of gorgeous coeds (I winced at the thought—I could have been arrested by the campus police just for thinking of them as "coeds") suddenly lurched toward me out of the darkness, each chattering excitedly into her cell phone. I lowered my eyes rather than risk a contemptuous glance and skulked into a dimly lighted pizzeria. There I drank a cup of miserable coffee from a styrofoam cup and tried to gather my wits about me. I wished I had a cell phone so I could call Elena. She was probably out at the theater or entertaining socially prominent dinner guests or maybe, God forbid, even in bed with her husband, but if I'd had a cell phone I would have called her anyway. The hell with the rules. Rules are for losers.

Then I noticed a pay phone on the wall. A pay phone isn't as fashionable as a cell phone but it will do in a pinch. I stepped over and boldly dropped a quarter into the slot, but I couldn't bring myself to dial Elena's number.

"You gonna use that phone or not?" It was a large man behind me who was waiting for a pepperoni and sausage pizza. Evidently he also wanted to use the phone.

"Yeah, sorry."   I dialed the only other number I could think of, which was Ernie's beeper. I'd been meaning to call Ernie ever since that afternoon, when I'd had to interrupt our research with my unceremonious exit. And now I was anxious to get him started on my latest idea, which had been festering in my mind since the wedding. The idea was to find the family secret lurking behind the murder. Yvette had given me the hint and Ken Gillingham had provided the name. I needed to find Irene Fluegfelter.

When I dialed Ernie all I got was a recording. I left the pay phone number and sat down to finish the swill in my styrofoam cup while the other man made his call. To my surprise, the phone rang as soon as he hung up and it was Ernie. I could hear loud music in the background.

"Ernie," I said, "I hope you don't mind me calling at this hour."

"No problem."

"I wanted to tell you what happened this afternoon. I ran into Art Valunos in the men's room, so I had to make a quick getaway."

"Yeah, I know. Valunos called the cops and they were all over the place. I didn't get out of there until about six."

I glanced around to make sure no one could overhear the conversation. "Did you tell them anything?"

"No," he said. "I told them I didn't see you. In fact I told them I don't even know who you are."

"Good work." I lowered my voice. "Ernie, I wanted to ask you something. Have you ever heard the story about how Babylon knocked up his secretary?"

"Fran Collins?"

"No, no.   Long before Fran. Her name was Irene Fluegfelter."

"That was before my time, man."

"I know. It was before my time too. It was about twenty-five years ago. Babylon knocked her up and had to buy her a car and send her to college to keep her quiet."

"I wasn't even born yet when all that happened."

"I know that, Ernie. I just thought you could talk to some of the women who've been around for a long time. Like Carol the receptionist or Mary Beth the office manager."

"No way, man."

"They must have known her. Maybe they're still in touch with her. I need to find her."

"No way, man. I don't mind finding files for you but I'm not going around asking questions. They'd fire me in a minute."

"All right," I conceded. "Fair enough. But keep your ears open."

"That I'll do. I won't even charge you for that."

Back at Madison's apartment I felt even lonelier and more self-pitying than before. Too exhausted to wait up for my hostess, I undressed and crawled into her bed as she had suggested. What a waste, I thought, for that beautiful creature to sleep in her roommate's bed while I pined away in this one! But again I reminded myself that I was not the type of man who would take advantage of a young woman in her position. And with those virtuous thoughts I drifted off to sleep.

I dreamed of the lovely Madison, and so an hour later it hardly came as a surprise when the woman of my dreams, still warm and moist from her shower, slipped into the bed and stilled my snoring with a kiss.

21.

Sex, sex, and more sex. That pretty much describes what happened next. The details are familiar, so I won't dwell on them. Suffice it to say that it was the next morning before we called it a night.

Exhausted, I finally fell asleep with Madison in my arms. Since all my dreams had just come true, I slept like I'd never slept before. The next thing I knew there was sunlight streaming into the bedroom and Madison stood beside the bed in a demure navy blue dress that was buttoned to the neck. She bent over to plant a chaste kiss on my forehead. I sat up in alarm. "Where are you going?"

"I'm going to church. See you later."

And off she went, leaving me breathless with a sudden new excitement. Sexuality and spirituality are inextricably linked in my perverse imagination. I don't know why. It probably goes back to those adolescent years when I lusted after the parochial school girls in their plaid skirts and braids, with those innocent crosses dangling over their breasts. Or maybe it's more philosophical, the idea that ecstasy—that sense of standing outside oneself—can arrive from seemingly opposite directions. Or maybe, I thought, it's just plain Freudian. If you think about sex enough, you find that it's inextricably linked to everything else, and isn't that very pervasiveness what spirituality is all about? Whatever it is, I always feel guilty just thinking about it. And just now I had to acknowledge another complication: During my most ecstatic transports of the night before it wasn't Madison or God that I was thinking about. It was Elena. Even though we'd never slept together, when I was in bed with another woman I felt as if I were cheating on Elena, because in truth she was the one I wanted to be with.

I glanced at the clock. On Sunday mornings Elena takes her mother to mass at St. Patrick's. Afterwards they pick up a few croissants at the bakery across the street and arrive back at Theresa's apartment a little after ten, where I usually join them for a cup of coffee. Right now it was 10:15, a perfect time to give Elena a call. But what was I going to tell her about where I had spent the night? I couldn't tell her about Madison. To her, Madison was just a stripper, little more than a prostitute. Elena would never respect me if she thought I'd gone home with a stripper. And not only was Madison sexy and beautiful, she was a good fifteen years younger than Elena. I guess it was part of my fantasy to imagine that Elena would be jealous.

"Pete," Elena said when she answered the phone, "I was worried about you. Where've you been?"

"Oh, I slept over at my buddy's house."

"Oh, really? Who?"

"Nobody you know. A guy I know out in the suburbs. Thought I ought to get as far away as possible."

"Well, I wish you could be here. Mom and I were just putting on a pot of coffee."

We talked about the wedding and my thrilling escape and Elena's problems with her kids and Theresa's swollen ankles and even a little about Elena's relationship with Geoff, which wasn't going well. It seems he was never home, and when he was he was short-tempered and mean.   Something was troubling him, and whatever it was, he was taking it out on his family. Like an idiot, I found myself defending him.

"I'm sure he doesn't mean to hurt you," I reassured her.

"You're probably right. Well, I've got to go now. My mom wants me for something."

"OK. I'll talk to you later."

"Give me the phone number of where you're staying and I'll try to call you this afternoon."

I panicked at the thought of Elena talking to Madison. "No, I can't do that. I mean, it wouldn't be a good idea."

"Why not?"

"Well, my friend's wife... She's coming home, and... I don't think you should call. They might recognize your voice."

"I thought you said I didn't know them."

"Well, they might know you."

There was what, in another situation, you might call a pregnant pause. "OK. But leave a message on my answering machine at work and let me know how you're doing. OK?"

"I'll do that," I promised.

"OK. Good bye."

"Good bye, Elena." I wanted to say "I love you" they way they do on TV shows whenever someone happens to be going out the door to take out the garbage or hop on a bus—not a passionate declaration but just an informative statement of fact, because it was true and we both knew it. But even that was taboo in our relationship. "Good bye."

It almost broke my heart to hang up the phone but in a few minutes Madison returned from church, and before I could say "Jack Rabbit" she had slipped out of her demure navy blue dress and wrapped her arms around me like a featherweight sumo wrestler. It was only a one-round bout, owing to our exertions of the night before, and after half an hour we were sitting up in bed contentedly sipping the excellent coffee she had picked up on her way home from church. I learned that she was a Presbyterian, a sect which I, in my ignorance, had always thought of as a little on the dour, thrifty side. It just goes to show how unreliable stereotypes can be.

"And what are you?" she asked.

"Me? I'm a Zen Baptist."

"Do you go to church?"

"No, that's against my religion. The last time I set foot in a church I passed out and had to be revived with smelling salts."

Madison had also picked up some spring rolls and fried wantons and ginger pickles, so after we finished our coffee we sat down at the table and enjoyed a nice brunch. "You know," she said, "I've been thinking about your investigation. I hope you don't mind me saying this, but I think you're going about it the wrong way."

"Really? How do you mean?"

"You've been focusing on the possible suspects instead of on the victim. Neil Babylon is the one who died. You should be focusing on him."

That seemed logical—after all, she was a Computer Science and Engineering major. "I'm still not clear on what you mean."

She took a dainty bite of her spring roll and smiled. "If you learn everything there is to know about a man, you will know how he died."

I thought about what she had said. On the surface it sounded tautological, like something you might read in a fortune cookie. If you knew everything about Neil Babylon, you would know who killed him. But wasn't that putting the rabbit in the hat?

"Let me show you what I mean," Madison said, stepping over to her computer. "Last summer I worked for a market research company. Their business is to know everything about everybody. I can show you on my computer how to find out everything you want to know about Neil Babylon."

I sat down beside her at the computer and we spent the next three hours learning things about Neil Babylon that he'd probably never known himself. We could not only survey his preferences—for example, he frequently paid for books, clothes and sundries with his credit card, all of which purchases were analyzed and classified in a market research database that accurately predicted subsequent purchases and enabled advertisers to target messages to his mailbox—we could also trace his physical movements. He had an "EZ Pass" transponder in his car that automatically paid the tolls on bridges and highways all over the Northeast, and by simply invading the EZ Pass database—which took Madison about two minutes of furious typing—we were able to track Babylon's car on numerous excursions to New York and around the Philadelphia area. For example, the day before he died he drove across the Ben Franklin bridge, entered the New

Jersey Turnpike at Exit 4 and drove north to Exit 8. On the way home one hour and forty-six minutes later he took Exit 6 and connected to the Pennsylvania Turnpike, from which he exited at the Mid-County tolls. From there he proceeded to a Mobil station in West Conshohocken and bought 14.8 gallons of gas. Before going home he stopped at the Rite Way Pharmacy in Bala Cynwyd and purchased a bottle of Vitamin C, a package of condoms and a prescription of Viagra. Nothing surprising there, since Yvette had already publicized his erectile dysfunction, but what was interesting was that the big man was apparently being treated for a number of other illnesses as well. The pharmacy database—which was a little more difficult for Madison to hack into than EZ Pass—revealed that Babylon was routinely purchasing a smorgasbord of other medications, which Madison (who was evidently an expert on pharmacology along with everything else) identified as treatments for high blood pressure, high cholesterol, enlarged prostate, smoking cessation and depression.

"This man was a walking medicine cabinet," I said. "Maybe he wasn't murdered after all."

"Oh, I wouldn't jump to that conclusion. We've learned a lot about him, but we haven't learned enough. We still haven't learned who killed him."

"Maybe that would be on the Neil Babylon Murder Home Page," I suggested jokingly.

"Oh, is there one? Let's take a look at that!"

She gave the keyboard a couple of strokes and the Neil Babylon Murder Home Page flashed before us with a newly revised list of Top Suspects. Alarmingly, my name had suddenly appeared at the top of the list, ahead of Osama bin Laden. Patsy Jessup was no longer on the list. The website had been updated to include a report on last night's wedding. There was a description of Yvette flitting around in her crimson gown, Alyssa and the groom being toasted by Art Valunos (who must have arrived after my departure), and even of Ken and Ruth Gillingham wandering around the hors d'oevres table. In addition to myself, several new suspects had been added to the list, most notably Oscar Feierabend, President of Third Millennium Bank, who had been seen dancing with Yvette on more than one occasion.

"Where is this website getting its information?" asked Madison.

"I wish I knew. Whoever it is seems to know the players and to have a bird's eye view of what's going on."

"Let's see what we can find out about it." Again she furiously hammered at the keyboard, probing deeper and deeper into cyberspace in search of a signal that would tell us where the website was coming from. "I'm not getting anywhere," she finally said. "They're using multiple firewalls."

"Computer experts?"

She shook her head. "Probably some fourteen year old kid. Given enough time, I could hack in and find out where that website is coming from."

"Before you do that," I said, glancing at my watch, "there's another person I've been trying to find. A woman named Irene Fluegfelter."

"That should be a no-brainer. How many Irene Fluegfelters can there be?"

As it happened, there were quite a few. But there were only three Irene Fluegfelters in Philadelphia and one in South Jersey. With a few flicks of the mouse, Madison brought up reams of information about each of them. The one in South Jersey was too old, the one in South Philadelphia too young, but in terms of age—I figured Babylon's former secretary would now be between 45 and 60 years old—the other two Philadelphians were just right. One of these candidates, however, owned a $600,000 house and held a Ph.D. in molecular biology, which didn't exactly fit the profile. That left one Irene D. Fluegfelter of Northeast Philadelphia. She was 47 years old, a graduate of Palermo Beauty College, and employed by Annie's Shear Beauty at Bustleton and Rahn. She subscribed to Soap Opera Digest and People Magazine, and her last purchase at Rite Way Pharmacy included a Weight Watchers Nutri-Pack and a 2-ounce tube of anti-fungal ointment. She drove a 1998 Chevy Malibu and lived with at least one Alpo-consuming companion at Castor and Loney Streets in the Great Northeast.

"Is this the woman you've been searching for?" asked Madison.

"All my life," I said. "I've got a thing for the overweight, fungal type."

"Is she a suspect?"

"She wasn't on the list. But you know"—I leaned down to kiss Madison on her smooth, high forehead—"if you don't mind, I think I'll drop in on Irene and say hello anyway." I kissed her again, this time on the mouth. "Promise me you won't be jealous."

22.

Sunday afternoons, in recent experience, are usually spent driving my kids around the tony suburbs of Philadelphia in compliance with an exacting schedule of games, practices, recitals, tournaments, sign-ups and try-outs, all of which take place simultaneously at various locations that are at least ten miles apart. This is what is known as quality time. Of course the ex-wife arranges this schedule to overlap exactly with my visitation hours, which spares unnecessary mileage on her SUV and has the added benefit of making my relationship with the kids as pointless and frustrating as possible. In their eyes I'm the chauffeur who never gets them anywhere on time, a bungling amateur who doesn't know his place, hugging them and annoying them with boring questions when all they really need is transportation. And so I can't say I was bitterly disappointed when Denise had said she was taking the kids to her mother's for a week. That gave me my Sunday afternoon off. Instead of heading out to the Main Line to gossip with the basketball moms, I found myself cruising up Roosevelt Boulevard into the Great Northeast to pay a call on Irene Fluegfelter.

She lived in a neat row house not far from Tom Riordan's equipment yard and the Big Boy where I hid in the men's room from McVeigh. The house was brick with wrought iron ornamentation and statues of dogs and dwarves on the tiny lawn. When I rang the doorbell I heard the sound of small dogs yapping furiously and a woman ordering them to stop as she unbolted the door. After a moment the door inched open, revealing a short, chunky woman of about fifty with a sallow, freckly face. She peered at me with a dull mixture of curiosity and distaste while a pair of enraged poodles hurled themselves against the storm door.

"Ms. Fluegfelter?"

She nodded warily.

"My name is Peter Cloud. Could I have a few words with you?"

"What about?"

"Neil Babylon."

Her eyes told me she knew he was dead. She leaned forward to nudge open the storm door. "Come on in."

The poodles expressed their outrage at this invitation but backed away as I stepped inside. She shouted their names a couple of times and they crawled under the couch, letting out just an occasional yip. When I told her why I was there and she realized that I was a potential recruit for the Neil M. Babylon Victims Support Group, she offered me a seat on an overstuffed armchair that looked like something out of a Dr. Seuss book. "So," she said, "Neil wasn't exactly a friend of yours."

"Not exactly. He screwed me to save his own skin."

She pursed her lips and nodded. "Sounds like Neil."

"How well did you know him?"

"I think you already know that or you wouldn't be here." She smiled for the first time and I caught a glimpse of the pretty young secretary who had charmed the young attorney and almost derailed his career. "He screwed you to save his own skin, he screwed me just because I was there and then later he thought about saving his own skin. How well can you know somebody like that?"

"Pretty well, I think."

"In that case I knew him pretty well. But that was a long time ago."

The poodles leaped into her lap and she pushed them casually back down on the floor. "Would you like something to drink? Some coffee or something?"

"Thanks. I'd appreciate that."

When she stepped into the kitchen I had a chance to look around. The living room was decorated like the Poodle Hall of Fame, with framed poodle portraits beaming down from every wall and popping up from every tabletop, poodle pillows cluttering the couch and poodle figurines dancing across the top of the large-screen TV. The actual poodles watched me carefully, as if ready to pounce if I touched any of the sacred relics.

"So what did you want to talk to me about?" Irene asked when she returned with my coffee.

"I'm trying to find out who killed Babylon. There's a mystery there and it's somehow connected with me. I think if I can clear it up I'll be able to get my life back on track."

"I hope you can do that."

"You don't sound optimistic."

She smiled again, this time with the calculated pride of an older woman. "You want me to say something bitter, but I'm not going to," she said. "I've got nothing to be bitter about. I've got this house and my son is in college in California. Next year he's going to medical school. And I love my dogs."

"Have you stayed in touch with Babylon?"

She shook her head. "I haven't talked to him in years."

There was something peculiar about this stubborn reticence. Here was an opportunity for a scorned, lonely woman to spill her guts out to a sympathetic listener and instead she seemed to be playing her cards very close to the vest. I decided to appeal to her vanity, suspecting that deep down the one saving grace of all her misfortunes was the possession of inside information. "So then you don't really know any more about Babylon's death than anybody else who reads the papers?"

My stratagem worked. "I work in a beauty shop," she said. "People talk."

"It was Yvette Babylon who suggested that I come to see you," I lied.

For the first time she seemed taken off guard. "His wife?"

"His widow."

"She's the prime suspect, isn't she?"

"She certainly had the motive."

"You bet she did."

"At least that's what everybody says," I agreed. "But I'm not so sure. Jealousy can only explain so much."

"It was a little more than jealousy, wasn't it?"

I must have given her a blank look.

"You know," she said. "The whole thing with the stepdaughter."

"The stepdaughter? You mean Alyssa?"

"Is that her name?"

"Yes. Alyssa. She got married last night. What about her?"

She seemed suddenly confused. "I don't know," she fumbled. "I mean, you know, don't you?"

"No. I don't know what you're talking about."

"I thought you already knew."

"Honestly, I don't know what you're talking about."

"Then you won't hear it from me."

"Won't hear what from you?"

"I thought you already knew."

"What are you talking about?"

She stood up as if to signal that our talk was over and snatched the empty coffee cup from my hand. "I don't spread those kind of rumors."

The poodles saw me out the door with a volley of hostility which now seemed to be shared by their owner. Darkness had fallen, a perfect reflection of my state of mind. What in the world was going on? If there was a family secret, I was beginning to realize, it was deeper and more sinister than anything I could have imagined. As I thought back on my encounter with Yvette Babylon in the Mutter Museum, it seemed that Yvette had sent me in search of Irene and the distant past in order to distract me from Alyssa and the present. How could I have fallen for such a transparent sleight of hand? By now Alyssa would be far away on her honeymoon, safely inaccessible until everyone but me would have stopped wondering why her stepfather had to die.

23.

When I left Irene's I felt like one of her poodles who'd been left too long at the groomer's. To calm my nerves I stopped at a bar along Roosevelt Boulevard that catered to the hockey crowd and tossed down a double Jack Daniels and a glass of beer. That made me feel better but I still needed to talk to somebody and that somebody was Elena. Madison was a nice girl but she seemed more like a fantasy figure than a real person, probably because she was from Generation X, Y or Z or whatever it was now. Just too young, I thought as I sat at the bar working on my second round. And too beautiful: maybe I couldn't perceive her clearly because I was blinded by my male wish-fulfillment fantasies. Or maybe I just didn't know her well enough yet, and our relationship would improve over time. But sometimes I wondered if she was holding something back, as if what I was seeing wasn't all there was. I never felt that way with Elena. With Elena I always knew where I stood—even if it was off on the sidelines, conspiring with her mother.

I knew Elena's routine on a Sunday night. If her Mom came out to the house for dinner, as she often did, Elena would drive her home about eight o'clock and sometimes stop in at my apartment to say hello when they came upstairs. Tonight, of course, I couldn't be there, but I decided that maybe Elena would check her office answering machine when she got to her mother's and then, if I left her the number, she could call me at Madison's. That could be dangerous, but I would easily be back at Madison's by then, or so it seemed, so I could take the phone call and avoid any contact between them. This was a major miscalculation. When I climbed the stairs to Madison's apartment, Madison was already on the phone with Elena.

"It's for you," Madison said with a pinched smile. "A mystery lady. Won't give me her name."

I took the phone and quickly arranged for Elena to pick me up at 30th Street Station on her way into town. "Hope you don't mind me giving out your phone number to a few people," I said when I hung up. "I thought I'd be home before she called."

"Is she your wife?"

"No. Absolutely not. I told you, I'm divorced."

"Your girl friend?"

"No, nothing like that. Honest. She's a good friend and, like you, she's trying to help me out of this situation I'm in."

"What's her name?"

It seemed harmless enough, just the first name. "Elena," I said. "Her name is Elena. She's a very nice person and I hope you can meet her someday."

Madison managed a smile. I took her hands and wrapped them around my back and hugged her tightly. "I hope so too," she said.

I had to hurry to get down to 30th Street by the time I'd arranged to meet Elena. It was a wet, foggy night and the cars seemed to rise up suddenly out of the fog and then disappear with a hush. I waited by the ATM across the street, where no cops would be likely to notice me, and after a few minutes the Land Cruiser hove into view with Elena driving and Theresa in the front seat. I climbed into the back seat and we floated through the fog down Market Street to 17th Street then across to Pine, where we turned left and circled back around on 16th to the Coolidge House. As we passed the building I kept my face away from the window and watched for anything that looked dangerous. "Drive slowly," I said.

"Who are you expecting?" asked Elena.

"I don't even know any more."

Sure enough, when we were fifty feet from the entrance to my building I noticed what looked like an unmarked police car standing in a no-parking zone with its engine running and its wipers on. From my cat-bird's seat in the Land Cruiser I could look down and see two white guys inside with matching bald heads who had to be plainclothes cops. "Cops," I said. "And they're looking for me. Don't even slow down."

"I've got to get Mom home."

"I know," I said. "But first let's go someplace where we can talk."

"How about the Melrose Diner?" Theresa suggested. "It's been a while since I had any of their eggs and scrapple."

"It's only been an hour since we had dinner," Elena pointed out.

"Anyway it's too public," I said. "I've got an idea. Head down to South Philly but take Oregon all the way east to the waterfront. There's a place down there we can park."

"Is it someplace I'll be allowed to smoke?"

"It's the kind of place where you almost have to smoke."

At the end of Oregon we ducked under the I-95 viaduct and turned right on Delaware Avenue that runs along the docks, the only car in the no-man's land between the dark warehouses on the river and the viaduct pounding over our heads. Suddenly the ghostly hulk of a ship loomed over us out of the fog like a monstrous visitor from another world. It was the tattered hulk of the U.S.S. United States, in its day the world's fastest ocean liner and now a gloomy apparition waiting to be sold to the Chinese or converted into a gambling casino.

"Holy Christ!" exclaimed Theresa in her foghorn voice. "Will you look at that?"

She jumped out as soon as Elena parked the car so she could smoke as she gazed up at the ship. I climbed into the front seat so I could talk to Elena. With the car windows open and the cigarette smoke mingling with the fog, I felt as though we had broken through time into some black and white movie from the forties.

"You look a lot better than you did yesterday morning," Elena said.

"Yeah. The swelling's down a lot."

"It was the cold baloney that did it," said Theresa, poking her head through the car window. She had always been one to give credit where credit was due.

"Probably was," I admitted. "That's probably what's been missing from my life lately. "Baloney.""

Elena shook her head. "Along with good judgment and common sense?"

"What do you mean?"

"Well, you started out trying to clear your name and somehow you've ended up on the most wanted list."

"It's been a busy couple of days."

Elena had already heard about my misadventures of the past two days—probably through one of Geoff's friends at the firm—including my encounter with Valunos and my hasty departure from Alyssa's wedding, with the police in hot pursuit. "I guess you haven't come any closer to finding the surveillance tape," she said.

"No."

"Why on earth did you go back up to the office?"

"Partly to see if I could find the tape or any reference to it in Babylon's files. And after what happened on Friday night I wanted to find out more about Riordan."

"What happened on Friday night? You mean getting beaten up?"

"No, I mean discovering that McVeigh works for Riordan."

Theresa was incredulous. "I thought McVeigh already got the Texas tranquilizer!"

"That was a different McVeigh. In fact this guy's name isn't really McVeigh. I just call him that."

"Refresh my recollection," said Elena. "Why is it so important that he works for Riordan?"

"Well, remember, the night before the funeral when I went up to Babylon's office McVeigh was in there acting like he was one of the maintenance men. Riordan must have sent him to look for something, probably the same tape that I've been looking for. And the more I find out about him, the more I'm convinced he's connected to the murder, if it was a murder. For example, was it just a coincidence that he came up the service elevator looking for Lockjaw the night Babylon died?"

"Wasn't Lockjaw the bartender at the cocktail party."

"He sure was. And Sproat was lurking behind the scenes just as the cocktail party was getting underway."

"Sproat?"

"I think McVeigh's real name is Norman Ezra Sproat."

Elena shook her head. "This just gets worse all the time."

"That's for sure," Theresa agreed. "I wish I could change the channel." She walked down to the edge of the pier and tossed her cigarette into the water.

"I read through all of Babylon's files for the past year that had anything to do with Tom Riordan," I went on, "and there were a lot of them. I'm pretty sure I found McVeigh in there, under the name of Sproat. Babylon kept him out of jail on a charge of abusing his former girlfriend."

"Too bad the case wasn't filed in my court."

"Sproat and Babylon also had a shouting match in Babylon's office. I don't know what about, but it was probably connected to one of Riordan's real estate deals called the Mists of Inverness."

"I was afraid you were going to say that."

Elena seemed rattled, as if a hundred vague apprehensions swirling through her mind had suddenly coalesced. "You know that Geoff's involved in that, don't you?"

"Yeah," I hesitated. "I just found that out yesterday. I didn't know whether you knew about it or not."

She turned in her seat to face me and lowered her voice. Her eyes told me that she was seriously upset. "Pete, are there things you've been hiding from me?"

"No."

"Are we having these secret conversations and there are things you're hiding from me?"

"No, there aren't."

"Are you trying to protect Geoff?"

"Why would I try to protect Geoff? Listen, I haven't been hiding anything. I just found out yesterday morning about the Mists of Inverness, when I went through Babylon's files."

Theresa had sidled back up next to the car. "The Mists of Inverness?" she said. "Wasn't that a mini-series?"

"No, it's a fancy real estate development that's about to go bankrupt."

"That was a different mini-series."

"Mom"—Elena was trying not to sound as desperate as she must have felt—"please let us talk about this."

Theresa stopped asking questions long enough to light another Marlboro, and Elena said to me, "Geoff was just a limited partner, wasn't he?"

"And a guarantor," I said. "Along with Senator Squires and several Rittenhouse partners including Valunos."

Theresa asked, "What the hell's a guarantor?"

"It's a person who agrees to be responsible for paying someone else's debt," Elena explained.

Her mother grimaced at me incredulously, as if hoping I could reassure her that there was no word in the English language for anybody that stupid.

"Another definition," I said, "is a shmuck with a fountain pen."

"That sounds like Geoff," Theresa nodded. "Though I don't know if he has a fountain pen."

"Mom!"

"O.K. I'll hold my tongue. Which isn't easy to do when you've got one of these cancer sticks in your mouth."

Elena was not amused by her mother's jokes, and I was afraid she blamed me for encouraging them. "I'm sorry," I said. "I know this is serious."

"Please go on." She sounded like a judge talking to a lawyer who was about to lose his case.

"Here's the bottom line: Geoff was more than a limited partner and even more than a guarantor. He was the attorney who represented the other limited partners at the loan closing. And apparently something went wrong. The guarantees were supposed to be limited to $100,000 but somehow the documents that the bank got are unlimited."

Theresa asked, "What does that mean?"

"It means they could be called for any amount of shortfall on the loan payments. And in this case the losses could be in the tens of millions before the bankruptcy's over."

Elena was trying to control her emotions by staying in her judicial mode. She sat there nodding her head slightly as she weighed the evidence—and there was probably evidence I didn't even know about, things she'd learned directly from Geoff or observations she'd made about him. She waited until Theresa had stepped away again and then she asked me, "Is the idea that Geoff made a mistake, or that he did this on purpose?"

"I don't know." I kept my voice down. "He might have been playing both sides of the street, trying to help Riordan get the loan closed by letting the wrong guarantee documents go to the bank. If everything went well, the guarantees would never be called and none of this would have made any difference. That seems to be what Babylon thought." I reached out and touched her hand. "But I know Geoff's not that kind of person."

"I'm not sure what kind of person Geoff is anymore."

"What do you mean?"

"I've told you: he's become very secretive, uncommunicative, short-tempered with the kids. I don't know. It just hasn't been a very good couple of months."

I didn't want to suggest that Geoff's involvement could be even worse than it appeared, that maybe Geoff was somehow connected with Babylon's death—after all, if Geoff was turning tricks for Riordan, anything was possible. And I could see Theresa padding back up from the water, so I decided to change the subject. "There's something else," I said, "another angle that I'm working on."

"What's that?"

"I think there's some kind of family secret lurking behind Babylon's death. I tried to talk to Yvette at the wedding. It turns out Neil had all sorts of health problems, including impotence, high blood pressure, heart disease, you name it."

"I hope he didn't take Viagra," said Theresa. She had already lit another Marlboro.

"He did. And Yvette knew all about it. She knew all about his womanizing, too, and it was pretty clear to me that she hated his guts. She wouldn't let me near Alyssa, but instead sent me on a wild goose chase to track down one of his love affairs from the distant past."

I described my visit with Irene Fluegfelter, adding enough background about her office seduction that Theresa, had she been on the jury, would have voted to convict. "She killed him, right?"

"No, she didn't strike me as the type who would have gone to the trouble of killing him after all this time. But she blurted out something about Babylon's wife, some rumor she'd heard in the beauty shop."

"What rumor?" Theresa asked.

"She wouldn't tell me. She totally clammed up when I tried to pry it out of her."

"But how did it come up?"

"It came up because she seemed to take it for granted that Yvette had killed him. But when I attributed it to jealousy, she said this had to do with a lot more than jealousy."

"What does that mean?"

"I don't know. But it was something to do with Alyssa. And when I thought back on it I realized that last night at the wedding Yvette sent me out in the direction of Irene Fluegfelter and the distant past in order to deflect me from Alyssa and the present, and now Alyssa's safely off on her honeymoon where nobody will be able to ask her until it doesn't matter anymore."

Elena had listened to this exchange with a darkening expression on her face. "You don't think Alyssa had something to do with Neil's death, do you?"

"I don't think anything yet. But there's some family drama going on here and I'm going to try to get to the bottom of it. Now that I think of it, Patsy said something when I was there the other day that hinted at some secret involving Alyssa. You never heard any rumors about that, did you?"

"No. But I don't usually hear rumors, except from Geoff."

"Oh, and the other thing I heard from Patsy was that Valunos—who tried to attack me yesterday with a shoe shine machine, by the way—announced at an Executive Committee meeting a couple weeks ago that somebody was going to have to die to pay off the bank loan."

Elena turned around in her seat and started the engine. "Can you believe anything Patsy says?"

"I don't know. Sometimes I think she's a compulsive liar and sometimes I think she's the most honest person in the city."

Theresa laughed. "Probably both," she said, flipping her cigarette into the river. "You haven't been in Philadelphia very long or you'd know that."

We drove up I-95 and Elena dropped me off at 30th Street before taking her mother back to the apartment. When I got out of the car she said something she had never said to me: "When will I see you again?"

24.

As Yogi Berra said, you can observe a lot by watching. I had enjoyed driving around with Elena and her mother on Sunday night, and on Monday morning I decided that what I needed was a change of scenery. So I asked Madison if I could borrow her Honda Civic for a drive out to Harrisburg, and after a lot of hemming and hawing she finally agreed. Madison was quickly losing her status as a fantasy figure and turning into a real person—with a past and a future I knew nothing about and motivations I was only dimly aware of—and this was not altogether an improvement. Her promise of lifelong devotion had been replaced by a grudging willingness to negotiate, and the reason, in a word, was sex. She was intensely jealous of Elena and spent most of Sunday night peppering me with questions about her, none of which I answered truthfully. The fictional Elena who emerged in my answers was an unattractive, overweight mother-substitute I'd met at a conference on toxic waste litigation. She was happily married to a police lieutenant who would tear me limb from limb if I looked at her the wrong way. My only interest in her was as a source of inside information from the police department, which she pried out of her husband and then passed on because she felt sorry for me. But the more I built up this picture of the fictional Elena, portraying her in the most unfavorable light I could imagine, the more alarmed Madison seemed to become. In a battle of brains and beauty she might have felt confident of victory, but how could she compete with this?

Truth be told, I was a little turned off by Madison's jealousy and possessiveness. Hadn't I just met this woman a few days before? But she served me a delicious late-night supper of lamb chops and potato salad, spent two hours helping me with computer research, and finally led me into her bedroom for another night of gourmet lovemaking. Of these activities, the only one that needs detailed description is the computer research. We focused on two things: the Neil Babylon Murder Home Page and Norman Ezra Sproat. Madison came up with the inspired idea of sending an email message to the Neil Babylon Murder Home Page, offering to disclose new information about the murder as a way of flushing out a reply from the webmaster and possibly locating the website in cyberspace. We crafted a tantalizing message suggesting that we had evidence against Art Valunos and that if the webmaster wanted this evidence he was going to have to pay for it. As for Sproat, it wasn't hard to find the court records of the conviction that almost sent him to jail. In fact he had quite a lengthy record in Pennsylvania for domestic abuse, terroristic threats, and other endearing habits—but oddly enough it only went back four years. I had written down the information I'd found in the Rittenhouse files, which indicated that Sproat was born in Oklahoma. So Madison created an official-looking website called the "MidAtlantic Regional Clearinghouse for Criminal Record Reporting." She copied the logos of the FBI and the Police Chiefs Associations of the various mid-Atlantic states, cited non-existent statutory authority and invented databases that we would never have access to. Using this website as our return address, we sent polite but urgent inquiries to various law enforcement agencies in Oklahoma, Texas, Arkansas, Kansas and Louisiana asking for any information they might have on Norman Ezra Sproat, born Stillwater, Oklahoma, March 6, 1973, who (we said) had been arrested in Pennsylvania on a weapons charge. Of course no answers were forthcoming on a Sunday night, but I was hoping we might get something back the next day.

The first thing I had to do on Monday morning, before I could take my drive out to Harrisburg, was to get Ernie's take on the rumor about Alyssa that Irene Fluegfelter had refused to tell me. I called his beeper and arranged to meet him in the parking garage under the Rittenhouse building. "I'll be sitting in a white Honda Civic on the lower level at 8:30," I told him. As I drove into the garage I kept my windows steamed up in case somebody I knew happened to be driving in at the same time. At 8:45 Ernie opened the passenger door and jangled into the car. I made a point to look at my watch so he'd know I noticed what time he arrived. The most I could afford to spend on this conversation was about ten bucks.

"Hey, man. Everybody's looking for you."

"Yeah, I'm very popular, but it's with the wrong set. You know what I mean?"

He didn't. "I think I can get those emails you wanted."

"You have them now?"

"No, I just figured out how to retrieve them. You wanted them on a disk, but I don't know if I can do that for all of them. We're in the middle of switching over to a new system. Some of them might be hard copy printouts."

"I don't care. I just thought a disk might be easier. But don't forget all that other photocopying you were going to do."

I turned the key so I could roll down the window. Ernie's sneakers were emanating a ripe smell reminiscent of week-old gorgonzola and I didn't know what I was going to tell Madison if I couldn't get the smell out of her car. "Listen," I said, coming to the point, "I want to ask you something. Have you ever heard any rumors about Alyssa Babylon?"

"Rumors?" He shook his head. "No. I don't think so."

"You sure?"

"She worked here for a while, that's all I know."

"Do you know her mother?"

"Mrs. Babylon? I've seen her around a couple of times."

"Any rumors about her?"

"I don't hear rumors, man. I stay away from that stuff."

Ernie was fairly easy to read. When he was being evasive he bobbed his head slightly from side to side, and this was usually because he was about to ask for money.

"Ernie, are you being straight with me?"

"You want files, I'll get you files," he said, bobbing his head. "I don't deal in rumors."

I was getting annoyed. "You've been lying to me and I don't like it."

"I haven't been lying."

"I've been paying you the big bucks, thinking you were on my side, and you've been lying to me. I'm not happy about that."

"I never lied to you."

"You were lying a minute ago when you said you never heard any rumors about Alyssa."

"All right," he shrugged.   "Everybody's heard those rumors."

The smell was getting worse as our temperatures rose. I used the power buttons to roll down all the windows, taking the chance that someone else from the firm might walk by after parking their car. Ernie squirmed in his seat. "Hey, man. Put the windows up. I don't want to be seen talking to you."

"That makes two of us."

"This is at the usual rate," he said, looking straight at me for the first time. "A hundred an hour."

"The clock doesn't start ticking until you start telling the truth," I said. "You were going to tell me about Alyssa."

"Yeah, Alyssa and her father. But I guess he was only her step-father, so it was all right."

"What was all right?"

"You know. Her sleeping with him."

"Is it true?"

"How should I know?"

"I only pay for facts," I said, tweaking him.

"You wanted to know if I heard a rumor, and I told you, yeah, I've heard a rumor. That's a fact." He was getting hot, and I was starting to feel asphyxiated. "I don't know if it's true or not."

I started the engine so I could run the air conditioner. "Ernie, you know everything about the firm. Is the rumor true or not?"

"I never believed it."

"Who else knows about this?"

"Everybody."

"Connie Liebman? Would she know about it?"

"Sure. Connie'd probably know all about it."

"What about Yvette Babylon? Do you know her?"

"Like I said, I've seen her around a couple of times."

"Would she know about this rumor?"

"I don't know."

"Can you get me the internet address of her home computer?"

"What do you need that for?"

"Let me worry about what I need it for. Can you get it?"

"If it's the same as Mr. Babylon's, I can. That'll take about five minutes."

"Good. Then I'll pay you for five minutes." I glanced at my watch. "And you've been telling me the truth for approximately one minute."

"Huh?"

"For a total of six minutes. That's a tenth of a hour, isn't it?"

I reached in my wallet and pulled out a ten dollar bill. Ernie accepted it reluctantly, as if he were the victim of a grave injustice.

"That's no fair, man," he whined. "Do you think the lawyers only charge when they're telling the truth?"

Now I understood why Yvette and Connie had been so anxious to keep me away from Alyssa at the wedding. Was this the little family secret that explained why Neil Babylon himself had to be kept away from the wedding? As soon as Ernie wafted his way upstairs I spiraled out of the parking garage with all my windows open and the air conditioner roaring and launched out onto Sixteenth Street where it was only about twenty degrees. Ernie's steamy emanations immediately froze onto the inside of the windshield and within half a block I had to stop in a no-parking zone to scrape a small clearing in the frost. I took this opportunity to fish around for Madison's cell phone, which she had loaned me along with the car, and dialed the main Rittenhouse number. I asked for Connie Liebman, and she answered in her usual cheerful, penetrating voice.

"Connie," I said. "It's Pete Cloud. I just wanted to thank you for saving my life the other night."

She lowered her voice about fifty decibels. "My pleasure."

"If you hadn't tapped my shoulder when you did, I would have spent the rest of the weekend in the wrong sort of hotel. You know what I mean? The kind where the service isn't very friendly and the decor's kind of cold and metallic."

She laughed. "When I saw those guys coming in with their walkie-talkies I had a hunch they might be looking for you."

"I wonder who called them. You don't suppose it could have been Yvette, do you?"

"I doubt it. Probably Art Valunos. He sent out a memo today instructing everybody at the firm to notify him immediately if they knew where you were. For a thousand dollar reward."

"Only a thousand dollars," I sniffed. "What does he take me for?"

"A psychopath."

"He says that in the memo?"

"That's one of his milder characterizations."

"Well, I guess I should be flattered to have a price on my head." With a thousand dollars on the table, I wondered how much longer I was going to be able to trust Ernie. "In any case, as someone once said to me, I owe you a lifetime of devotion."

"Wow! Will that get me a cup of coffee?"

"How about dinner tonight?"

"Where?"

"It'll be a surprise." A surprise for me as well as for her—where in the world could we go where we'd be sure that no one would recognize us?

"I need to know what to wear."

"All right. But first tell me the truth: are you going to turn me in for the reward?"

She giggled. "I don't know. That depends on where you take me to dinner."

The drive out to Harrisburg was pleasant and mindless, like Harrisburg itself. I listened to the country music station and tried not to think about anything. Of course Elena was never very far from my thoughts. I remembered our encounter of the night before and what she'd said as she dropped me off. She must have realized that I was staying with a woman near 30th Street, not with one of my friends in the suburbs as I'd told her. But if she was jealous she didn't want me to know about it. And if she was feigning indifference she let the truth slip out with her parting words—"When will I see you again?" It was a question which, in a normal relationship, could have led to something. But for us there was no place to go and no way to get there, and the conversation kept surfacing in my mind like the aftertaste of a missed opportunity. The whole subject of Elena was too painful to think about.

The other thing I tried not to think about was the story about Babylon and his stepdaughter, which apparently I'd been the last person in Philadelphia to hear. I felt like a fool when I'd finally pried it out of Ernie that morning in the parking garage. Everyone else I'd talked to in the past several days— Patsy, Yvette, Connie, Art Valunos, even Irene Fluegfelter— had known about that rumor while I was stumbling around asking questions about Tom Riordan's construction projects. Personally I doubted if it was true. Babylon was a womanizer but he carried on his affairs with a certain gallantry and discretion and always associated with women close to his own age. And I knew something which perhaps the others didn't know—I knew about his liaison with the Senator's wife, which I assumed was of recent vintage. Of course even if the rumor was false it could still hold the key to his death. But at the moment I couldn't bring myself to think about any more possibilities than the ones I'd been dealing with. My mind was near the boggling point.

After two hours on the Turnpike trying not to think about all the things I was thinking about trying not to think about, I paid my toll and glided into our historic state capital. Harrisburg is a middling city that always looks as if a neutron bomb had exploded there the day before. It has everything a city of its size usually has except people. What people it has are state employees who stand behind counters waiting for an opportunity to ignore members of the public in need of their services. At the State Banking Commission I was greeted by a flinty-eyed matron of about fifty who kept her right hand concealed beneath the counter as if she had a gun and was prepared to shoot me if I asked too many questions.

"Excuse me," I said, "could I see the file on—"

Apparently one question was too many. "Check the docket on the computer," she interrupted, eyeing me carefully. "When you have the case number, come back."

I escaped without being shot and found the computer on a nearby desk, where I searched the docket for matters involving Harrison State Bank. As I'd expected, there was a proceeding pending that concerned the bank's application for approval of a proposed merger with Third Millennium. I wrote down the case number and ventured back to the counter, where the woman slapped a file requisition form down in front of me as if she were serving my death warrant. Her right hand remained hidden beneath the counter.

"Go back and fill this out," she said. "Then come back."

When I returned with the completed form we had a discussion about my "Reason for Requesting File." I had written "Interested member of the public" but evidently this wasn't enough.

"You have to have a reason," she said. "Why do you want to see the file?"

"I'm an interested member of the public."

"Are you an attorney?"

"No."

"Media?"

"No."

"Commission staff?"

"No."

"What are you then?"

"Just an interested member of the public."

She squinted back at me to make sure I wasn't just being smart. "Wait here."

After a few minutes she returned with a portly man wearing a short-sleeved checkered shirt and a plaid tie who peered at me through a pair of thick eyeglasses while I stood there trying to look as much as possible like an interested member of the public. Apparently neither of them had ever seen one before. But my impersonation must have been successful, for after a thorough inspection the man nodded approvingly, handed the requisition form back to the woman and waddled back to his desk. The woman returned to the counter and wrote her initials on the form. "Take this to the file room," she said. "Second door on your left."

In the file room I had another long wait while a pair of skinny girls in matching Penn State sweatshirts searched for the file. They lugged matching armloads of files up to the counter and dumped them in front of me. I signed for the files and carried them to a secluded table near the window, where I spent the next two hours reading the record of the Pennsylvania State Banking Commission proceedings on the proposed merger between Harrison State Bank and Third Millennium, including the transcript of a hearing which had taken place about six weeks before Babylon's death.

One of the main issues at the hearing involved the loan from Harrison State Bank to Tom Riordan to finance construction of the Mists of Inverness. It was a complicated issue addressed at the hearing by a lot of boring testimony from accountants and bank examiners. My eyes almost glazed over permanently when I read it. To make a long story short, it seemed that the whole financial viability of Harrison State Bank depended on whether the guarantees given by the limited partners were limited or unlimited. If the guarantees were limited, as Third Millennium argued, then Harrison was financially weak and approval of the takeover by Third Millennium was necessary to avoid a bank failure. If the guarantees were unlimited, as Riordan insisted, then Harrison had more then adequate collateral for the loan and there was no compelling reason for the Commission to approve the merger.

The last witness at the hearing was Geoff Goodwin, and that was when things got interesting. Geoff testified that the guarantees had always been intended to be limited to $100,000 per partner and that he had delivered limited guarantees at the closing, suggesting that the loan documentation had been tampered with by Riordan or the bank after closing. Riordan called him a liar and Babylon intimated that Geoff had been bribed by Third Millennium or coerced by "political pressure" into lying under oath.   Babylon asked for a recess in order to develop some additional evidence, and a month later—about two weeks before he died—he dropped a bombshell on the Banking Commission. He filed the affidavit of one Charles W. Scofield, an officer of First Delaware Valley Title Insurance Company who had attended the closing on the Mists of Inverness loan.   Scofield swore in his affidavit that the guarantees were unlimited and that he discussed this fact with Tom Riordan and Geoff Goodwin at the closing.   More ominously, Scofield asserted that Geoff Goodwin had approached him shortly before the Banking Commission hearing and tried to persuade him to have a memory lapse on the subject of the guarantees. When Scofield insisted that his memory was quite clear, Goodwin first offered certain "incentives" that could be made available to Scofield if he cooperated, and when this was unsuccessful began to threaten him with "political repercussions" that would put him out of business in the state.

Suddenly I understood why Senator Squires, who stood to gain by a couple of million dollars if the merger was approved, had found it necessary to "Call Geoff G" after that Executive Committee meeting. In the flush of excitement I returned the files to the two skinny clerks, who looked at me as if they were expecting a tip. The flinty-eyed matron watched coldly as I passed her desk but she did not shoot.

Outside, I cleared my mind with a walk around the block— a solitary walk, as you'd expect in Harrisburg, since there are no people there even in the early afternoon. Speculations about Neil Babylon, Tom Riordan, Senator Squires and Geoff Goodwin darted in and out of my thoughts in no particular order. I needed time to sort them out, in an atmosphere more conducive to reflection than a state office building. Bureaucracy! At least I was done with that, I thought, for the two hours it would take me to drive back to Philadelphia. But in this I was wrong—I still had to stop for gas.

On the outskirts of Harrisburg I pulled into a recently remodeled Gypsoco station with a convenience store and a canopy roof over the self-service gas pumps. When I slipped my Visa card into the slot on the pump, a disembodied voice boomed at me from a loudspeaker above. It was one of those phony corporate voices that sound like Big Nurse humoring a psychotic. *At Gypsoco, our customers come first. We're here to make sure you know you're Number One, twenty-four hours a day, seven days a week.*

I tried to concentrate on what I was thinking about but it wasn't easy with all that fake sincerity dripping down on me from the canopy roof. I didn't know what to make of the Scofield affidavit. Who was lying, Goodwin or Babylon? Or were both of them lying about something I still couldn't imagine? Whatever it was, it involved Tom Riordan and Senator Squires, and the stakes must have been high.

We are committed to you, our customers, to provide the outstanding service that you deserve. Our customers are never wrong!

What, if anything, was I going to tell Elena about her husband's involvement in this mess? Should I tell her about the affidavit that accused him of perjury? If he'd been bought, as Scofield indicated, was it Senator Squires who paid the freight?

The loudspeaker messages seemed to be getting louder and more insistent, and I was getting more and more annoyed. Now a man's syrupy voice was telling me how much the Gypsoco corporation cared about my perspectives and concerns and how eagerly they wanted me to share them with their customer service representatives. By the time I'd finished pumping my gas I was seething. Why should I have to listen to this propaganda just in order to pump my own gas? They weren't even giving me any service! Look at that dirty windshield!

I replaced the gas cap and strode into the convenience store, where a young man who appeared to trace his origins to the Indian subcontinent idled behind the counter. "You know those messages they keep beaming down about how they love the customers and how much they want the customers to inform them of any dissatisfaction?" I asked pleasantly. "Well, I'm a customer and I'm dissatisfied. I find these messages extremely annoying."

The clerk gave me a blank look. Perhaps he didn't understand English.

"So do me a favor," I went on. "Tell the owner I said that."

He pointed to the ceiling, from which a new message blared as if on command. *And while you're here, why not try a delicious hot dog or a cup of steaming hot coffee?*

"The messages go on all the time," the clerk said in crisp, perfect English. "There's nothing you can do about them."

"Well, I'm a customer and I'm Number One, twenty-four hours a day, seven days a week. And I'd like you to tell the owner I don't like those messages."

He looked offended, as if I had complained about his religion. "Most people like them," he said. "Why don't you like them?"

"I find them annoying. And since I'm a customer, and I'm never wrong, that ought to be enough."

"That's not a reason."

"You're not supposed to argue with me about it. This is my perspective and concern, so I'm sharing it with you. All I want you to do is tell the owner."

"I'm not going to do that."

"You don't have to agree with me. Just tell the owner what I said."

The clerk seemed to be carefully considering his next move. "Sir," he finally said. "The messages are there. There's nothing you can do about them. So if you don't like them, why don't you buy your gas somewhere else?"

On the long drive home I turned off the radio and tried to think, but my mind had passed the boggling point and all I succeeded in doing was putting myself to sleep. On any other highway that would have been fatal, but the Pennsylvania Turnpike, which opened in 1939 as America's first superhighway, was designed by railroad engineers who assumed that a road should span the shortest distance between two points. As a result it follows a surprisingly straight course for hundreds of miles, carving its way across hillsides and tunneling through mountains instead of zigzagging over them. Naturally it lulls you to sleep, but when you doze off you can survive as long as you keep going in the same direction. There's a lesson in that, I mused as I struggled to keep my eyes open. If only I could find a direct approach to what I was doing, instead of a circuitous route that took me all over the map and never reached its destination. If only all this evidence I was gathering would fit together into a coherent pattern instead of a continually expanding web of confusion. Every explanation I could think of for Babylon's demise seemed to lead to two more equally plausible explanations, which in turn, if I thought about them enough, led to two more. How could I escape from this maze?

A trucker leaned on his horn behind me, blasting me out of my reverie into a state of battle alert. My heart was pounding in my teeth and for the rest of the trip I was as wide awake as a tightrope walker. And when I paid my toll and headed back into Philadelphia, I remembered another thing Yogi Berra said: When you come to a fork in the road, take it.

25.

Climbing the stairs to Madison's apartment, I wondered which Madison would be waiting for me that afternoon. The delightful Madison who was all sweetness and light—or the jealous Madison who would scratch my eyes out if I used them to look at another woman? I was hoping to avoid the jealous one, since I'd arranged to take Connie Liebman out to dinner and I wanted to be able to read the menu. Luckily Madison was working that night, and so I had reason to believe that if I played my cards right I would be able to get through the next three or four hours without serious injury.

As it happened, the Madison who greeted me at the door was the one I was hoping to see. She kissed me so sweetly that I wondered what I'd been thinking of when I hesitated on the stairs. Then she sat me down at the table and served the most delightful Thai dumplings, noodles in peanut sauce and shrimp curry I ever tasted, all of which she had cooked herself that afternoon. "I made this for you," she smiled. "Did you have lunch?"

I shook my head. "I drove back as soon as I finished what I was doing."

"I knew you'd be back."

She poured me a glass of white wine and I told her about my adventures at the Gypsoco station. I think she sympathized with the attendant but she was careful not to say so. After the jealousy and suspicion of the night before, she was going out of her way to show how trusting and sympathetic she could be.

"Do you have to work tonight?" she asked.

"No. Sunday and Monday are my nights off."

"I have to start work at seven. Do you think you could drop me off so I don't have to take the train?"

"No problem."

"Are you sure it's OK? I mean, you've been driving all day. You must be tired."

"It's OK. Really. I'll even pick you up when you're done." It sounded magnanimous but actually I was being a cad. If I gave Madison a ride, I'd have the use of her car and could still be on time to pick up Connie at seven o'clock.

After our meal we sat together on the couch and exchanged a few affectionate kisses while we finished our wine. "How long have you been a jazz musician?" she asked.

"I don't consider myself a jazz musician. I'm just a cocktail pianist, that's all. Not a jazz player, really. Not like a Bill Evans or an Oscar Peterson. If my audience wasn't drunk they'd toss me out."

"But you've always made your living that way?"

"Oh, no. I used to be a lawyer."

"Really?"

"Really. Until I got disbarred a couple of years ago. Before I went to law school I was a high school history teacher. And wrestling coach."

She peered at me playfully out of the corner of her eye. "You're a Renaissance man."

"Well," I demurred, "maybe late Middle Ages. One thing that's definitely been lacking in my life is perspective."

Madison shifted sideways on the couch so we could see each other without craning our necks. "Is that why you're so interested in Neil Babylon? Because you used to be a lawyer?"

"I used to work at his firm. He was the reason I got disbarred."

"Oh! Doesn't that make you a suspect?"

"There are people who think so. Unfortunately some of those people are the cops."

We talked about a lot of things, the way people do when they're getting to know each other. I gave her my capsule autobiography—home town, high school, college, marriage, divorce. My parents, my brothers, my sisters and my cousins and my aunts. Even my deadbeat Uncle Frank who was responsible for my introduction to both music and law. "You see," I explained, "Uncle Frank owned a tavern in Pittsburgh where they had a piano bar. It was really a console piano but it had a bar built in back of it the shape of a grand piano. He was always on the verge of going broke, and one day when I was about ten years old he showed up at our house, which was about a hundred miles from Pittsburgh in a little Appalachian mining town, driving a truck filled with furniture—tables, chairs, barstools, and that rickety piano bar. His creditors were after him and he had taken the precaution of absconding with their collateral in the middle of the night. He needed a place to hide it until he could borrow enough money to pay off what he owed. My parents let him unload the tables and chairs onto our front porch but the only place with room enough for the piano bar was the dining room, which until then had been furnished with a formica-topped dinette set. My father and Uncle Frank rolled the piano bar into the dining room and surrounded it with barstools, and from that day forward our family ate its meals perching around the piano bar like a bunch of drunks at the American Legion hall."

Madison listened impassively as I spoke, as if such families were commonplace where she grew up. "Then you learned to play the piano... while your family got drunk?"

"Oh, no. They didn't drink at all. I learned to play while they ate their macaroni and cheese."

We both had a good laugh over that. "But how did you learn to play the piano?"

"There was an old man in town named Eustace Garnett who'd played in Fletcher Henderson's band in the thirties. I used to mow his lawn and in return he taught me everything I know about playing the piano."

She stood up from the couch and walked over to the kitchen with our empty wine glasses. She put the wine glasses in the sink and turned back around to face me, framed against the afternoon light sifting in through the window behind her.

"Where are you from?" I asked, and her impassivity began to harden into something even more impenetrable. "China?"

She shook her head. "Thailand."

"Thailand! That's a beautiful country, isn't it?"

"Yes. Very beautiful."

"So why did you leave?"

"This is a beautiful country too."

"Did you come here with your family?"

"I don't have a family. I grew up in an orphanage."

Suddenly I understood and admired her in a new way. The orphanage explained how she could be so loyal and resourceful, and yet at the same time so jealous and insecure. I could only imagine what her fate would have been if she had stayed there. She sensed what I was thinking.

"Thailand is still a man's country" she said. "In this country a woman can be herself. Strong. And independent."

"Is that what you're looking for? Independence."

She lowered her eyes. "That's one of the things."

"What's the other?"

"Security."

"Sometimes those two things don't go together."

"I know."

I stood up and stepped over to her and gave her a hug. "But sometimes they do," I said, and she pressed her body closer to mine. I wanted her to know that she could be strong and independent and I would still be there for her.

She dug her fingernails under my shoulder blades and pulled me closer, reaching her lips toward mine. But I raised my head and kissed her chastely on the forehead. There are times, even at moments like this—or maybe I should say especially at moments like this—when it's best not to follow the path of least resistance.

And besides, there was a piece of business I needed to attend to before she left for work. On the way home from Harrisburg I had called Ernie to see if he'd been able to obtain Yvette Babylon's email address. After a little haggling, he told me he had confirmed that Yvette's email address was the same as Neil's. In other words, the Babylons had shared the same email address at their home computer, and Ernie read it to me over the phone. Now I was anxious to enlist Madison's help in some research into how that computer had been used.

"Madison," I said, pulling away from our embrace, "before you go to work I need to ask you something: If you know the email address of someone's home computer, can you find out what web sites they've visited?"

"Indirectly." She smiled, seemingly amused by my abrupt change in direction, and reached up to smooth her hair away from her face. "Every computer has a unique identifying number, so when someone uses their computer to access a website there should be a record of that visit somewhere in the server. The trick is to locate that record."

"How do you do that?"

"Well, first you have to get into the server. Once you're there, you might be able to use the email address to figure out what identifying number belongs to that computer, and then track what websites the computer visited through the identifying number."

"Do you think you can do it?"

She glanced at her watch. "We have to leave at 6:30. But I think we at least have time to get started."

In her own way Madison was as much a master of the keyboard as Vladimir Horowitz. She sat down at the computer and I sat beside her like a page turner as she clicked and scrolled her way from one incomprehensible screen to another at a breathtaking pace. After about ten minutes she had a complete summary of every website visited by Neil and Yvette

Babylon's computer during the past six weeks. There were many of them, and a quick spot check on the internet revealed that most were unrelated to anything I was interested in. But finally, just as Madison was about to turn the computer over to me so she could take her shower and get ready for work, we found a string of visits to a website that started the bells going off in my mind.

"That's it!" I exclaimed. "Druginteractions.com. Stop there!"

She clicked back to the website that caught my eye and stopped. "What are drug interactions?"

"That's what happens if you take two different drugs at the same time. You might take one drug for headaches and another one for high blood pressure—individually they're safe enough but if you take them together you could get dangerous side effects."

"But why is that so important?"

"Remember the other day when we traced Babylon's movements? You got into his pharmacy records and he was taking about half a dozen different drugs."

"All I remember is that one of them was Viagra."

"Right. And this shows that while Neil was gallivanting around the countryside, stopping at every other drug store to pick up his Viagra and a pack of condoms, his lovely wife Yvette was at home obsessively trying to understand how all those drugs interacted with each other and with everything else under the sun. Look at this: On January 23—that was a week before Neil died—she went through this website looking for interactions with Viagra. And not just with the other drugs he was taking. They have information here about all kinds of other things—alcohol, amphetamines, aspirin, even certain kinds of poison."

Madison immediately saw the fatal flaw in my argument. "But how do you know it was Yvette? It could have been Neil. This was his computer, too, and he was the one who was taking all the drugs."

"Can you tell what time of day these website visits were made?"

"Not without a lot more work." She stood up and headed for the bedroom. "Which is going to have to wait. Right now I have to get ready."

Madison left me stalled in frustration at the computer. She had made a telling point. All I really knew was that somebody in the Babylon family—it could have been Neil, or Yvette or even Alyssa—had spent a lot of time researching drug interactions. For a minute I'd thought I had found the smoking gun, but Madison was right. Without a lot more research, how could I know if what I saw was smoke or just the fog of my own confusion?

26.

Connie and I had dinner at Freddy Harvey's, a jazz club on North 7th Street in a neighborhood of abandoned factories and low brick apartment houses known as Northern Liberties. In spite of its grim appearance, it's a relatively safe neighborhood where none of the Rittenhouse partners would be caught dead, which was also what I was trying to avoid doing.

Connie seemed skeptical about the neighborhood at first, but we were able to park directly across the street from the club and once inside she appreciated the unusual ambiance. The room is long and narrow with a bar in the front and a small bandstand along one wall, where the same jazz group has performed for many years. Actually it only seems to be the same jazz group—many different musicians have passed through over the years, some of them very fine players, but there is always one common denominator, and that is Freddy Harvey, the club's owner. Freddy is an alto sax player of limited talents who eventually realized that he would never get a steady gig in any club he didn't own. So he bought an abandoned brewery and turned it into an excellent bistro with a resident band. In fact, the only downside about Freddy Harvey's is having to listen to Freddy Harvey play the alto sax. I was hoping we could finish our meal and slip out before he mounted the stage.

Connie looked lovely in a turquoise sweater and a pair of black leather pants. She's a strawberry blonde with a ready smile and cheeks that blush to a rosy glow after a couple of drinks. "How does it feel to be having dinner with a man who has a price on his head?" I asked her as we dug into our salads.

"Well, they say every man has his price."

"And mine's only a thousand dollars. Hardly worth turning me in for, is it?"

"Oh, I don't know. I've got my eye on a new pair of skis."

We laughed and joked for a while about all the things she could do with the bounty Valunos had put on my head. Valunos was such a cheapskate I almost felt like making an anonymous call to the *Inquirer* and offering a more generous reward for my own capture.

"Everybody at the firm assumes that you killed Babylon," Connie said.

"What do you think?"

"I don't know. I'm not convinced anybody killed him."

"You ought to know."

"What's that supposed to mean?"

"You were there when it happened."

"I was?"

"At the cocktail party. If anybody killed him, it was probably right there. And the very first thing I heard about that cocktail party was that Babylon made a pass at you and there were some heated words between the two of you."

Connie seemed to lose a little of her composure. "What am I, a suspect? I thought this was a date!"

I laughed and signaled to the waitress for another round of drinks. "You have to be careful when you go on a date with a psychopath."

Smiling, she pulled a cell phone out of her purse and laid it on the table. "You know," she said, "I'm only ten digits away from a thousand dollars. So try to keep your psychosis under control."

Our entrees arrived and we had a lively conversation about various goings on at the firm and around town and some of the people we'd both known for one reason or another. Before we finished eating the band started to play and that ended our conversation, and as we listened I glanced at Connie from time to time to make sure she was enjoying herself and not reaching for her cell phone. She seemed a little lost in thought, and when the band stopped she leaned toward me and spoke in a low voice.

"OK. You want to know what happened?" she said. "Neil was always making passes at me. He thought he was God's gift to women, and since I'm single I was fair game. But that night he was more aggressive than usual. He was leaning close to my face when he talked to me, touching my arms." She demonstrated by reaching out and squeezing my forearms in a decidedly affectionate manner. "I kept trying to get away and he just came closer and closer, until finally he actually had his hand around my waist and was sort of sliding it downwards. I pulled away and went over to the bar for a drink, and he followed me and pretended to be leaning over the bar but he was really—well, I hate to say it."

"What?"

"He had an erection and he was pushing it against me."

"No kidding!"

"No kidding. That was when I sort of went ballistic and pushed him away and yelled at him. Everybody turned around and stopped talking. Neil looked really embarrassed. His face was as red as a lobster and he cracked some stupid joke so everybody laughed and that broke the tension. But a few minutes later he disappeared. I guess he went back to his office."

"Did anybody go with him?"

"I don't know. I didn't see him leave."

"Then what?"

"I never saw him again. They found him dead the next morning. In his office, in the same suit he was wearing that night. They said he'd been dead for eight to twelve hours, so he must have died not too long after the cocktail party."

I drained the last of my wine. "Would you like another glass of wine?"

"No thanks."

"What was Neil drinking that night?"

"I don't know. Probably scotch. That's what he usually drank. Yeah, I remember seeing him swirling the ice cubes around in his glass."

"Did he say anything about it tasting funny?"

"You think he was poisoned?"

"It's possible. Who was bartending?"

"It was Lockjaw, as always. I remember him handing me a drink."

The busboy snatched our plates off the table and the waitress returned to offer dessert and coffee. "No dessert for me," Connie said. "Just coffee."

"Was Neil's wife there?" I asked after the waitress had left.

"Yvette? I don't think so. Why would she have been there? It was a firm function."

"Just wondering. What about Alyssa?"

"Alyssa might have been there. But you know, she was getting ready for her wedding, so I sort of doubt it."

"Did you ever hear any rumors about Alyssa and her father?"

Connie stared at me for a long, tense moment. "What kind of rumors?"

"You know, about anything strange going on between her and Neil?"

"I guess you've heard them."

"Everybody has."

She slapped her hand down on the table in a flash of anger. "Well, they're complete crap. Compliments of our resident witch, Patsy Jessup."

"Patsy made the whole thing up?"

"I think she did. She claimed to have proof, but nobody ever saw it. She also claimed she had walked in to Neil's office when he was in there with Alyssa and his pants leg was stuck in the top of his sock."

"Did you ever talk to Alyssa about it?"

Connie nodded solemnly. "We're close friends."

"She heard about the rumors?"

"She heard a couple of the secretaries gossiping about it. She was very upset, to put it mildly. And then Neil heard it and he was beside himself."

"I've heard about his reaction," I said. "Who do you think told Neil about it?"

"The place is a sieve. You know that. Everybody hears everything."

"What about Yvette? Did she hear about it?"

The rosy glow had drained from Connie's cheeks. Her eyes were darting from side to side as if she were looking for an escape route. "I shouldn't be telling you this."

"It's too late. You already did. And besides, I've already heard most of this from other people."

"Yvette heard about it—I assume through Patsy. You know, Patsy spied on Neil for Yvette all the time."

"What did Yvette do?"

"She was devastated. She believed everything she'd heard, no matter how much Alyssa denied it. And she kept asking Alyssa if Neil had videotaped it."

"Videotaped what?"

"The sex they supposedly had. And Alyssa would say no, we didn't have sex, and Yvette just kept asking if it was on videotape. Evidently that was one of Neil's hobbies. Home movies."

I knew that, of course, but I didn't want Connie to know I knew it. "So Yvette didn't believe Alyssa?"

"No. She was totally incensed. She threw Neil out of the house. Wouldn't let Jennifer near him."

"Jennifer?"

"Alyssa's younger sister. You saw her at the wedding. She's sixteen."

"Did you say Yvette threw Neil out of the house?"

"That's right."

"So he wasn't living there? When did that happen?"

"I don't know. Maybe a month ago."

The waitress arrived with our coffee, and not a minute too soon. I was afraid Connie was about to hyperventilate. She gulped down her coffee as if it were a glass of water. I was excited myself, particularly at the revelation that Neil stopped living in the Babylon house—and having access to the household computer—as long as a month ago. The web searching on drug interactions was much more recent than that, and this confirmed my original hunch that Yvette was the one who carried it out.

"What did Neil do when he heard that this rumor was going around?" I asked Connie.

"Well, naturally, he was furious. And that's important—he was furious, not ashamed, because he knew it wasn't true. So he started an investigation to find out where it was coming from. Various lawyers and secretaries were called into his office and interrogated, myself included, and eventually the finger pointed to guess who? Miss Congeniality herself, Patsy Jessup. We didn't really need much of an investigation to find that out."

"Then what?"

"Well, Neil called Patsy into his office and reamed her out. He threatened to fire her, have her disbarred, send her to jail—

you name it. People could hear him bellowing all over the 43rd floor."

"But he didn't do any of those things?"

"He didn't have a chance."

I watched her carefully as I thought about what she had just said. "So you think maybe Patsy killed him before he could carry out his threats?"

"I don't think anything."

"Maybe it was Alyssa."

She shook her head insistently. "Alyssa wasn't angry at him, because the rumor was false and she knew it."

"What if it wasn't false?"

"It was false. But even if it were true, that wouldn't have been a motive for Alyssa to kill him all of a sudden. Obviously if it were true it wouldn't have come as a surprise to Alyssa."

"Maybe she did it out of revenge. Or embarrassment. Or to protect her little sister."

"That's ridiculous."

It seemed obvious that Connie had given a lot of thought to this subject, and I wondered how far her speculations had taken her. "But it wouldn't have been such a ridiculous motive for Yvette, would it?" I asked.

"Why not?"

"Because unlike Alyssa, Yvette didn't know the rumor was false. And think about it—if she believed this sort of thing about her husband, maybe in her mind he needed to be deposited safely inside a small brass canister before the wedding took place."

Connie shook her head wearily. "Believe me, if Yvette wanted to kill him, she would have done it long ago. She didn't need any more reasons. She already had plenty."

"None quite like this. To be scorned by your husband in favor of your own daughter, with the kid sister waiting in the wings. It's like a Greek tragedy."

Connie picked up her purse and stood up. "I have to go to the ladies room," she said, a little severely. "And when I come back I want to talk about something else. I spent half the morning going over all this with Art Valunos and I'm sick of it. I wouldn't have gone out with you if I'd known it was going to be a grand jury investigation."

While Connie was gone I asked the waitress to bring the check and watched with growing apprehension as Freddy Harvey mounted the stage with his alto sax. A short, wiry man with black-rimmed glasses and a mop of curly dark hair, he looked like an accountant in disguise. He waved to me and I waved back, pointing to my wristwatch to let him know I was in a hurry. Whatever happened, I wanted to be out the door before he started to play.

"I'm sorry, Connie," I said when she returned. "You've been a good sport, letting me ask you all these questions. If I decide to turn myself in, I'll let you make the call so you can claim the reward."

She picked up the cell phone and ran her fingers over the buttons. "If I don't earn it sooner."

"Can I ask you one last question?"

"All right. But if you ask more than one I'm going to dial 911."

"Who else knew about the videotaping?"

"What do you mean?"

"Did anyone else know that the sex that supposedly took place between Neil and Alyssa was videotaped?"

"Well, it wasn't, because there wasn't any sex."

"OK. But was the videotaping part of the rumor?"

"I don't know. I don't think so. I think I only heard that from Alyssa." Connie smiled her nicest smile. "Now do you have any more questions? If so, ask them now, because I really have my heart set on those new skis."

There was no sign of the waitress or our check. I added up the bill in my mind, calculated a generous tip, and laid two fifty dollar bills on the table. We waved good-bye to Freddy just as the first strains of his alto sax assaulted our eardrums.

27.

It was Tuesday morning and I had another rendezvous scheduled with Ernie in the parking garage. I felt unaccountably positive toward Ernie that day, almost avuncular, as I reflected that almost in spite of himself he was evolving into a full-fledged assistant. He wasn't exactly Dr. Watson, who so far as I know had no body piercings and rarely if ever wore sneakers that smelled like overripe gorgonzola. But Watson never gave his boss any valuable information he didn't already have. Ernie, by comparison, was a gold mine of information, without which my investigation would never have left the ground. The two of us had learned to communicate in spite of his monosyllabic inclinations. And yet I was dissatisfied with our relationship, for his sake as much as for my own. I wanted to get him more involved in the investigation, give him more of an idea of what I was looking for and why. I wanted him to take something away from this experience beyond the money he was always extracting from me, because—strange as it may seem—apart from his greed, his body odors and his ungodly appearance, I was actually starting to think of him as a human being.

To my relief, that morning he was not wearing his sneakers but a pair of hiking boots, with which he imprinted a treadlike design on the dashboard of Madison's Honda Civic. He'd arrived in the garage with a carton of documents, mostly photocopies of the files I requested on Saturday. Setting the carton on the back seat, he pulled out a sheaf of papers which proved to be print-outs of email messages he'd retrieved from the firm's computer system, and gave me a floppy disk with many more he'd been able to copy electronically. I flipped through the papers to see if there was anything especially interesting. "Any good stuff in here?"

"I don't know, man. Depends on what you're looking for."

I decided to try the positive reinforcement approach. "You've been doing a great job, Ernie," I said, "coming up with a lot of valuable information that I couldn't have gotten anywhere else. By now you probably have a sense of what I'm looking for."

He looked at me skeptically.

"For example, did you call the insurance agency and ask them about that call from Valunos the week before Babylon died?"

"Sorry, man. I didn't get around to that."

"But remember, I told you exactly what to say."

He squirmed in his seat, and I could see that I was expecting too much of him. "That's all right," I said. "Maybe you can call them today."

"Yeah. Look, I put the emails in alphabetical order."

Ernie must have subscribed to a different alphabet than the rest of us, possibly one that had been imported from his native planet. "Valunos," which an earthling might have expected to find near the bottom of the stack, was actually somewhere near the beginning. It turned out he had grouped Valunos's messages under "A" for Arthur, which had a certain logic, but in his version of the alphabet "A" came before "B" and just after "D."

There was one message that caught my attention immediately. It was dated a week before Babylon's death—the day after the Executive Committee meeting at which Valunos had made the remark about someone having to die to pay off the bank debt, and the same day as his call to the Albert Wrubel insurance agency. This is what it said:

> *From: Arthur P. Valunos*
> *To: Louis J. Squires*
> *Re: Insurance*
> *Lou—*
> *10MM insurance is up for renewal 3/1. Physicals needed. Payoff next week.*
> *Art*

I was excited. "Did you see this one?"

Ernie shrugged. "Yeah, I think so."

"Read it again. This was what we were trying to find out from the insurance agency. Valunos called them up and asked them when the life insurance had to be renewed, and whether the individual partners would need physicals. The answer must have been yes."

"So?"

"Valunos knew about Neil's health problems and knew he'd never pass the physical. So if someone had to die to pay off the bank, and that someone was Neil, it would have to be soon. Payoff next week."

Ernie shrugged again. "Speaking of payoffs," he said, "are you paying me for this time?"

I hesitated. How could I afford to get Ernie more involved in the investigation if he was going to nickel and dime me like this?

"I mean, I don't mind listening to all this. You can tell me your life story if you want to as long as you're paying my hourly rate."

That one cut me to the quick. My mind flashed back to the sign on the wall at ZuLu's: NO, I DON'T WANT TO HEAR YOUR LIFE STORY. That put me in the right category. I was to Ernie what a middle-aged voyeur was to the girls at ZuLu's: a shmuck with a wad of one-dollar bills. "I'll make sure you get your share of the reward money," I said.

"The only reward I know about is the one Valunos is offering for you."

"There's another one," I lied. "Much bigger than that one, that's been offered by Babylon's daughter. I'll cut you in on it if you stick with me."

"Sure, man," he laughed. "I'm not going to turn you in."

I flipped through the pages until I came to "P," which was just after "Q," and found a group of messages from Patsy Jessup to Neil Babylon. The most interesting looked like this:

From: Patsy L. Jessup
To: Neil M. Babylon
Re: Document

Neil—

I located that missing document you've been looking for. Please let me know when you would like the settlement discussions to begin.

Patsy

This one was even more exciting. "Wow!" I exclaimed. "She's located a 'document' that Babylon was looking for. And she's asking him when he wants to start talking "settlement." This could be the smoking gun!"

Ernie took his hiking boots off the dashboard and shifted in his seat, groping for the door handle. He seemed anxious to get out of the car.

"Wait a minute," I said.

"You paying me for this time?"

"Yes, I'm paying you. Look at me."

He turned to face me and I could see his eyes rolling away as if he was still trying to escape.

"You know anything about this?" I asked him.

"A little."

"Let's hear it."

"You still owe me for yesterday, and all the time I spent getting these email messages."

"Don't worry. I'll pay you."

"OK, man. I'll tell you." He sat back in his seat and lodged his hiking boots back on the dashboard. "One day Mr. B called me into his office. I was sort of surprised, because I didn't know if he knew I even existed. He said Patsy and him were working on a case together and would I go down to

Patsy's office and look around for a videotape that they were going to use at the trial. I thought it was a little funny because why didn't he just call her secretary? So I said that."

"You said what?"

"I said, why don't you just ask her secretary? She could look for it."

"And what did he say?"

"He was like, No, I'd rather you keep the secretary out of this. It's a highly sensitive document and I just want to get it back as soon as possible."

"So what did you do?"

"So I went down there like he said and looked through the office. The secretary was sitting outside but she didn't pay any attention, probably just thought I was fixing the computer or something. I searched all over the office, in all the drawers and bookshelves, you know, and even behind the books because Mr. Babylon told me it was such a sensitive document that Patsy might have stashed it somewhere out of the way. But I couldn't find it anywhere."

"So you went back and told Babylon you couldn't find it?"

"Yeah, and then—well, this is where it starts to get a little weird."

"What do you mean?"

"Well, he was like, Maybe she's got it in her house up in Bucks County. He wanted to know if I would go up there with him and look for it."

"What'd you say?"

"I asked him if he had a key, and he said no, we might have to break in, but it would be all right because he had Patsy's permission. I didn't believe him."

"Why not?"

"It just seemed so fake, and he was nervous and sort of whispering like he didn't want anybody to hear. So I said no, I couldn't help him with that."

"You refused?"

"Not exactly. I said I was busy."

"So then what happened?"

"Nothing. That was the last I heard about it."

I couldn't believe I was just hearing about this for the first time. "Ernie, why didn't you tell me about this before?"

"You didn't ask."

"I didn't ask! For Christ's sake!"

"Is it so important? I didn't know it was so freakin important."

"Just let me think about it for a minute."

This revelation put a whole new spin on the story. There was blackmail going on here and people react to blackmail in strange ways. Was this the surveillance tape showing Riordan breaking in to the DEP archives? Or was it a tape showing sex with Alyssa, as Yvette had feared? Or was this `document' the tape Babylon had made of the Senator's wife? Ernie hadn't searched farther than Patsy's office, but if this was the one with the Senator's wife, then someone else must have searched for it, because I had found it in Babylon's office the day after he died. In any event, Patsy was suddenly pushed onto center stage—and so was Yvette, because according to Connie it was Yvette who was so obsessed with Neil's videotaping habits.

"Listen, Ernie," I said. "I asked you about Yvette Babylon. Do you know her?"

"I told you. I've seen her a couple times. I don't know her."

"But you'd recognize her?"

"Sure, I'd recognize her."

"Did you see her in the building on the night Babylon died?"

"No, I didn't see her, but—"

"But what?"

"But whether I saw her or not doesn't prove anything because I left early that night. And anyway Mrs. Babylon wouldn't come up the freight elevator and through the mail room."

"She might if she didn't want to be seen."

"Well, I didn't see her."

"But you did see that skinhead guy."

"Yeah, the guy Babylon was yelling at. I saw him just as I was leaving."

I was annoyed with Ernie, but I wanted to give him another chance. "Is there any way to tell if Yvette was here?"

He pursed his lips and nodded his head from side to side, the way he always did when he was thinking about money. But this time—and it was a first—he was actually thinking about the case. "There might be," he said. "There might be."

"I'll pay," I entreated.

He shook his head, as if to say that money wasn't the issue.
"We could ask Building Security."

"What would they know?"

"They have electronic records of the people with monthly
garage passes. If you have a monthly pass they have a sensor
for your car. Like those things they have on the Turnpike."

"EZ Pass?"

"Yeah, like that."

"So how do we find out?"

"Follow me."

With a new sense of determination he spun out of the car
and marched me through the garage in his hiking boots with
his earlobes and eyebrows jangling like sleigh bells, and after
winding our way through an endless congeries of SUVs and
BMWs and Mercedes Benzes we came to a brightly lighted
booth inhabited by a man in a uniform who sat smoking a
cigarette while he watched TV. On closer inspection I could
see that he was monitoring a bank of closed circuit TV screens
that showed fascinating views of modern life such as closed
doors and deserted staircases. He snuffed out his cigarette
hurriedly when he noticed us approaching.

"Hey, Dan," Ernie said.

"How ya' doin?" asked Dan.

"Good. Hey listen, we're doing a little investigation. You
know, for the firm."

"Ah!" Dan nodded gravely in my direction, evidently
assuming that I was a senior official from the firm. "That was
a shame about Mr. Babylon."

"Sure was," said Ernie. "Say, do you know Peter Cloud?"

I almost choked. What was this idiot doing? Introducing me to the security guard?

"I've heard of him," said the guard knowingly. "Used to work in the building, didn't he?"

"Yeah. Did you know him?"

"I'm sure I'd recognize him."

"Well," said Ernie. "Turns out he's a psycho."

"A psycho?"

"A real nut case." Ernie turned to me for confirmation. "Isn't that right?"

"Nutty as a fruitcake," I agreed.

"Just between you and me," Ernie confided to the guard, "Cloud probably killed Mr. Babylon. We don't know how. Anyway, Mr. Valunos is offering a reward."

The security guard looked awestruck. This was the moment he'd been waiting for in a lifetime of closed-circuit TV screens. "A reward? For finding the killer?"

"Just for finding Cloud. Probably the same thing."

"So what do you want me to do?"

"We're tracing his movements, and we need to know if he drove into the garage that night."

"In here?"

"Yeah. He might have been right here."

"Right here," the guard repeated.

"If we give you a serial number, can you look it up and tell me if that car came through the sensor on a certain night?"

"Sure. Year, day and time, to the second. What's the account number?"

"I don't have it with me. But I'll call you when I get back upstairs.   What's your phone number down here?"

As we walked away from the guard station I wanted to put my arm around Ernie's shoulder and congratulate him.   It was a masterful performance. "You deserve to be paid for that," I said.

"Just put it on my tab," he grinned.

"Now what?"

"Now I go upstairs and look up Yvette's account number in the firm's computer.   Then I call down here to Dan and he tells me whether she was here that night."

"Brilliant," I said.

He grinned again, and for the first time I saw the glow of some real pride and intelligence in his usually glassy eyes. Maybe there's hope for the brain dead after all.

28.

My next challenge was how to get into my own apartment building without being recognized or caught. I was determined to see Elena and the only way I could do that was to have lunch at Theresa's. How was I going to get past the police?

Back when I was practicing law one of my favorite clients was a toxic waste company called Toxicops. They're the ones who send out the men in moon suits when there's a toxic waste spill or a radiation scare. The manager of the local office is a wild Welshman named Owen Owens who's been through enough scrapes with the law that I knew he wouldn't mind helping me out of a jam. He also owed me fifty dollars as the result of a drunken bet he'd made during the World Series a few months before. I knew very well that my chances of ever seeing that fifty dollars were somewhere in the range between minuscule and infinitesimal. But I also knew that Owen, though a deadbeat when it comes to money, is a man of honor—he will always square his accounts if it doesn't cost him anything. "Owen," I said when I'd reached him from a pay phone on Lombard Street, "can you help me out with something?"

"You name it, friend," he said. "You name it and it's yours."

"I want you to send a couple of men in moon suits over to my building to check out some possible contamination. One of the old ladies says there's something in the laundry room that glows in the dark and looks like it might be coming to life."

"Are you making this up, Cloud?"

"It's sort of a belated Ground Hog Day joke. And I forgot to mention—one of those men in the moon suits is going to be me."

Within an hour Owen's van had picked me up for an emergency call on the Coolidge House, which we found still under observation by the two plainclothesmen with matching bald heads. The officers could not have been more accommodating to the two men in moon suits who emerged from the van to deal with the crisis. They interrupted their vigil for the diabolical Peter Cloud—conducted from a Mercury Grand Marquis parked inconspicuously in a no parking zone in front of the building—and escorted us into the lobby, beyond which, we warned them, it would be unsafe to proceed. Owen left after a few minutes but advised the officers not to go inside unless I called for their assistance. He would be returning with a relief crew in a couple of hours.

Dealing with the police was a simple matter compared with the challenge of getting into Theresa's apartment in my moon suit. "That does it!" she cried, trying to push the door closed after I was half inside. "I'm calling 911."

"No, listen. It's me. I—"

"I knew this was coming! Elena!"—She threw her whole ninety-five pounds against the door—"He's finally cracked up! Help me with the door!"

Fortunately Elena was able to persuade her mother to let me in, and after I removed my head gear and Theresa had administered a complete neurological examination, including shining a small flashlight in my eyes and forcing me to recite the Pledge of Allegiance while balancing alternately on one foot and then the other, she relented on her threat to call the police and I was allowed to take my seat at the kitchen table, letting the rest of my sweltering moon suit crumble to the floor. Theresa retreated to the stove to inspect her simmering pots.

Elena squeezed my hand and smiled. It was the sort of smile I love to see on her face, especially when aimed at me. Humorous, fond, tolerant—maybe even a little admiring—of my shortcomings. "Would you like some coffee?"

"I'd love some."

Elena poured me a cup of coffee, and while Theresa dished out our lunch, I filled her in on everything I'd learned since Sunday night. And there was plenty: the rumor about Neil having sex with his stepdaughter, Yvette's obsession with whether he'd videotaped it and her research into drug interactions, Patsy's blackmail messages about the "missing document," Ernie's search of Patsy's office at Babylon's request and the attempt to get him to search her house. It was probably more than Elena could digest at one sitting—not unlike the lunch, which consisted of spaghetti with marinara sauce, hot Italian sausages, roasted red peppers, a salad of canned artichoke hearts drenched in olive oil, Italian bread and a little antipasto plate of cheese and cold cuts—and even so, I left out what I'd learned about Elena's husband at the State

Real Estate Commission. I was still wrestling with whether I would ever need to bring that up.

"All that stuff sounds like an episode of 'Days of Our Lives,'" Theresa observed as she refilled our cups with hot coffee. "About six months ago. You know how it turned out?"

"How?" I asked.

"The stepdaughter got pregnant and tried to stab the old man with a fork."

"This isn't a soap opera," said Elena.

"No," Theresa agreed—sarcastically, as if in response to Elena's dismissive attitude toward soap operas—"it's a law firm."

"So instead of a flesh wound," I said, "the old man ends up dead."

"Probably had a better offer," Theresa said.

"What do you mean?"

"Well, when one of the characters on a soap opera dies it means that the actor wanted to leave the show. Usually because he got a movie deal."

"Mom, this is real life. Neil Babylon is really dead. He's not just playing some different part in Hollywood.

"How do you know that?"

"I went to the viewing."

"Did you see the body?"

"No, he was cremated."

"Ha!" Theresa exulted. "All I can say is, when you go to a viewing and there's nothing to view...." She ended with a flourish of upturned hands suggesting that the conclusion was inescapable.

Elena looked like she was tempted to shove a fistful of hot Italian sausages down her mother's throat to keep her quiet. "Now here's something interesting," I said, changing the subject. "I asked Connie whether videotaped sex was part of the Alyssa rumor that was going around the office, and she said she didn't think it was."

Elena frowned quizzically. "And?"

"Anybody who heard the rumor knew about the alleged sex between Neil and Alyssa, but not everybody would have suspected the videotaping. Yvette did, because she was his wife and she knew about his voyeuristic tendencies. Alyssa knew, because Yvette asked her about it, and Connie knew because Alyssa told Connie."

"All right."

"So if someone else knew or suspected the videotaping, they must have gotten the idea from one of them. In other words, from Yvette, Alyssa, Connie or Neil."

"Don't forget the Senator's wife," Theresa interjected. "Babylon videotaped her, didn't he?" Theresa always seemed excited when that subject came up.

"Good point. I forgot about the Senator's wife. What's her name?"

"Marianne," Elena answered. "Anyway, where were you going with this?"

"Let's assume for the moment that Patsy suspected that the sex with Alyssa had been videotaped. Where would she have gotten the idea? Not from Alyssa or Connie—they hate her, and they deny that there was any sex in the first place. Not from Neil, and certainly not from the Senator's wife."

"So that means she got the idea directly from Yvette?"

"That's what I think. According to Connie, Yvette used Patsy to spy on Neil at various times in the past. And Yvette must have heard the rumor from somebody, and that was probably Patsy. Especially if Patsy made it up, which is what Connie thinks."

Having finished my salad, I soaked up the remaining olive oil with a piece of bread and started working on the antipasto. After a few bites, it occurred to me that there was something a little too familiar about the baloney. "Theresa," I said, "this isn't the same baloney that you plastered all over my back the other night, is it?"

"You think I'd just throw it out?"

"Mom!" Elena coughed a half-eaten slice of baloney into her napkin. "That's disgusting!"

Theresa enjoyed a good laugh before admitting that she was putting us on. "Don't worry, dear," she said to Elena. "You think I'd do a thing like that? I gave that baloney to Mrs. Sedlak next door."

Elena found a clean napkin and turned her attention back to the antipasto, though I noticed she avoided the baloney. "All right," she said. "This is starting to come into focus. Patsy hears the rumor—or starts the rumor—and reveals it to Yvette. From Yvette she learns about Yvette's concern that the sex would have been videotaped. So Patsy, either on her own or at Yvette's request, searches Neil's office and what does she find?"

Theresa waved a videocassette. "This "

Elena and I looked back uncomprehendingly.

"It's the videotape of Babylon having sex with the Senator's wife."

Elena jumped out of her seat. "Where did you get that?"

"I lifted it out of your purse the other day. It's not safe for you to be walking around with this, you know."

I stepped between Elena and her mother to keep them from coming to blows. "All right," I said, trying to keep the discussion on track. "To Patsy this videotape is a gold mine. Babylon's on a rampage looking for the person who started the rumor. He's already called Patsy into his office and threatened her with everything short of decapitation. But now she has a trump card. She lets Neil know she has the tape and begins negotiations with him over a 'missing document.' Who knows what she was trying to get out of him for that one? Neil fights back. He recruits Ernie to search Patsy's office for the tape, but Ernie doesn't find it. He tries to get Ernie to search her house and he refuses. So what does he do next? He hires our friend McVeigh, aka Norman Ezra Sproat, for whom breaking and entering is a lesser included offense in his everyday routine."

"Would Babylon have trusted Sproat with the videotape?"

"No. He wouldn't have given Sproat a chance to watch the tape and make a copy of it. He would have driven up to Patsy's with Sproat and taken possession of the videotape as soon as it was found. And it's clear that Sproat didn't have a chance to make a copy of the tape, or he wouldn't have been up in Babylon's office the night after he died looking for it."

"He was searching for the tape even though he didn't know what was on it?"

"He knew that whatever was on the tape was important enough that Babylon hired him to break into Patsy's house to get it back."

Theresa had taken a seat at the table to smoke a cigarette and listen to the conversation. For some reason I realized at that moment that in all the times I had been to her apartment, which usually involved her serving a meal to Elena and me, I had never seen Theresa eat. I'd seen her drink enormous amounts of coffee, I'd seen her cook enough food and smoke enough cigarettes to kill the Chinese Army, but I had never actually seen her eat. No wonder she was all skin and bones.

I offered her the antipasto plate. "Care for some baloney?"

"Nah," she said. "Not while I'm smoking."

Elena looked at her watch and poured herself another cup of coffee. "Let's assume Sproat or somebody else got the tape back from Patsy," she said. "Then what happened?"

"Patsy thought she was sitting pretty. She was blackmailing Babylon not to carry out his threats, and suddenly she discovers her house has been robbed and she's lost the tape. Patsy's not dumb. She must have realized what a dangerous situation she was in. She knew Babylon was diddling Squires's wife and making movies of it. And when she lost the tape she must have realized that in effect it had been her life insurance policy."

"So she killed Babylon?"

"She was afraid for her job, her career, maybe her life. That's a powerful motive to kill somebody."

"If he's really dead," Theresa added.

Elena rolled her eyes. "Do you think she and Yvette were in on it together?"

"That's a possibility," I said. "I'm checking out Yvette's movements to see if she was in the building on the night of the cocktail party. And of course there's evidence that Sproat was in the building. I don't quite know what to make of that. Maybe he brought some drugs for Patsy to put in Neil's drinks. Yvette was apparently fascinated with drug interactions, specifically those involving the drugs Babylon was taking."

"How do you know that?"

"Somebody who had access to the Babylon home computer spent a lot of time online studying the subject. And it couldn't have been Neil. According to Connie, Yvette kicked him out of the house when she heard the rumor about Alyssa."

Theresa, who had been sitting quietly puffing on her Marlboro, crushed it out in her saucer and immediately reached for another one. "I don't want to be a spoilsport," she said in an unusually croaky voice, "but there's something wrong with this picture."

"What?"

"I don't know what it is, but there's something wrong with it. For openers, it's a completely different picture from the one you were talking about the other night down by the waterfront. What happened to the Mists of Inverness? Last time it was all about the Mists of Inverness and limited partners and that shmuck Geoff with his fountain pen. No offense, dear."

Elena chuckled.. Evidently her own opinion of Geoff hadn't improved much since Sunday night.

"And before that," Theresa went on, "it was this Valunos creep and Tom Riordan and Timothy McVeigh come back from the dead. If you don't mind my saying so, it almost seems like you have too many suspects. Are you sure you really know what's going on?"

I felt my self-assurance starting to seep away. "You're not convinced?"

Theresa shook her head regretfully.

"How about you?"

Elena smiled with that polite but skeptical smile a lawyer hates to see on the face of a judge. "Not beyond a reasonable doubt," she said. "Sorry."

"Why not?"

"I've got to get back," she said, standing up to leave. She leaned over and kissed me on the cheek. "Let's meet for lunch again tomorrow and I'll explain the weaknesses in your argument."

As it turned out I would see Elena sooner than that. Events were starting to speed up.

29

After Elena left I chatted with Theresa for a while and made a few phone calls. First I called my friend DuWayne Hastings, who had covered for me at the Pickwick on Saturday night, and learned that Niko had made it clear he would not be welcomed back. Evidently Thelonious Monk was not what Niko had in mind for the piano bar.

"Niko is a weird little human," said DuWayne.

"Assuming he's human."

DuWayne seemed to be giving the question some thought. "Yeah, man. But anyway the cat says from now on he'll accept no substitutes, you know what I mean?"

"Not exactly."

"He says he could hire anybody he wants to play his piano, and he hired you, not me or anybody else. Long story short, if you don't show up tonight you're out of a gig."

Life on the lam was starting to take its toll. I felt like a caged bird and I wanted to fly back to the Pickwick Club, if only to assert my independence. Theresa advised me to stay out of sight until the police and the mob forgot I ever existed.

"That could be a long time," I said.

"Years," she agreed.

"What am I supposed to do in the meantime? I can't work or go anywhere or do anything?"

"I know people who've been in hiding since the fifties. It can be done."

That settled it. I called Niko and told him I'd be back at work that evening. Then I slipped back into my moon suit and rode the elevator down to the lobby, where a nervous crowd had assembled behind a barricade of yellow police tape. "Everything's under control," I announced. "It's safe to come in now."

Owen's van stood waiting at the curb. I opened the back door, waved appreciatively to Tweedledum and Tweedledee in their Mercury Grand Marquis and climbed into the back of the van. We glided away like a lunar module returning to the mother ship, laughing all the way. By the time we were five blocks away at 18th and Chestnut, I had morphed back into a mild-mannered piano player and recovering lawyer who could easily disappear into the Center City crowds. I thanked Owen profusely, forgave him his debts, and spent the rest of the afternoon running errands and enjoying my freedom. It was a clear, crisp winter day and there were hundreds of people on the streets, going about their business without getting arrested or gunned down or beaten up, and for the time being I was one of them. Nobody seemed to be watching.

At five o'clock I arrived back at Madison's but found that she had already left for work. After a shave and a shower, I went online and found a message from Ernie. He had confirmed with Building Security that Yvette Babylon entered the parking garage at 4:52 on the afternoon of her husband's death and left at 6:22. I printed out the message and sat staring at it with a feeling of suspended excitement, like a hunter watching the movements of his quarry through a gun sight. The last few blanks in the puzzle were filling in.

And there was another amazing message from Ernie. The police had identified the webmaster of the Neil Babylon Murder Home Page. It was, as everyone had predicted, a fourteen-year-old kid in the suburbs. What was amazing was that the teenager's name was Josh Taconelli and he was Rick Taconelli's teenage son. Evidently he'd been getting his information by eavesdropping on conversations between his parents.

Before I could react to that development my attention was grabbed by another message that appeared on Madison's phony website for the Mid-Atlantic Regional Clearinghouse for Criminal Record Reporting. It was from the State's Attorney for Bexar County, Texas, and it concerned Norman Ezra Sproat in response to our inquiry. The message resolved any doubts that Sproat was McVeigh, because it was accompanied by two large color photographs, one frontal and the other in profile, and the subject was not smiling and saying cheese but wearing a number around his neck. Sproat was an ex-con wanted for armed robbery and attempted murder in Texas, which was not really surprising, but I felt almost sick to my stomach when I scanned to the bottom and saw the note: "Also wanted for questioning in the murders of three exotic dancers in San Antonio and Dallas."

I grabbed the phone and called ZuLu's. The bartender said Madison was dancing and couldn't come to the phone. He took a message which said, "Stay there. Don't leave. Wait for me. Peter." I made him read it back to me twice and promise to give it to Madison as soon as she sat down. Then I hurried off to the Pickwick, planning to hop over to ZuLu's on my first break.

Niko greeted me at the door with a hostile nod. I hung my coat in the hall near the kitchen, opened the piano and sat down to play my first song. It was a Tuesday night and the crowd was sparse. But halfway through that first song, I glanced up and saw the unmistakable hulk of Bardahl looming over the piano, shrouded in cigarette smoke like a genie waiting for the right moment to announce his presence. That moment came even before I finished the song. Bardahl cleared his throat—with a sound that could have been mistaken for an avant garde sax solo—and leaned closer so I couldn't pretend not to hear him.

"I'm here to recommend that you turn yourself in," he said.

"Turn myself into what?" I quipped. "A pumpkin?"

"If you don't, they're going to come after you with all they got. You won't like it."

"What am I charged with?"

"Murder one."

As if that wasn't bad enough, the next thing I saw was another shrouded figure perching on one of the barstools like a bird of evil omen. It was Patsy Jessup, sipping a double scotch, and I wondered what ill tidings she could bring that would be worse than what I'd just heard from Bardahl.

Luckily I was not without benefit of clergy. Father Brian O'Dolan parked himself boldly between Patsy and Bardahl, as if he were confident that he could overpower the evil forces that surrounded him. He raised his wine glass and looked straight at Patsy. "Young lady," he said—perhaps he was already drunk—"do you realize what drinking scotch whiskey can do to your bowels?"

Patsy ignored him and looked at me. "The Lesser Evil knows where you are," she said.

"Evil always knows where you are," O'Dolan agreed. "And if you think—"

"He wants to have you committed."

"Committed!" O'Dolan repeated. "Committed to evil!" He seemed delighted by the idea. "You know"—he turned to Bardahl—"the modern world no longer believes in God, but it still believes in the Devil."

Just as he said that, another repeat customer took a seat at the bar and gestured to the cocktail waitress. It was my friend the Mafia undertaker, accompanied by two unsmiling assistants in dark overcoats who stood behind him with their hands in their pockets and their eyes on me.

"Quite frankly," said Patsy, "if I were you I'd get out of town."

Time out for another sax solo as Bardahl cleared his throat. "That's a bad idea," he finally said.

Patsy squinted at Bardahl as if noticing him for the first time. "I've never had a bad idea," she said.

"Cloud," said Bardahl, ignoring Patsy, "I've gone to bat for you to keep anything from happening for another twenty-four hours. Like a little stay of execution, so to speak. This way I could talk to you."

I nodded, to let him know I was listening.

"I told them I could convince you to come in now and avoid a hassle."

"But I'm innocent."

"Innocent!" O'Dolan echoed.

"It doesn't matter if you're innocent or not," said Patsy, "once the Lesser Evil has you locked in his clutches."

O'Dolan leaned toward the smiling mortician. "I feel as though I'm witnessing a struggle for this man's soul." He looked to his right at Bardahl and then to his left at Patsy, sizing up the capabilities of the antagonists. "Or is it just for his body?"

"His body," said the undertaker.

The assistants made some unintelligible noises that sounded like dogs barking. In retrospect I think they were laughing.

"At least that's what I'm interested in," the undertaker added. "His body. Heh heh."

More barking. The undertaker ordered a drink from the cocktail waitress. "You see," he said to O'Dolan, "there's a funeral tonight and the piano man's invited. We came to pick him up."

"Maybe he's got other plans," said Patsy.

"Attendance is mandatory," the undertaker said. "Isn't that right, Mike?"

The larger of the two assistants nodded and grinned, displaying a front tooth of solid gold.

"Heh heh. Here's a riddle: What if they had a funeral and nobody came?"

He looked from one impassive face to another. "Get it? No *body*."

Patsy spoke to me. "You should just get out of town. These creeps wouldn't lay a finger on you in front of the police."

"There's still time to accept my offer," Bardahl said. "We'd protect you."

All eyes were on me, and all I could think about was how stupid I was for walking into this trap. The only certainty in my mind was that I couldn't let anything stop me from getting over to ZuLu's to warn Madison about Sproat. And they all would stop me if I gave them half a chance. Bardahl wanted to arrest me, the undertaker wanted to bury me, and Patsy wanted to scare me out of town. Each, in their own way, must have felt me closing in. Patsy was looking out for herself, as she always did, though she might have had other purposes, such as protecting Yvette. The undertaker was undoubtedly getting his orders, if not his jokes, from Valunos. And Bardahl was a riddle wrapped in an enigma inside a mountain of flab and a cloud of cigarette smoke. He said he wanted to help me, but he was about as trustworthy as a Saturday night special. All I knew was I had to escape from the lot of them or I would never get to ZuLu's.

I played one tune after another as I brooded over how to get away. When I was close to despair, I happened to catch the eye of Brian O'Dolan, the only person at the bar who didn't have capturing or eliminating me on his agenda. He sat brooding over his wine glass with an agitated look on his face, something I had never seen before. Perhaps his years as a priest had given him a sense of when people are in trouble. When our eyes met he raised his eyebrows in a clear signal that he wanted to help me. I couldn't signal back, but when I came to the end of the song I stopped playing instead of launching right into the next tune. The undertaker and his assistants scrutinized me carefully.

"This one's for a priest I once knew named Father O'Dolan," I said, assuming that none of my enemies would know that he was sitting at the bar with them. "It's a special request."

The song was "Dancing In the Dark," and Brian O'Dolan might have been the only one there who was old enough to recognize it. After a few more minutes of brooding he took the hint. He stood up unsteadily and set his wine glass down on the bar. "Don't let them take my drink," he said to Patsy. "I'm just going to use the facilities." And he staggered off toward the men's room.

I pictured Brian O'Dolan's motions in my mind's eye as he disappeared behind me. First he'd pick his way through the crowded tables toward the main bar. Then he'd take a left and head down the hallway toward the kitchen and the rest rooms. Along that same hallway stands a utility closet containing the electrical control box for the entire premises. Once inside that closet, which is not kept locked, it would be a simple matter to find the master circuit breaker. Let the dancing in the dark begin!

When the lights went out I leaped away from the piano and bolted toward the kitchen. It was a trip I'd made many times, unlike my pursuers, and apart from knocking down a few patrons and at least one waitress carrying a tray, I navigated it successfully while everyone else stumbled around dancing in the dark. There was a lot of screaming and shouting but when all was said and done I was out in the alley behind the kitchen, running in the general direction of ZuLu's without anybody chasing me. Unfortunately I had to circle around in order to get to the ZuLu's entrance, and by the time I did that the undertaker's assistants were tearing after me as if they were going to embalm me on the spot. I ran straight ahead, across the traffic on Sixteenth Street and into the lobby of the Hotel Lamartine, where I'd worked years ago as a busboy. Back through the kitchen, out into the alley and again in the opposite direction from the one I wanted to be going, and all the time I could hear the assistants tramping after me and shouting at the top of their lungs. On Sansom Street I found a sleepy bar named Alexander's, where I hid in the men's room until I couldn't stand it any longer. I was getting to be a connoisseur of nonfunctional toilets, and I would have to rank this one as slightly worse than the one at the Big Boy.

A little before ten I ventured out to the street and was relieved not to find anyone who was trying to kill me. It was several blocks to ZuLu's and I arrived there about ten minutes after ten. Madison was nowhere in sight.

"Where's Madison?" I asked the bartender.

He peered at me through his tinted glasses. "She went home."

"Didn't you give her the note?"

"Are you the guy that called?"

"Yeah, and you were supposed to tell her to wait for me."

"She left with her boyfriend."

"Her boyfriend? What did he look like?"

"Tall white guy with a shaved head."

"You bastard!" I grabbed him by the collar and almost pulled him over the bar. "You didn't give her the note, did you?"

"I gave her the note! Now let me go!"

I dropped him and ran out before anyone could stop me. In front of the Warwick Hotel I found a taxi which took me out to West Philly and left me in front of Madison's building. The lights were on in her apartment on the fourth floor. I rang the buzzer and got no response, and so I kept ringing it and all the other buzzers until somebody finally let me in. As I ran up the stairs I thought I could hear a scream. I pounded on her door until people started coming out of their apartments to see what was going on. Just as I was about to kick in the door, it flew open and Sproat came out at me brandishing an empty whiskey bottle.

"Get out of here!" he shouted.

I could hear Madison crying inside the apartment. "What are you doing to her?"

He broke the whiskey bottle on the door jamb and waved it in front of me. "Get out before I mess up your face!"

I felt like I was in a movie but couldn't remember my lines. What do they usually do after the psychopath breaks the whiskey bottle? I ran back into the stairwell, where I remembered seeing a metal trash barrel. With this raised in front of me I ran back toward Sproat, who stood in the hallway guarding Madison's door. The whiskey bottle was no match for the trash barrel, which flattened him against the door frame and pinned his arms at his sides. I yanked the barrel upwards under his jaw and pushed it against his throat until he dropped the bottle. Then I pushed him into the apartment and shoved the barrel out of the way so I could get at him with my hands.

Sproat seemed to find this amusing. He spun around and started flailing at me with his fists. I took a few punches before getting my elbow around his neck for a stranglehold, and then almost bent him in half as I watched his face turn the color of an angry plum.

Madison huddled on the couch crying, her face red and swollen where he'd punched her. I eased off on the stranglehold to keep Sproat from suffocating.

"Madison," I said. "Do you have a rope or an extension cord? Let me have it. And shut the door." I had no interest in a visit from the police while I was still there. My plan was to hog tie Sproat and drag him down to the laundromat and call the police from there.

"What do you care about this whore?" he growled.

"Watch your language."

"I picked her up on a sex tour of Thailand. Take my word for it, she's a whore."

"Madison, give me that cord! And bring me a pair of socks."

I shoved the socks in his mouth and had him completely immobilized by the time the cops arrived. One of the neighbors had dialed 911. The Batman routine, in which the hero slips out the back way before anyone can recognize him, didn't work. The neighbors told the cops that the fracas began when I tried to break in to the apartment. Before I knew it they had me in cuffs and were loosening the cords around Sproat.

"That guy's the one you want," I protested. "He beat up the girl and he's wanted for murder in Texas."

This information didn't earn me any better treatment from the police, but at least they had the decency to arrest Sproat along with me. We rode to the station in separate police cars.

30.

The knowledge that you are going to be hanged the next morning is said to concentrate the mind wonderfully. I might add that spending an entire night in a locked jail cell is a mind-concentrating experience second only to being hanged. There's much to observe and to think about. For example, I learned that contrary to the typical prison movie, where everyone seems to be groping his way around in the dark, a real jail—at least the Philadelphia County Jail, where I was privileged to spend the night at the taxpayers' expense—is harshly lighted at all hours of the night, like the cage of a laboratory rat. Your clothes are confiscated and you're issued a blaze orange jump suit that makes you look like everyone else. There may not be a bed or any other furniture in your cell, except for a toilet which, in keeping with recent trends, is nauseating in its emanations. Your cell mates, who might be pleasant enough fellows if you met them over cocktails at your country club, in the prison setting can have a deranged, menacing quality that puts solitary confinement in a whole new light. For example, one irascible young man with whom I spent part of the evening—and who had just been awarded an extended stay at Graterford Penitentiary—kept insisting that he should have been acquitted because there was too much evidence against him. With that much evidence, he argued, it should have been obvious that the case was a frame-up.

That set me to thinking—could there ever be too much evidence in a case?—but in spite of my wonderful mental concentration I couldn't keep from dwelling on the miseries of my own broken heart. The bruises I'd suffered at the hands of Norman Ezra Sproat were nothing compared to the pain I felt at realizing that Madison had been deceiving me from the moment she walked into the Pickwick and gave me that first passionate kiss. The exotic beauty who promised a lifetime of devotion had turned out to be a fraud. She'd known Sproat for a long time. She was evidently his girl friend or whatever a girl is called when she's brought back from a sex tour of Thailand. In all likelihood she was in cahoots with whatever evil scheme he was perpetrating, and all her innocence, all her tenderness, all her devotion—even her jealousy of Elena—had been a sham. For me it was a bitter realization, arousing emotions which I hope I will never feel again.

But a broken heart can also concentrate the mind wonderfully, and certainly with more practical effect than being hanged. By the time my name was called out by the guard and I was shoved down the hall to my bail hearing the next morning, I was convinced in my own desperate, sleepless mind that I was close to solving the mystery of Neil Babylon's death.

I was still in for a few surprises, though, the first of which awaited me in the courtroom where they took me for my bail hearing. It was one of those old-fashioned courtrooms with lots of dark paneling and heavy wooden tables and chairs for the parties and their lawyers. One of the tables was already crowded with Norman Ezra Sproat and his handlers: Tom Riordan, Art Valunos and Rick Taconelli, all wearing conservative dark gray pinstripes that contrasted with their client's blaze orange jump suit. Sproat growled at me when I walked in and seemed ready to attack until Riordan laid a hand on his shoulder. At the other table sat a young Assistant D.A. dressed in plaid with a balding head and a baby-like face who I soon learned was named Larry Schildkraut. There was also the usual assemblage of tired-looking bailiffs, guards and court reporters. But the person who got most of my startled attention was the judge.

"All rise!" shouted the bailiff. "The Court of Common Pleas of the City and County of Philadelphia, the Honorable Elena M. Fiore presiding, is now in session."

There she was in her black robe and her hair pulled back, as beautiful as ever but with a dark, pitiless expression on her face that made me want to run back to my cell and try to burrow out with a spoon. Not that her expression was aimed at me. She never looked at me, and I knew at that moment that she could have sentenced me to the electric chair without so much as a glance in my direction.

"Matters of Norman Ezra Sproat and Peter W. Cloud," intoned the bailiff. "Nos. 345695 and 345696."

Elena peered at the Assistant D.A. over the tops of her reading glasses. "Mr. Schildkraut?"

"If it please the Court, Your Honor," began Schildkraut in an awkward, tentative manner, "these two men were arrested last night. After a fight. It was in an apartment in West Philadelphia. The police were called by a neighbor, who—"

"Whose apartment was it?" asked the judge.

"The tenant is a young woman named Kandsadar Nim, 23 years old.   She was treated for bruises and abrasions at University Hospital."

"They were fighting with her?"

"No, Your Honor—"

"Your Honor," said Rick Taconelli. "Mr. Cloud broke into the apartment—"

"Have you entered your appearance?"

"I beg your pardon, Your Honor.   Richard Taconelli, Rittenhouse Poole & Babylon, appearing for Mr. Sproat. Mr. Cloud broke into the apartment and attacked Mr. Sproat and the young woman.   He overpowered Mr. Sproat, who was trying to protect her, and then he tied him up and beat Ms. Nim with his fists and a heavy metal garbage can."

"Your client was protecting the woman from Mr. Cloud?"

"Yes, Your Honor.   Apparently Mr. Cloud had been living in the apartment—"

"Living there?"

"Yes, Your Honor. They were having some sort of relationship. Mr. Sproat was an old friend, and Ms. Nim asked him to come over and be there when Mr. Cloud returned, because she feared for her life."

Art Valunos stood up beside Rick Taconelli and spoke to Elena in a familiar, unctuous fashion, without bothering to state his name or enter his appearance. "Your Honor, Mr. Cloud is a former employee of our firm. I believe that he is seriously in need of psychiatric evaluation.   During the past week, for reasons best known to himself, he has broken into our offices on at least two occasions.   On one such occasion he threatened me and I felt fortunate that I was able to escape without serious injury."

I had sat in stunned silence during Rick Taconelli's comments, unable to summon the words to defend myself. When Valunos joined in I lurched to my feet. "Your Honor—"

"Mr. Cloud," Elena interrupted, "are you represented by counsel?"

"No, Your Honor. I don't need a team of suits standing here—"

"Then let me advise you that you have no obligation to say anything at this hearing. Whatever you say will be taken down and could be held against you. I strongly advise you to remain silent."

"While they take turns lying about me?"

"It's your choice."

"None of what they've been telling you is the truth. And none of it's admissible evidence. They weren't there last night. I was there and Sproat was there. I don't mind testifying if he does."

Taconelli brushed that offer aside. "Mr. Sproat declines to testify at this hearing."

"Do you want to testify?" Schildkraut asked me.

"Sproat beat the girl up and I went there to stop him. He met me at the door with—"

"This isn't testimony, Your Honor," Taconelli interrupted. "If he wants to testify he should be sworn as a witness."

The judge agreed. "That's correct, Mr. Cloud. Do you want to testify or not?" She looked at me directly for the first time. "Again, I'd strongly advise you not to do so."

I stood there thinking it over for a minute or two while Valunos and Taconelli coughed and shuffled their feet. Elena's warnings seemed more than perfunctory, more emphatic than what she might have said to someone else in the same situation. There were probably a hundred reasons why I'd regret not keeping my mouth shut, but at the moment I couldn't think of any. Fortunately, before I could respond, we were interrupted by a familiar voice croaking from the back of the courtroom.

"Your Honor—" Everyone turned around.

There he was, my dark guardian angel, in his black trench coat with all the belts and buckles that no one could make any sense of. "Lieutenant Alvin Bardolski, Philadelphia Police Department. I think I can provide some testimony that the court will find helpful."

"All right, Lieutenant. Please have a seat up here."

Bardahl was duly sworn—it was all the bailiff could do to hold on to the Bible when Bardahl laid his hamlike right hand on it—and proceeded to identify himself and lay the foundation for his testimony. Schildkraut's questioning was so inept that the judge started asking the questions herself.

"Did you observe either of these suspects last night?"

"Yes, Your Honor. I've had Cloud under surveillance for the past week on another matter. What Mr. Valunos says is true. Cloud did make unauthorized entry into the Rittenhouse offices on several occasions."

Valunos nodded smugly and whispered something to Riordan and Taconelli. Sproat watched me with a murderous expression in his eyes.

"It is also true that he was living with the Nim woman. He has been driving her car, a 1996 Honda Civic. She is employed as an exotic dancer at ZuLu's."

Elena's brow darkened but she kept her eyes on Bardahl. "I see."

"However," Bardahl continued, "Cloud's account of what happened last night is substantially accurate. I had Cloud under direct surveillance until approximately nine o'clock. I then lost contact with him until he appeared at Ms. Nim's apartment building at approximately 10:45. Mr. Sproat was already there. Eyewitnesses report that Sproat met Cloud at the door with an empty whiskey bottle that he broke it and threatened him with it."

Valunos glared at Rick Taconelli, and Taconelli stood up. "Your Honor, I'm going to object. It's unclear whether this witness is testifying from personal observation or hearsay statements that were collected by the police."

"Overruled."

Bardahl went on, "Ms. Nim could be heard crying inside the apartment. Cloud found a garbage can in the stairwell and used it to dislodge Sproat from the doorway. There was a fight inside the apartment, and Cloud finally subdued Sproat and tied him up with an electric cord. When the police arrived Cloud was dragging Sproat out the door and Ms. Nim was crying on the couch."

"Your Honor!" Taconelli seemed ready to explode.

"She stated to the officer that it was Sproat, not Cloud, who had beaten her."

"Objection, Your Honor!   This is the purest form of hearsay. If the prosecution intends to rely on Ms. Nim, she should be here testifying as a witness."

Elena gave Taconelli a look that would have withered every leaf in a sizable forest. "I understand she's not here because she's in the hospital, recuperating from a vicious beating."

"It's my understanding that she's been released from the hospital."

"Then is it your understanding, Mr. Taconelli, that a victim of abuse is obligated to limp down to the courthouse to testify as soon as she's released from the hospital or face the risk of getting beaten up again by the time she gets home?"

"It's a question of evidence, Your Honor. This type of testimony—"

"This is a bail hearing, Mr. Taconelli, not a trial. The purpose is to determine whether there is sufficient evidence to bind the suspects over for trial and how much bail should be required, and in an abuse case the evidentiary standards are different when there is an imminent threat to the victim's safety. Objection overruled."

Elena turned back to Bardahl. "Is that all, Lieutenant Bardolski?"

"Yes, Your Honor. To sum it up, I would say all of the eyewitnesses agree that Mr. Cloud, far from being guilty of abuse, acted heroically and at considerable risk to himself to put a stop to the abuse being perpetrated by Mr. Sproat. In all my years on the force—"

"Thank you, Lieutenant."

I rose slowly to my feet. "May I ask the witness a couple of questions?"

"Certainly."

"Lieutenant Bardolski, have you learned any more about Mr. Sproat since last night. About his previous record?"

Taconelli never seemed to know when to stop. "Your Honor," he blurted, "this is not an inquiry into Mr. Sproat's previous record. He's not testifying as a witness and he can't be impeached—"

"The fact is," I interrupted, "Mr. Sproat was the subject of a consent judgment about six months ago—at which time he was represented by the Rittenhouse firm—arising from his abuse of his ex-girlfriend, probably the same woman, and he's wanted for armed robbery and attempted murder in Texas—"

"Your Honor, this is objectionable and highly prejudicial to my client!"

Elena glanced at Sproat, who sat staring dully into space as if we were all talking about someone else, and then gave Rick another of her withering looks. "Mr. Taconelli, I agree that it's highly prejudicial, and deservedly so. Let me make something clear, if I haven't done so already. This court attaches a particular seriousness to cases of domestic violence. There is no excuse for it, and this court will not tolerate it. You seem to be suggesting that Mr. Sproat, who has been the subject of a prior injunction regarding his abuse of this very woman, should be released so that he can go beat her up again."

"No, Your Honor, of course not."

"But you think I should release him?"

"Yes, Your Honor, but—"

She cut him off and glared at Riordan. "Mr. Riordan, what is the reason for your presence here this morning?"

Riordan swallowed hard and answered in a weak, throaty voice. "Mr. Sproat is one of my employees."

"Do you like what you've heard about him this morning?"

"No, Your Honor."

"Then I would suggest that you pay more attention to the kind of people you have working for you. It could rub off."

"Yes, Your Honor."

"Mr. Schildkraut, where is Ms. Nim?"

Schildkraut looked around the courtroom, as if he expected to see Madison sitting in the audience. "I don't know, Your Honor. I assume she's back in her apartment. She was examined at the hospital and released."

"This case illustrates the way our legal system is failing to address the seriousness of domestic violence. The issue here is whether one or both of these men abused a young woman, and we have the spectacle of half a dozen men arguing about it without the woman being present or even consulted, so far as the court can determine. Where is the woman?"

It was a rhetorical question, but Schildkraut make the mistake of trying to answer it. "Your Honor, as you pointed out earlier, we didn't think it was necessary for her to be here. She was injured and quite upset and—"

"All right then," Elena cut him off, " I'm ready to make a provisional ruling. Mr. Sproat will be retained in custody without bail until any outstanding warrants in other states can be checked—"

"Your Honor," objected Rick Taconelli, "there aren't any outstanding warrants. Mr. Cloud is just making that up. He doesn't have standing to testify about outstanding warrants so as to justify holding Mr. Sproat in custody—"

"Don't interrupt, Mr. Taconelli. The argument is over. This is my ruling. Reporter, please read back what I just said."

The reporter read back, "Mr. Sproat will be retained in custody without bail until any outstanding warrants in other states can be checked," and Elena continued: "and Mr. Cloud will be released on his own recognizance, subject to the following. Neither Mr. Cloud nor his attorney (if he retains one) nor Mr. Sproat, Mr. Riordan or any member of Mr. Sproat's defense team or any other employee of Mr. Riordan will have any contact with Ms. Nim, either verbal or physical, in person or by telephone or by any other means of communication, without prior notification and approval of this court. Is that clear?"

It was time for the little unison chorus of acquiescence by the lawyers that ends every hearing. "Yes, Your Honor."

As always, I wanted to have the last word. "Your Honor, may I ask a point of clarification?"

"Certainly. And by the way, Mr. Cloud, if Lieutenant Bardolski's testimony is accurate, you're to be commended."

"Thank you, Your Honor. I do have one problem, though. As Lieutenant Bardolski testified, I have recently been staying in Ms. Nim's apartment because my apartment was ransacked and is uninhabitable. May I have permission to contact Ms. Nim in order to make arrangements to retrieve my belongings?"

"No, Mr. Cloud. You may not. Not without my approval, which at this time is denied without prejudice to any future request."

She peered over the assembled faces with that glow of arbitrary power that every judge exudes when he or she has made a decision. "Are there any further questions?"

And so before the morning was over, Sproat was comfortably behind bars and I was out on the street. One of the cops escorted me to the Processing Room, where I changed my clothes and retrieved my wallet and other personal effects, and from there to the exit. When I stepped outside I was in for another surprise. The same officer who had served as bailiff in the courtroom stood waiting for me on the sidewalk. As I started to walk away he sidled up beside me and asked for a light.

"Sorry," I said. "I don't smoke."

"Neither do I," he said. "But I have a message for you. Walk down Race to Chinatown and stand at the corner of Tenth and Race. Be there at noon."

Not having any better place I could go, I did as I was told. Not much was going on in Chinatown at that hour of the day. But a few minutes after noon the big Land Cruiser with the tinted windows pulled up to the curb and I climbed in. Elena had taken off her black robe but her face still wore the look of a hanging judge.

"Where are we going?" I asked.

"West Philadelphia. What's her address?"

31.

The drive out to West Philly was like a continuation of my bail hearing, only the questioning was more hostile and relentless. "Why didn't you tell me you were living with this go-go dancer?" Elena asked as we shot through a red light and headed up Arch Street.

"I had the feeling you might not want to hear it."

"You said you were staying with some buddy of yours out in the suburbs."

"I wasn't under oath."

Trying to lighten things up with a joke was evidently the wrong thing to do. She whipped the Land Cruiser around a corner and almost knocked a little old man off his bicycle.

"Just kidding," I explained.

"What else have you been lying to me about?"

"Nothing much. There are things I don't tell you about, if I think they'd upset you."

"Why do you think your living with this girl would upset me?"

"It seems to be upsetting you now." That was an understatement. She was driving like an escaped convict. Fortunately we were bottled up in traffic, so the amount of damage she could do was minimal. "Maybe you're a little jealous or something. I don't know."

"I'm not jealous," she said. "I'm just a little shocked that you would stoop so low. How old is this girl?"

"About twenty-three. She's an engineering student at Drexel."

"Twenty-three? What kind of 'relationship' have you been having with her?"

"The usual kind."

There were several minutes of awkward silence as we made our way in a series of violent fits and starts up Market Street. I felt a little thrill as I realized that Elena really was jealous of Madison, and that her jealousy was sexual.

"I haven't taken a vow of celibacy, you know."

She made no response.

"And you're not in a position to complain about Madison."

That one drew a response. She slammed on the brakes and pulled over to the side of the street. "What do you mean I'm not in a position to complain? Because I won't sleep with you?"

"Well, if you would, obviously things would be different. I may not be celibate but I am monogamous."

Conflicting emotions swirled in her eyes like the colors in a kaleidoscope: anger, apprehension, jealousy, maybe even a little bit of love.

I took her hand. "Elena, I love you. I've told you that before. At the least sign of encouragement I would do anything you asked me to do. I'd sell everything I own—

"You don't own anything."

"I know, but if I owned anything I'd sell it and move to China if you asked me."

"You've always wanted to go to China."

"I know, but you know what I mean. I'm yours for the asking. But you can't expect me to sit around my apartment— or your mother's apartment!—by myself while you live your life with your husband and your kids."

"I know," she said quietly. "You're right."

We drove the rest of the way in silence until Elena parked the Land Cruiser in front of Madison's apartment. "Are there things you've found out about Geoff that you haven't told me about?" she asked.

"Not really."

"You're lying again."

"Well, maybe I am. But I still have some self-respect. I wouldn't win your heart by turning you against your husband."

She smiled. "How noble!"

"You heard Bardahl. I'm practically a mythic figure."

"Peter," she said, suddenly serious, "at least tell me this: The stuff you found out about Geoff—it's just business stuff, isn't it? I mean, it's nothing really bad, is it? Or anything... that has to do with me?"

"No. It's just business, that's all it is. Cutting a few corners here and there. Geoff's not a bad guy."

We went up the stairs and there was another awkward moment when I introduced Madison to Elena. The poor girl looked terrible. Her face was bruised and her eyes were almost swollen shut.

"I wanted to make sure you were all right," I said.

"I'm all right. Come on in."

"Madison, this is my friend Elena."

They shook hands. "Nice to meet you," Elena said.

"You're the judge, right?"

I had never told Madison that Elena was a judge. In fact, as far as I could remember I had never told her anything about Elena.

"Yes. I am a judge," Elena answered.

We sat down on the couch and Madison served us some tea with thin cookies. The conversation was even thinner. After a long time I said, "It was true what Sproat said, wasn't it? That he brought you back from Thailand?"

"That was a long time ago."

"Why didn't you tell me you knew him?"

"I was afraid."

"Afraid of him or afraid of me?"

She lowered her eyes. We drank some more tea.

"I could tell you didn't want to know the truth about me," she finally said. "You wanted me to fit your fantasy image of what you wanted me to be. That's all. Just like all the men at ZuLu's."

Elena squeezed her hand and the two of them shot a triumphant blaze of female solidarity in my direction. I felt about two feet tall. "By the way," I said, changing the subject. "I think I've got the murder solved."

Madison's swollen eyes widened. "You do?"

"I'm pretty close. I just have to make one or two phone calls and I think I'll have it nailed down."

She stood up and hurried over to her computer. "Wait till you see the latest thing on the website." She sat down facing the screen. "It's a picture of the webmaster. He identified himself."

Elena and I watched over her shoulder as she navigated to the website. On the home page there was a link to the "Webmaster" and when she clicked on it, we saw the face of a smirking fourteen-year old replica of Rick Taconelli. "Look familiar?" I asked Elena.

"I heard about this yesterday," I told Madison. "I didn't get a chance to tell you. He's the son of one of the Rittenhouse partners."

She flipped through a few screens to the page headed, "Did the Murderer Go to the Funeral?" There were a number of small photographs which could be enlarged by clicking on them. She clicked on one and it expanded to fill the screen. "There you are," she said, pointing to the picture of Elena at the funeral. There was something hostile, almost accusatory about the way she said it.

"Yes," Elena admitted. "I was there."

"And I know that guy too," said Madison. She was pointing at a picture of Elena's husband, who stood directly behind her in the photograph.

"You do?" Elena's voice sounded weak.

"Sure. He comes to the club all the time."

"The club? You mean the place where you... work?"

"Yeah, ZuLu's," Madison nodded. "He's got a thing for one of the other girls. Amber."

Elena took a step backwards. "I don't believe this."

We sat back down on the couch. "Don't jump to any conclusions," I said. "A lot of men go to those places. It doesn't mean anything."

"It does in his case," said Madison. "He takes her out, which is against the rules."

"Takes her out?"

"Oh, yeah. He's got it bad. We've been a little worried he's another Craig Rabinowitz."

"Oh, my God!" Craig Rabinowitz was a local celebrity of a few years back, a wealthy suburbanite who drowned his wife in the bathtub after he fell in love with a topless go-go dancer. At the mention of his name Elena started sobbing uncontrollably. I put my arm around her and held her and comforted her until she stopped crying. Madison watched quietly but said nothing. Her swollen eyes remained dry.

I walked Elena to the door and turned around to say goodbye to Madison. She had let me down but I wanted to kiss her one last time.

"I guess I'll come back for my stuff," I said.

"Maybe you ought to take it now."

32.

I put Elena in the Land Cruiser and drove home to the Coolidge House. It was risky but Elena was sobbing and I decided the only safe place for her to be was at her mother's. As it happened, there was nobody waiting to pounce on me when I drove into the building garage. My fifteen minutes of fame had passed. I parked the Land Cruiser in the garage and after Elena had composed herself we took the elevator up to her mother's apartment, hoping for a nice bowl of soup or a plate of fresh pasta. But Theresa was nowhere to be found, and the stove, for the first time I could remember, was cold.

"I remember now," Elena said. "She was going on a bus trip to Atlantic City with her Bingo Club. She won't be back till late tonight."

Elena opened a can of soup and heated it up. She had stopped crying but she was very quiet, saying nothing until we sat down at the table to eat our soup.

"I should have known," she said. "In fact, I guess I did."

"What do you mean?" I asked gently.

"I'm not surprised he's having an affair. I guess I'm just shocked at what kind of an affair he's having. An exotic dancer named Amber."

"Don't be so hard on him. I'm no better."

"Yes, you are."

"No," I insisted—I don't know why I felt the compulsion to defend Geoff. "Look at me, running around with Madison."

"You're not married," she said. "You're not another Craig Rabinowitz."

After lunch I slipped into Theresa's bedroom to use the telephone. Those dour saints who prayed perpetually over her bureau gave me the evil eye as I sat on the bed fumbling with the old fashioned rotary phone. I had to make three calls to get the right number, and then I was on hold for another five minutes before I finally reached my party. But by the time I walked out of that bedroom I knew who had killed Neil Babylon. I was brimming with excitement, but something told me it wasn't the right time to give the news to Elena. She was sitting on the couch sobbing uncontrollably into her handkerchief.

I sat down beside her and held her hand to try and comfort her. "I know you and Geoff haven't been getting along that well," I said.

"It's been a long time since we've gotten along at all."

"I didn't realize that."

"It's been a long time since I've felt loved." She managed a sheepish smile. "That sounds like such a cliché."

"No, not at all."

"Maybe just because I've thought it so many times." The crying had stopped but there was still a lot of work to be done with the handkerchief. When that was finished she turned to face me with a look of embarrassed innocence in her eyes. "But there's a little twist. I guess you could call it guilt."

"Guilt?"

"I feel that I shouldn't be surprised if Geoff doesn't love me. I made the conscious decision to stay with him not because of who he is but for the marriage and the kids. That's not something you would love a wife for, is it?"

"I don't know. If my wife had made that decision I'd probably still be with her."

"Do you still love her?"

"No. I'm not so sure I did even then."

I folded her in my arms and gently rocked her like a frightened child. "What do you feel guilty about?"

"I don't care if he loves me or not."

We sat together like that for over an hour, and I have to admit that although I tried to understand Elena, most of the time my thoughts were elsewhere Dealing with convoluted emotions, whether my own or someone else's, is not my strong point. And after everything that had happened in the last twenty-four hours—the fight with Sproat, the breakup with Madison, my sleepless night in the Philadelphia County Jail, and now the solution of the Babylon murder—I didn't have a lot of mental capacity left over to deal with Elena's guilt about her husband. I fell sound asleep with her in my arms, dreaming a nightmarish replay of my bail hearing in which Valunos and Sproat and Madison all took the witness stand and proved beyond a reasonable doubt that I was a menace to society who should spend the rest of his life behind bars, and when I woke up the judge was kissing me quite seriously on the mouth.

"I've made a decision," she said.

"They're all lying," I protested.

"It's about you."

"I hope you haven't decided to increase my bail, because—
"

"I've decided I would like to sleep with you."

I blinked a few times to make sure I wasn't dreaming. "You woke me up to tell me that?"

She laughed. "Did you hear me? I want to sleep with you."

She started to unbutton my shirt. "Are you sure about this?" I asked her.

"I've been working on this decision for a long time."

"What about your family?"

"I'm friends with all the other judges. I'll get the kids."

"And Geoff?

"He can have Amber."

We sat on the couch making out like a couple of teenagers while I adjusted to the realization that my dreams had finally come true. The woman in my arms was not some ordinary woman, not even some unusually beautiful or desirable woman. This was Elena, the mate that fate had me created for.

"Oh, wait a minute!" She jumped up and ran into the kitchen and started digging around in the refrigerator and the cupboards.

"What are you looking for?"

"Champagne. I think we ought to celebrate, don't you?"

"Sure. But... does your mother usually keep champagne in the apartment?"

"No, I guess not." She looked suddenly crestfallen, as if the whole momentous occasion turned on whether we had champagne or not.

"Hey," I said. "No problem. I'll just run down to the store and pick some up." I rebuttoned my shirt, slipped on my jacket and gave Elena a long goodbye kiss. "Be back in a jiffy."

Out the door and through the hall and down the elevator into the lobby—if there was a floor in that building, I didn't know it because I was walking on air. No need to rush—these were moments I wanted to savor, like the champagne I would soon be toasting Elena with. The street was jammed with cars honking and jostling with each other because a funeral procession was blocking one of the cross streets, but I hardly noticed the commotion. I took my time navigating through the stalled traffic toward the state liquor store on the next block.

As I picked my way across Locust Street, a black funeral limousine lurched in front of me and its doors flew open. The undertaker's burly assistants climbed out solemnly as if they were there to pick up a corpse. I tried to squeeze between the limousine and a couple of trucks but before I could go ten steps the assistants had me pinned from behind. They dragged me back to the limousine and pushed me inside, shoving me down between them on a rear-facing seat. Across from me sat the smiling undertaker.

"Whose funeral?" I wondered out loud.

The undertaker's smile widened. "You have to ask?"

33.

My captors did nothing to prevent me from observing where we were going. We turned west on JFK and after a few blocks we glided down the long ramp into the sub-basement of the Rittenhouse building, where we came to a stop near the freight elevator I had used as my private entrance to the firm. As the undertaker pulled out his cell phone he made sure I noticed the gun sticking out of his belt. He dialed a programmed number. "Art," he said, "we got him. No problem. Down in the garage, by the freight elevator. Yeah, we'll bring him up. But we don't want any incidences, you know what I mean? Could you send down some reinforcements?"

We waited about five minutes until the elevator doors opened and Valunos stepped out with Lockjaw and Ernie at his side. The undertaker's assistants yanked me out of the car, each wrapping himself around one of my arms as they dragged me up to the loading dock. I probably could have smashed their heads together but I was afraid the undertaker might decide to use his gun.

"Tell these buffoons to let me go," I said to Valunos.

"We're not making that mistake again."

I turned to Lockjaw and then to Ernie—"Are you guys going to let them get away with this?"—but they both looked away as if they didn't recognize me.

"Come on," said Valunos. "Bring him up to the Hieronymus Bosch Room."

That sounded worse than it really was. In a tradition dating back to Mrs. Clarence Rittenhouse, who came from money and eventually went wherever money goes, all the conference rooms at the Rittenhouse firm are named after famous artists—Leonardo, Donatello, Raphael and a number of others. Although the firm's current artistic sensibility is at the paint-by-numbers level, the conference rooms have retained this quaint nomenclature to the present day. I'm sure most of lawyers assume they were named after the Ninja Turtles.

We made the long ride to the 43rd floor in silence, except for a series of angry outbursts by Valunos every time the door opened and someone tried to use the freight elevator for its intended purpose. "I'm being kidnapped," I told a befuddled maintenance man who tried to get on at the thirtieth floor. "Call the police and send them to the Hieronymus Bosch Room at the Rittenhouse firm."

The man looked at me incredulously and started to say something, but Valunos cut him off. "He's crazy," Valunos told the man. "Pay no attention." And the door closed in his face.

On the 43rd floor we bypassed the mail room and headed down the hall. "As it happened," Valunos said to the undertaker, "we were just about to read Neil's will when you called. Everyone's here. The timing couldn't have been better."

The Hieronymus Bosch Room is a spacious but dimly lighted room furnished with a long conference table surrounded by padded arm chairs. Its walls, as you might expect, are decorated from one end to the other with visions of sin, degradation and eternal torment—a fitting venue for the reading of Neil Babylon's will. And there they were, the whole cast of victims and demons, sinners and tormentors who had populated Neil's Garden of Earthly Delights. At the head of the table stood an empty chair which must have belonged to Valunos. In the next seat Senator Squires huddled whispering to a nervous-looking Rick Taconelli. To his right sat Yvette Babylon—legs crossed, head erect, hands folded in front of her—striking a pose of fashionable discomfort, and beside her sat the beautiful Alyssa, who had evidently interrupted her honeymoon to attend the reading of her stepfather's will. Patsy Jessup perched next to Connie Liebman on the other side of the table, drinking coffee out of a stryrofoam cup, and next to Connie I could see Tom Riordan smirking with his amiable hostility. Babylon's secretary, Fran Collins, frowned at me from a chair near the window with a steno pad on her knee. The only person I was really surprised to see was Geoff Goodwin, Elena's husband, who occupied the seat next to Riordan. He did not look happy to be there.

In fact none of them looked happy to be in the Hieronymus Bosch Room just then. They looked like a jury deliberating in a capital case, and something told me I'd arrived just in time to be the defendant.

Valunos closed the door behind us and took his seat at the head of the table. The Senator flashed an unpleasant smile at the undertaker. "Where did you find him, Dominick?"

"Caught him trying to block a funeral procession," said the undertaker, whose name was evidently Dominick.

"Good work."

I tried to shake off the assistants, but they held my wrists behind my back. "Get these two gorillas off me!"

Valunos waved them aside and they let me go, backing into a menacing orbit between me and the undertaker, who had planted himself beside Fran Collins's chair. "Lockjaw," said Valunos, gesturing toward the door, "you and Ernie stand over there in case he tries to escape." My ex-friends from the mail room took up positions like Roman centurions on either side of the door.

Valunos didn't offer me a seat. "A lot of people have been looking for you," he said. "Including the police."

"So I've noticed."

"We were just discussing what to do about you. Of course you'll eventually be turned over to the police, but now the time and place are under our control."

"Heh, heh," the undertaker said in his peculiar comic-book voice.

Valunos shot him a glance that warned him not to interrupt. "The problem is," he said, "you're a menace to the firm. First you killed Neil Babylon—we don't know exactly how you did it, but the truth will come out in due course—and then you tried to destroy the firm by making it look like one of us was the murderer. Obviously this is something we can't let happen."

"And that's why you've had your Mafia buddies trying to kill me."

Valunos and the Senator exchanged smirks. "Believe me," said Valunos. "If I had any Mafia buddies and they tried to kill you, they would have succeeded."

"So what do you want me to do?"

Valunos smiled with a labored benevolence. "Confession is good for the soul, Pete. And it would bring closure for the family." He nodded respectfully toward Yvette and Alyssa.

For a moment he must have imagined that I was going to cooperate. "You can do it right now. Fran can take your confession down in shorthand and type it up for you to sign."

I glanced at Fran. She sat poised like a court reporter, looking at the floor to avoid distraction while she recorded my confession. The others watched me expectantly. "Do you mind if I sit down?" I asked Valunos.

"No, not at all."

I pulled out a chair and sat facing the Senator and Yvette. "I can understand why you'd want me to confess," I said. "In fact I can understand why just about everybody in this room would want me to confess. The trouble is, I have nothing to confess. I didn't kill Babylon, and as you well know, there isn't any evidence that I did. But as you also know, there's a lot of evidence linking most of the people in this room to the murder. And he was murdered."

That threw a chill over the proceedings. I studied their faces. Most of them felt a sudden need to take a sip from their styrofoam cups or to fiddle with the papers in front of them. Valunos glared at me as if he were going to leap over the table and pluck out my eyes. Only the Senator, accustomed as he was to playing for high stakes, seemed capable of dealing rationally with the situation.

"What evidence are we talking about?" he asked blandly. I was expecting him to take the bait. He had to know what I had that could link him to the murder.

"Well," I started to answer—but Valunos cut me off.

"Lou," he said to the Senator, "let's not go down that road. We've got him, let's just get it over with."

The Senator glared at Valunos with ill-concealed contempt, and I realized that he, not Valunos, would be playing the judge in these proceedings. Valunos had been cast in the role of slightly hysterical prosecutor.

The Senator took his time and then looked back at me. "I want to know what evidence is out there," he finally said.

"Lou –"

"Let's hear it."

"That's a wise precaution, Senator," I said. "It's not a pretty story, and you wouldn't want to be reading about it on the front page of the *Inquirer.*"

"Let's hear it."

His tone of voice told me that, like any judge, his patience was not unlimited. For an instant I flashed back to my days in the Public Defender's office and relived the harrowing experience of defending a jury case. The withering stares of the judge, the sneering attacks of the prosecutor, the maddening impassivity of the jury. The dry mouth, the queasiness, the sweat pouring off your forehead as if your life were at stake—and the will to overcome all these obstacles and somehow argue your case as if you knew you deserved to win.

If I could do it then, I could do it now. But this time it was different. My life really was at stake, and this strange assortment of humanity that sat in front of me—this roomful of shysters and scoundrels, with at least one murderer among them—was going to be the jury of my peers.

And the Senator, like all judges, was running out of patience. I had about two minutes to put the prosecution on trial.

I couldn't argue my case sitting down, so I stood up and used the back of one of the chairs as a lectern. Valunos's eyes darted nervously toward the assistants, who positioned themselves between me and the door. "It's a story that goes back a long way," I began.

"Let's hear it," said the Senator.

"Art Valunos and Neil Babylon were the best of friends. But as everyone knew, they hated each other's guts."

"In other words," Patsy quipped, "they were law partners."

I took the interruption in stride. "Precisely," I agreed. "And a little more than that. There'd been a power struggle going on between them for the past twenty years. Nick's ambitions were held in check as long as Babylon was bringing in the big clients. But when Art recruited you, Senator—when was that, about five years ago?—Babylon saw that as a step in Nick's long-range plan to consolidate power for himself."

Valunos rolled his eyes. "Do we have to listen to this?"

"Go on," said the Senator.

"Thank you." I found myself pacing between the tables, searching their faces in hopes of finding a sympathetic juror. There was Valunos scowling and ready to explode, Patsy squirming in her seat and darting her eyes around the room, Rick Taconelli looking as vain and hostile as he always did, Tom Riordan sneering like an executioner. The only face where I could detect some glimmer of sympathy belonged to Geoff Goodwin, whose wife, but for my own stupidity, I should have been in bed with at that very moment.

"Babylon responded with his famous attempt to defect to Morgan Lewis and almost brought the firm down," I said to Geoff. "Art never forgave him for that. It was partly pride on Art's part—he's always been more loyal to the firm than Neil ever was—but it was also a matter of economics. All the partners are individually liable on the bank debt and the lease. If Neil had gone to Morgan Lewis with a dozen hand-picked Rittenhouse lawyers and took a few of the big-money clients with him, the partners who were left behind wouldn't have been able to service the debt."

Valunos started to interrupt but the Senator overruled him with a sharp glance.

"So Neil allowed himself to be brought back from the brink, but at enormous expense to the firm. His salary and perks went up and his client base went down. The firm ended up owing ten million dollars to Third Millennium which could never be paid off. And Art never forgave Babylon for what he did to Rittenhouse Poole."

"Lou—"

"Now let's jump ahead three years. The ten million dollar note to Third Millennium was coming due. Fortunately the firm—at the bank's insistence—had taken out 'key man' life insurance covering each of the senior partners up to ten million dollars, so if any one of them died the loan would be paid off. Everyone knew that was the only way the debt was ever going to be paid. And if the partner who died was Neil Babylon, then Art Valunos would be the top partner in the firm."

Valunos couldn't restrain himself any longer. "This is unbelievable!" he yelled. "I can't believe that we're sitting here letting this psychopath psychoanalyze me!"

"It's not only believable," I said. "It's true. And it gets worse."

"What are you talking about?"

"In early January there was an Executive Committee meeting. And at that meeting, Art, you were quite explicit about the need for one of the senior partners to die in order to pay off the debt."

Valunos almost jumped out of his seat. "Who told you that? I want to know who told you that!"

"What difference does it make who told him?" the Senator asked Valunos.

"It was a joke, for God's sake!"

I smiled knowingly at the Senator. "Maybe it wasn't unusual for the partners to make morbid jokes about each other dying in order to pay off the debt. But when a joke about someone dying is followed up by a call to his life insurance agent, you've got to wonder."

"This has gone on long enough! Rick, pick up the phone and—"

"No," said the Senator. "Let him finish."

"Shortly after that executive committee meeting Art Valunos picked up the phone. He dialed Albert Wrubel, the insurance agent, to ask him if the life insurance was still in effect and whether the individual partners could cancel it or change the beneficiary. The agent told him no, the partners couldn't do either of those things without the bank's consent, and the policy would be coming up for renewal in a couple of months."

I paused. "And then Art asked him another question: Would they require physical examinations of each partner at the time of renewal?"

"That was a routine question that you would ask any insurance agent!"

"Or maybe you'd ask it because you knew about Babylon's deteriorating physical condition. You were the only one at the firm who knew he'd just been diagnosed with serious heart problems. If he was going to die, he'd better do it quickly— that's how it seemed, isn't it, Art?—because in another month he'd fail that physical and the insurance wouldn't be renewed."

At last Valunos rose to his feet. Even in this position he wasn't much taller than the Senator, who remained seated. "I'm not going to listen to this any longer," he said evenly. "Lou, I'm going to insist that we put an end to this nonsense."

"Is that all?" the Senator asked me.

"If Art doesn't like where this is going, we could change the subject," I suggested. "For instance, we could change the subject from Art Valunos to Tom Riordan."

Riordan's reaction was immediate and physical. "You son of a bitch," he snarled, pounding the table and rising half way out of his chair. Fortunately the chairs were jammed together and by the time he was standing the two assistants had blocked

him in, responding to a signal from Dominick. Riordan sat
back down. "You son of a bitch, you say one lying word about
me and I'm going to break your goddam neck!"

"I won't tell any lies about you, Tom. We're good buddies,
remember? We did a lot of work together, back before you
had me disbarred. Back then you were trying to buy that
property down along the riverfront just in case casino gambling
ever came to Philadelphia. Well, you lost out on casino
gambling, so you decided to settle for the next best thing, a
piece of the banking industry. You decided to go for control
of Harrison State Bank. Unfortunately, Oscar Feierabend at
Third Millennium had the same idea. He wanted to get control
of Harrison too, but you had a minority stock interest and you
were blocking the way, with litigation assistance from your
other buddy, Neil Babylon."

"Babylon's services didn't come cheaply. What was his
billing rate? Five hundred an hour? And everybody knows he
charged a billable hour for every martini he guzzled at those
long lunches at the Four Seasons. Now all that wouldn't have
been so bad under normal conditions. You've stiffed plenty of
law firms on their fees over the years. But Babylon was
different. He had something on you. He had those
surveillance tapes that showed how you stole the asbestos
inspection records that I got disbarred for having in my office.
He was holding them over your head—an attorney's lien is
probably what he called it, but blackmail might be a more
accurate description—and he was making you pay your bills as
they came due. But he wasn't getting the results you wanted,
was he, Tom?"

"I swear to God—"

"Don't say any more than you have to, Tom, or I'll tell them all about what you had Sproat doing here at the office."

Riordan growled a little more but said nothing. "And then there was the little matter of the Mists of Inverness. That was a messy situation, wasn't it, Geoff?" Geoff Goodwin stopped slouching and sat up in his chair, trying to look like an innocent bystander. "You know, that problem with the guarantees. Were they limited or unlimited? Depends on who you ask, doesn't it?"

Geoff Goodwin said nothing. "You have the right to remain silent," I said. "And Neil Babylon—now he has no choice but to remain silent, does he?"

I turned to the Senator. I knew I had to be careful because I was about to turn my attack on him. "You probably remember when Oscar Feierabend came to the firm with a proposal. He knew the firm was vulnerable because of the ten million dollar loan coming due, so he proposed a simple plan: If Babylon would drop Tom Riordan and stop representing him against Third Millennium, and if Senator Squires would help persuade the Banking Commission to give them a favorable ruling so they could acquire Harrison State Bank, Third Millennium would extend the term of the ten million dollar loan and bring a substantial amount of legal business to the firm. But Riordan would have to go."

"This is just typical law-firm stuff," the Senator said. "A couple of partners squabbling over clients and conflicts of interest. Big deal. And for the record, I never intervene with state agencies. That would be unethical."

"This is a little different from the usual conflict case, though. In this case there's a ten million dollar debt that's an individual claim against all the partners. And there's no other way around it. A default by the firm, and an ensuing dispute with Third Millennium, would be fatal to the firm and damaging to the reputations of the people associated with it. And there would be political fallout too."

The Senator tried to laugh but only managed to scoff. "I've survived worse things. That was nothing."

"Oh, and I forgot to mention: Under the Feierabend proposal you would have gotten forty percent of the fees from the Third Millennium business."

He looked accusingly at Valunos, as if I had acquired that information directly from him. "There's no such formula," he said. "I work for a living and get paid just like any other partner."

"I have your handwritten calculations, Senator."

This time he tried to scoff but only managed to sneer. "Art, if you want to pull the plug on this guy, that's all right with me. Go ahead and make your call."

"But then of course you had other, more personal reasons to hate Babylon and to want to eliminate him."

He was suddenly very red in the face. "What are you talking about?"

"Do you really want me to say?"

He glared at me with murder in his eye and I knew enough to stop.

"As you know, Senator," I said, "there's proof, and I stumbled on it, and you shouldn't imagine that getting rid of me will make it go away. There's more than one copy and it's in a safe place, and that's where it will stay unless something bad happens to me."

"I'm telling you, Lou," said Valunos, "this guy is a psychotic. There's no telling what kind of story he might make up."

The Senator just kept glaring at me, furious but speechless.

It was time to move on to another target. "Everybody has his personal hot buttons," I said. "For Neil Babylon, it was his beautiful stepdaughter Alyssa and the nasty rumor that started going around last summer about the nature of their relationship."

No one looked at Alyssa, who blushed and stared straight ahead. Yvette tensed visibly and added her own glare of hatred to the others that surrounded me. My jury was turning into a lynch mob.

"I was glad to see Alyssa here today," I went on. "I'd been told that she was honeymooning in Bermuda, but probably this is more important. Her mother's here and so is her best friend—or maybe 'big sister' would be a better term—Connie Liebman. Connie is important for another reason as well. She's the one who had the little altercation with Neil at the cocktail party right before he died."

Connie grimaced to cover her embarrassment, and I continued, again addressing my remarks to Geoff Goodwin, who at least wasn't a member of the family. "A few months ago Alyssa ran into Connie's office in tears. There was a rumor going around the firm that she was sleeping with her stepfather. Alyssa swore to Connie that it wasn't true, and

Connie believed her. But somehow both Neil and Yvette also learned of the rumor. Neil could be heard bellowing all over the 43rd floor, and he pulled out all the stops to track down the source of the rumor. Of course he had the advantage, which Yvette didn't have, of knowing whether it was true or false."

"We're not going to sit here and listen to this," Yvette began, but the Senator cut her off.

"Yvette, please," he said. "I know this is painful, but I want to know what's out there. You don't need to worry."

"Yvette was beside herself," I went on. "Not just for her own sake—she was used to her husband's philanderings—but for the sake of Alyssa and her younger sister Jennifer. Rightly or wrongly, she believed that Neil had seduced Alyssa and that Jennifer would be next. She had often thought about divorcing him. Now she thought about killing him."

"I did not."

"She tried to figure out a way to do it without getting caught. As his wife, she knew things about him that most people didn't. She knew about his health problems and she knew what medications he was taking. She did some investigating on the internet about drug interactions and overdoses and fatal side effects that she might be able to bring about."

"He's making this up."

I ignored her. "Meanwhile Neil did some investigating on his own—it probably didn't take much—and traced the nasty rumor to Patsy Jessup. He called Patsy down to his office and did some more bellowing, which this time was heard as far away as the forty-second floor or maybe even Atlantic City. He could have fired Patsy on the spot and made sure no other Philadelphia firm would ever hire her, probably could have had her disbarred like I was. But he didn't do any of those things. Why not?"

Everyone looked at Patsy as if she would provide the answer. But she peered at me with a strangely quizzical expression in her eyes, paying no attention to anyone else.

"Obviously Patsy had something on him," I said. "It might have been evidence that the nasty rumor about Alyssa was true. Or it might have been something else. Something else she knew that he couldn't risk being exposed."

I took a few steps toward Patsy but she didn't flinch. "Neil was no saint, but he didn't seduce his daughter, did he, Patsy?"

Patsy looked a little sheepish. "No, I never really thought so."

"So what Patsy had over him must have been related to something else, something of a very embarrassing or dangerous nature. Embarrassing to someone else, perhaps, and dangerous to Neil. I think I know what that was, and I think you do too, Senator. And when he got that back from her— and I know that he did, because I found it in his office—she had nothing over him."

The Senator looked a little sick. "She killed him over that?"

"At that point Neil Babylon became very dangerous to Patsy," I said. "Didn't he, Art?"

Valunos squirmed in his chair but said nothing.

"Art has his sources in the Attorney General's office—"

"They never said it was Patsy."

"No," I agreed, "but they said it was a partner, didn't they? They said they had evidence that it was a partner."

"I never believed them."

"But if it turned out to be true, the whole firm could go down the tubes. And when you questioned Connie and Alyssa and found out all about the nastiness and the blackmail and the threats between Patsy and Neil Babylon, you started to wonder, didn't you? Because you realized that Patsy, along with just about everybody else in Philadelphia, desperately wanted to see him dead."

34.

A tense silence filled the room. Everyone had been looking at Patsy, especially the Senator, but when I finished their eyes drifted away. No one wanted to be the first to speak.

It was Patsy who finally broke the silence. "We can't all be guilty," she said.

There was another long pause, and then Geoff Goodwin said, "That's just what I was thinking. First I thought you were trying to prove that Art did it. Then it was Tom Riordan, and then Lou, then Yvette, and now Patsy. And there's a plausible case to be made against each one."

"There's an even more plausible case to be made against him," Valunos insisted, pointing at me.

"Exactly," I said, ignoring Valunos.

Geoff hesitated. "What do you mean, 'Exactly'?"

"I mean that's exactly right—all these people can't be guilty—and that's exactly how it dawned on me who the killer really is."

"Lou—"

"Wait a minute, Art," said the Senator. "Go ahead."

"It occurred to me, as Patsy suggested, that even though the evidence against each one of you is overwhelming, you can't all be guilty."

"That's right," said Valunos. "We're not guilty. You are."

"And since not everybody can be guilty, it means that some of the evidence, or maybe all of it, has been manufactured. Or at least assembled and interpreted in such a way as to point the investigation away from the killer and towards everybody else."

"That's exactly what you've been doing."

"Not me, Art. I've been scrupulously objective in my investigation. But I haven't been alone. I've had help, every step of the way."

I had their undivided attention. "For example, I've had a lot of help from Patsy. She was the first person I talked to here at the firm after the murder. She fed me a lot of information that she wanted me to know, for reasons of her own. Most of it turned out to be false or misleading."

"Are you accusing me of killing Neil Babylon?" she asked.

"No, not at all. You could have been the murderer, you had every reason to kill him, and I'm sure you wanted to. But I know you didn't do it."

"Then who did?"

"There was someone else, someone who had no apparent motive to kill Babylon and for that reason never landed on anyone's list of suspects." I glanced at Geoff Goodwin, who had his motives but had kept them secret. For the first time he looked uncomfortable. "A person who had a reputation for hard work, resourcefulness and reliability."

Patsy shot a glance at Rick Taconelli. "Well, that rules you out, Rick."

Nervous laughter rattled through the room, but Rick didn't join in, especially when everyone turned around and glared at him as if guilt were written all over his face. His forehead was dripping like a tall glass of iced tea on a hot summer day.

"Not really," I said. "Rick was in a privileged position, with access to a lot of highly confidential information. He was in a position to abuse that information for his own ends."

"Listen, there's no proof of any of this!" Rick exclaimed. He appealed to Valunos. "If he's accusing me, he's going to have to speak to my lawyer!"

"Luckily," I said, "I'll be spared that ordeal, since I'm not accusing you of anything other than being an insufferable jackass."

More brittle laughter. Rick was so relieved that he nodded in enthusiastic agreement and laughed along with everyone else.

"No," I continued, "the person I'm talking about, though regarded as a hard working model employee, actually spent less time on work than on surreptitiously gathering and intercepting information about Neil Babylon. Information that could be found in various places, but mainly in the firm's own records."

I took a few steps to the right, toward Fran Collins, whose icy stare said that she was expecting me. She laid down her steno pad and stopped taking notes. "As everyone here knows, Neil conducted all his personal business from the office. He paid his bills from the office, made his medical appointments from here, booked his vacations, bought gifts for his family. Isn't that right, Fran? Or course, Neil didn't do any of this for himself. He never did anything for himself, did he, Fran? It was Fran who did everything for him."

"Of course I did," she said evenly. "He didn't have time for those things. He was an important man."

"For how many years did that go on? For how many years did you do all those things for him?"

"Eighteen years," she replied.

"And that included listening in on all his personal phone calls, didn't it?"

"Well, not all of them. But he did want me to listen to quite a few."

"And you opened his personal mail?"

"That was part of my job as his secretary."

"So you probably knew more about the man than most of his partners, didn't you?"

"I'm sure I did. But if you're implying that I used any of that information improperly, or did anything else...that I shouldn't have done..."

"No, I'm not implying that at all. You did an excellent job of running his life for him, right up to the end. And I'll bet it was a lot harder in the old days, before everything was computerized. Now everything is done on the computer. All the travel arrangements, the bills, the doctor visits..."

"Of course."

"So if you had access to the telephone calls and the mail and the firm's computer system and really knew how to use it—between that and all the data available on the internet—you could have found out just about anything you wanted to know about Neil Babylon, couldn't you? For example, recently you could have learned that Neil had been diagnosed with serious heart disease, clogged coronary arteries complicated by arrhythmia. The lab results came back to the doctor's office from the lab via the internet, and the doctor forwarded them to Neil. You could have learned that the doctor wanted to do a quadruple bypass operation but because of potential complications it couldn't be done right away. And you would have known that Neil wanted to put it off in any case, until after he got his appointment to the Federal bench."

"I didn't know any of that," said Fran.

"No, perhaps not," I said. "But all that information was right there, wasn't it? And someone with access could have learned all that and more."

"I suppose so." She glanced over towards Valunos as if hoping that he would object to the line of questioning.

"Where are you going with this?" asked the Senator impatiently.

"Let's take a hypothetical example," I said, speaking directly to the Senator. I knew I had to come to the point or I would lose my audience. "If a person came to work at the firm—let's say, in the mail room—and kept his eye on the ball, pretty soon he might be in charge of sorting the morning mail and distributing it to the attorneys. It would be easy for him to intercept items of interest about any particular attorney, Babylon for instance. And if he also knew his way around computers, he could intercept Babylon's email messages and track all the sites he visited on the internet. He could get into the firm databases and use the internet to search for information about Babylon. With a little bit of electrical ability he could tap into your phone, Fran, so he could listen in on Babylon's telephone conversations. In this way he could learn all about Babylon's medical condition and the drugs he was taking. He could learn not only about the heart disease but about a few other things as well. For instance he could learn that Babylon had a prescription for Viagra. Did he need it? I don't know, but he used it as some men do to enhance his performance. That's a dangerous thing to do when you have heart disease."

One by one, the people around the table were slowly turning toward the door and the two men standing on either side of it. I kept my focus on the others, but when I glanced toward the door I saw both Lockjaw and Ernie staring at me with murderous intensity.

"If you were this hypothetical mail room employee," I went on, "you would know all this and you could use it when the opportunity presented itself. At one of those firm cocktail parties. You wouldn't be bartending. That's a little obvious. Better let Lockjaw do that. No, but you could run in to bring Lockjaw a few supplies, being careful not to be noticed. But that's not hard. You've never presented a high profile around the firm. So you just slip in long enough to pour a special drink for Neil Babylon. A little nitroglycerin for his heart and a little Viagra too, and maybe a little amphetamine that you picked up on the street. Who would notice any of that in a glass of Scotch?"

Lockjaw turned his towering frame toward Ernie and took a step forward, but Ernie stood his ground and kept his gaze fixed on me.

"The results would be predictable. The Viagra would take its effect subconsciously. Neil was a ladies man, but he was no cad. He didn't usually go around cocktail parties with his hands on the women, let alone other parts of his anatomy. But that's what happened that night, isn't it, Connie? And then even he was embarrassed and escaped back to his office just in time to have a massive heart attack. If anybody had done an autopsy they would have found the Viagra and the heart medicine and even the amphetamines in his bloodstream, none of which would have been surprising. Just a freak accident. Drug interactions. You can read about them on the internet. You can take a warning on the label and turn it into a recipe for murder."

Ernie tried to laugh. "You're accusing me? You've been going around the room accusing everybody, like some perverted joke. And now it's my turn?"

"That's right, Ernie. Only in your case it's not a joke."

"This is stupid."

"No, it isn't. It's you who's been spreading all the trumped up evidence against everybody else."

"I don't know what you're talking about."

"It was you who started the whole rumor about Babylon and Alyssa. Isn't that right, Patsy?'

Patsy nodded grimly.

"And it was you who planted the phony trail in Yvette's computer of internet searches on fatal interactions between the drugs Neil was taking."

"What?" demanded Yvette.

"And this was your big mistake, because I knew how to find out if it was true—it was you who tried to convince me that Yvette had secretly come to the office the night of the cocktail party."

"I can't believe this," said Yvette.

"But why?" asked Valunos. "Why?" He looked like a broken man.

"Yeah, why?"

"You've got some explaining to do," said Lockjaw. Contrary to his name, his jaw was quivering visibly.

Ernie ignored them and spoke to me. "If you think you know why, you better listen to me. I've been spying on you too. It was me who trashed your apartment, in case you were wondering. I know a lot of things about you that nobody else knows. I've been watching and I know it all. Who, what, when and where—and I'm not talking about the Asian porno princess. I'm talking about the other one. The voice on the telephone tape. In fact I've got a whole website ready to launch about that situation."

"What do you want?"

"I want to make a deal. One woman for another. You get what I mean?"

"I think so."

"You gotta be sure."

"I'm sure. It's a deal."

"Okay."

And then he turned to the others and delivered an astonishing rebuke that no one in that room will ever forget. "You're all just as guilty as I am," he said calmly. "Every one of you. You spend your two thousand billable hours a year figuring out how to ruin people's lives without actually killing them. But Neil Babylon—you wanted him dead, every one of you, and you know it. You just didn't have the guts to do what I did. So don't stare at me like I'm some kind of a wacko. I was just acting out your fantasies." And he backed out the door and disappeared.

Lockjaw started to run after him but Valunos called him back. "Let him go," Valunos said. "I don't want any more... incidents here." He turned to Rick Taconelli, who looked like he was about to lose his lunch. "Better call building security—no, let's let him go."

You could practically see the wheels spinning as Valunos tried to figure out some way to pretend this never happened. He looked sharply at me as if I had made it all up. "What was this deal you just stuck with him?"

"I don't know," I said. "I was just playing along with him because he's obviously crazy."

"He's beyond crazy," said Patsy with authority. "He's evil."

A few minutes passed in which no one said much. I think everyone was too embarrassed. Then the Senator stood up and slipped out without saying a word. "He wasn't here," Valunos told the rest of us, his eyes darting around nervously.

"None of us were," said Yvette.

After a few more minutes Valunos looked at his watch and stood up like a teacher dismissing a class. "It's probably all right now," he said. And then, led by Lockjaw, we trooped down to the mail room in a kind of morbid curiosity to visit the scene of the crime.

What we found was a shocking sight. Ernie was lying dead on the floor next to his computer with two bare electric cords wrapped around his wrists. His eyes were wide open and little electrical impulses were crackling up from his body piercings. There was a stench in the air. Connie Liebman started to vomit and ran out of the room.

I noticed the little telephone answering machine tape on the desk next to Ernie's computer. It had a little yellow sticky with my initials on it. Next to it was a small framed picture of a woman I recognized. I slipped both of them into my pocket while the others gasped and turned off the power and rolled Ernie over on his back. With the cords disconnected he looked as normal as he had ever looked.

"What a shame!" cried Valunos, groping for the positive spin he would try to impart to this gruesome scene when the police arrived. "How could something like this happen? He was so young!"

Naturally I couldn't keep my mouth shut. "Perfectly healthy man drops dead," I shrugged. "Happens all the time."

And then Valunos finally lost it. After all that time preening and posturing and watching his whole world view unravel before his very eyes, he finally couldn't take it any more. I heard a shriek and saw him skittering towards me with an agility I didn't know was possible in a man with his billing rate.

"You!" he shrieked again, jabbing his quivering forefinger about three inches in front of my face. "Get the hell out of here!"

35.

By the time Valunos chased me out of the office it must have been after six o'clock. People in the elevator were talking about a snowstorm that was supposed to hit Philadelphia later that night. "The storm of the century," one woman called it.

"Which century?" I asked.

The woman chuckled but I was dead serious. In the past twenty-four hours I'd brawled with Sproat, spent a sleepless night in the Philadelphia County Jail, broken up with Madison, won Elena and lost her again. I'd been kidnapped by an undertaker and put on trial for a murder I didn't commit, solved one crime and committed another in the process. I didn't know what time it was, what year it was or what century it was. And the way I felt, I didn't really want to know.

The worst part of the whole thing was what had happened to Ernie. True, the goal of any detective is to confront the murderer in front of all the other suspects and trick him into confessing. But I had to ask myself, was this really necessary? Did it really matter to the world whether Ernie was caught and punished? And did his punishment fit the crime? As the elevator arrived in the lobby, I closed my eyes and all I could think about was Ernie lying on the floor sparking and fizzling like a malfunctioning appliance. Maybe I wasn't cracked up to be a detective.

Once outside I stopped thinking about Ernie and concentrated on finding Elena. I hurried back to my building and went straight to Theresa's apartment. There was no answer to my knock, no wary eyeball peering through the peephole in the door. Theresa was still out with her Bingo Club and Elena must have gone home long before. She'd left no note on my door or at the concierge's desk downstairs, no sign of how long she'd waited after I went out to get the champagne or whether she'd guessed why I never came back. I felt like crying.

My apartment still looked ransacked but now that seemed appropriate, a fitting metaphor for the wreckage of my life. And I knew now it was Ernie who had done it, in proud and prophetic revenge for what I would do to him. There was poetic justice in that, though not real justice. I called Elena's chambers and left an incoherent message on her answering machine, downed a couple shots of Jack Daniels and fell dead asleep on top of the bed without changing my clothes.

I woke up about twelve hours later. It was light outside but eerily quiet. The storm of our young century had settled in overnight, muffling the city in a blanket of fresh snow. I turned on the TV and learned that it was a weather emergency, possibly the greatest such crisis our city had faced since the last Ice Age. The whole city was shut down while the mayor and his snow removal crews worked around the clock to keep essential services from being interrupted. For me this was good news, or at least indifferent news. All I wanted to do was stay in bed in my ransacked apartment and get drunk and sleep it off. I left another message for Elena but she never called back. A little before noon Theresa knocked on the door and said Elena called to say she wasn't coming into the city today.

"You look like you got hit by a train," Theresa told me.

"Good," I said. "That's better than how I feel."

Unfortunately there was one thing that had to be done. I shaved and showered and put on my dark suit and my dark topcoat and walked out to the garage to find my car, in violation of the mayor's order to avoid all unnecessary travel. But this trip was not unnecessary.

I had the streets to myself. The snow removal crews, which were supposed to be out in full force, were nowhere to be seen. There was at least a foot of snow on the streets, but I didn't care. My Toyota Corolla has front wheel drive and it slid over the top of the snow like a sled. The city was so quiet and desolate, I imagined that I was in a science fiction movie set in some distant, post-nuclear future. I kept to the city streets and avoided the Expressway as I wended my way toward Northeast Philadelphia. There was no traffic on Roosevelt Boulevard or Bustleton Pike. Without too much looking I found the little row house on Loney Street and picked my way up the unshoveled walk past the frozen dwarves, who I knew were giving me the evil eye from under the snow. This time the dogs didn't bark when I knocked on the door. When Irene let me in they huddled under the couch whimpering like a pair of lost souls.

"I wondered if you'd come," she said. Her eyes were as empty and desolate as the streets I had just driven through.

"I wanted to bring you this," I said. I handed her the little framed picture I'd taken from Ernie's desk. "He kept it on his desk."

She laid it carefully on the coffee table. "Do you want to sit down?"

The room looked different than I remembered it. In place of the Poodle Hall of Fame, everywhere I looked there were pictures of Ernie: Ernie as a baby, Ernie as a toddler, Ernie as an altar boy, Ernie in his cap and gown when he graduated from high school—all the pictures that had been removed in anticipation of my first visit. And Irene, with a little prompting, filled in all the details. Ernie was Neil Babylon's son, of course, and she never kept it a secret from him, though now she felt she'd made a mistake in letting him know the truth. He became obsessed with it after he finished high school and found himself at the bottom of the economic heap. He started collecting newspaper clippings about the doings of his successful father. Then he took a job at the Rittenhouse firm without telling Irene and without disclosing his true identity to the firm. For a while he contented himself with spying on Neil from a distance and collecting more information about him from within the firm. It was Alyssa's arrival as a privileged employee that sent him in a more dangerous direction. She wasn't even Babylon's daughter, he complained to Irene (who by this time knew he where he worked)—why should she be treated like a princess while he slaved in the mail room?

After a while he wrote a letter to Babylon, identifying himself as his son but still not revealing that he worked at the firm, and then he started calling him on the phone. Neil humored him at first but refused to meet him or send him money. Ernie became increasingly insistent and belligerent, as Irene witnessed on several occasions when he called from home. Ernie never made it clear what he wanted, probably because he didn't know himself. But Neil assumed it was money, and after several unpleasant exchanges he stopped taking the calls. Then Ernie started leaving messages that amounted to blackmail. By this time he knew enough about his father's private and professional life that the transition to blackmail was almost effortless. He threatened to sabotage Babylon's chances for appointment to the Third Circuit by going public with some of the things he'd learned about him that nobody was supposed to know.

"The next time Ernie called him," Irene said, "Neil said a lot of insulting things about me. I don't know what they were. Ernie wouldn't tell me, but he was furious."

"What did he do?"

"I begged him to just let it drop, find another job somewhere and forget he ever heard of Neil Babylon. But he had to stay there."

"And?"

"I guess he made up the story that Neil was sleeping with Alyssa and told it to somebody at the office. One of the female attorneys."

"That would be Patsy."

"Yeah. And she was a patsy. She spread the story around and Neil almost went berserk. When he traced the story back to her he called her in and threatened to have her whacked."

"Whacked?" I repeated. "Killed?"

"Yeah, killed.   Neil came from the coal mining country and he has some pretty rough friends up there."

That was an angle I'd never thought of.   In my self-centered way I had just assumed that the treatment I'd received from Neil was the worst he was capable of.   No wonder Valunos thought Patsy had killed him. I asked Irene, "Did Patsy tell Neil where she first heard the story about Alyssa?"

She kept her eyes down, as if I had asked her to acknowledge her own complicity. "I don't know," she said softly. "But Ernie was afraid she did, and he was afraid Neil would realize who he was and take it out on me."

"Neil knew where to find you, didn't he?"

"Sure. He'd been sending me money for twenty years."

While Irene and I were talking the two poodles had crept toward me, whining occasionally, and now they were both sniffing up my pants leg and wiggling their tails in the cautious hope that I would prove to be a friend. I reached down to pet them and they both rolled over and gazed up at me with a look of instant devotion. If only life were so simple, I thought.

I stood up and started to pull on my overcoat. "I guess that explains it," I said. "If anything does."

"Nothing does." Her eyes were still cast down.

I waited for her to look up. "Ernie and I made a deal," I said.

"What was that?"

"To keep you out of it. I'm the only one who knows who he was. I'm not going to tell anyone."

She stared at me for a long time with her vacant eyes, as if she had to start at the beginning of her life and think the whole thing through in order to know how to respond. "Thank you," she finally said. "Not that it matters a whole lot."

I said good-bye and trudged sadly out into the night. My tracks had been covered by fresh snow and I had to spend ten minutes shoveling my car out. I turned on the radio to the classical station and floated back through the unreal city to my apartment. By now it was almost seven o'clock and for the first time I remembered that I was supposed to have gone to work the night before. And I was supposed to be going there now, if I still had a job. Not that it mattered a whole lot.

36.

I parked in the building garage and slogged through the snow over to the Pickwick Club, expecting it to be closed for the duration of the weather crisis. Surprisingly it was not only open but crowded with the usual cast of characters.

Niko greeted me at the door with more than ordinary hostility. "Where were you last night?"

"I don't know," I said unconvincingly. "It's a long story."

"You're fired."

"Fine. Do you mind if I just have a drink?"

"Not if you pay for it."

"And if I feel like it, would it be all right if I played the piano for a little while?"

He calculated his chances of getting something for nothing. "You're not getting paid."

"I understand." I slipped past him and headed for the bar.

"You should be paying me," he called after me. "You should be paying me to come in here and play my piano."

I ordered a double Jack Daniels at the main bar and chatted with Doug while I nursed it down. On the other side of the room, the piano bar made for a curious sight. The piano stood silent, yet the regulars huddled around it, drinking the same drinks and having the same conversations they had every night.

"What's the matter?" asked Doug.

"For some reason," I said, "I've always thought that the presence of a piano player was an essential part of what went on at the piano bar."

"You were misinformed."

Without saying a word, I stepped over the piano, sat down at the keyboard and began to play. The song was "I Got a Right to Sing the Blues" and I played it like I'd never played before. The laughter and conversation faded and for the first time the regulars actually seemed to be listening to the music. When I finally stopped after twenty minutes I looked up and they were all staring at me as if they'd been hypnotized.

Rhoda the bird woman daubed tears from her eyes with a handkerchief. "What happened?" she wanted to know. "What happened that you're suddenly playing so beautifully?"

"That time," I said, "I meant it. And I'm not getting paid for it."

She burst into a fit of sobs. "That's so beautiful!"

Brian O'Dolan coughed and took a sip of his wine, and Jim Hively cradled his head in his hands as if the pain were unbearable. The only one who didn't seem to be moved was Bardahl, who sat enveloped in the usual cloud of smoke at the far end of the bar. He walked over and leaned toward me to avoid being overheard.

"Why did he do it, Cloud?"

"What do you mean?"

"You know what I mean. Why did that kid in the mail room kill Neil Babylon?"

"I wish I knew."

"You know."

"If I did, I probably wouldn't tell you."

He scowled and started buckling up his trench coat. "What about the surveillance tape?"

"What about it?"

"You know where it is?"

"No, and I'm done looking for it. You've got nothing over me now. You're going to have to find some other way to bring the Senator down."

Bardahl leaned so close to my face that I almost fell backwards off the piano bench. "You've got the right to remain silent," he growled, "and the right to be represented by counsel. But you know what, Cloud?" He backed away and gave me one last bitter scowl before he walked out. "You *don't* got a right to sing the blues."

I played another song and by the time I finished, Connie Liebman sat perched on the nearest barstool. She looked pretty in her ski sweater with her rosy cheeks from the cold air outside. It made her look like she was blushing. I was glad to see her. Out of the whole sick crew at the Rittenhouse firm, she had come out looking pretty good.

"Hi," I said. "What brings you out on a night like this?"

"I just needed a little fresh air. It's only a couple of blocks."

"So what's new?"

"You were right about Ernie," she said. "People are starting to remember things that he did, things they didn't notice at the time because they thought he was such a nonentity."

"Like what?"

"Like seeing him at the cocktail party. A few people have said they remember seeing him that night."

"Did anybody see Yvette? Or Sproat?"

She shook her head.

"I didn't think so. He made all that up."

"They found his notebook about the drug interactions. The police are pretty sure that's how he did it. Just like you said."

I shrugged. "Well, nobody at the firm's going to be asking me about it. Or anything else, for that matter."

"I will," she smiled. "You're not persona non grata with me."

"Thanks."

"By the way, everything is working out OK for the firm. The insurance proceeds came through to pay off the loan, and Riordan and Valunos have reached some kind of settlement on the bank takeover."

"That warms my heart."

She glanced at her watch. "Hey, I've got to run. Give me a call. Do you have my home number?" She wrote her phone number on a cocktail napkin and pressed it into my hand. "Bye now."

Seeing Connie gave my spirits a lift, and I think my next song was a little less self-pitying. But for the regulars, unfortunately, I had set a tone of existential angst from which they may never recover.

Brian O'Dolan ordered another drink for himself and the still-sobbing Rhoda and stared fearlessly into the abyss. "Either there is a God who created us and loves us as his children and will preserve our souls for all eternity," he said, "or we are insensate lumps of matter careening through space, soon to be swallowed into nothingness when our pointless little lives sputter to an end."

Jim Hively suddenly looked a little more depressed than usual. "Isn't there a middle ground?" he asked.

"No," said O'Dolan. "Those are the two alternatives. There's no middle ground."

Hively thought about it for a moment. "Well," he finally said, raising his glass to propose a toast, "I guess it's pointlessness then. I don't think I could stand eternity."

O'Dolan laughed as he raised his glass. "What makes you think you have a choice?"

In my own little world there was one last bit of entropy that still had to be attended to. The time and place were more or less predetermined: noon the next day at Theresa's apartment, when Elena arrived at her mother's for lunch.

I was already there, sipping a cup of hot coffee at the kitchen table. I had just finished telling Theresa the whole crazy story—except the part about Elena—when Elena tapped on the door and walked in. We hugged and kissed like long-lost friends but it only took a second to notice what was missing.

Theresa poured Elena a cup of coffee and she sat down across from me. "I guess you heard what happened," I said.

She nodded. "Geoff told me all about it."

"They grabbed me when I went out for the champagne. Valunos was going to turn me over to the police because he'd made up his mind Patsy Jessup had killed Babylon and he didn't want to risk losing the insurance proceeds. I'm sorry."

"I am too," she said.

There was an awkward pause, the first of many. "When Geoff came home that night," she said, "he was like a different man. It was as if he'd seen a part of reality he'd been blocking out for a long time. He couldn't get the image of Ernie out of his mind."

"Neither can I."

"We stayed up talking all night like a couple of college kids."

Theresa had turned on the TV to watch "Days of Our Lives" but now she grabbed the remote and clicked it off. "Who needs a soap opera when you've got this going on in your own apartment?"

Elena gave her a look. "Go ahead," Theresa said, hurrying into the kitchen to stir her spaghetti sauce. "I'm not listening."

"What about Amber?" I asked.

"Amber's one of his pro bono clients. She has a drug problem and a couple of disabled kids."

"And he's been sleeping with her?"

Elena stared into her coffee cup for a long time as if trying to remember some obscure detail from a past life. "Until recently," she finally said. "He told me all about it. How it started, where it led, how it ended. The whole sordid tale."

"Is that what college kids stay up talking about these days?"

"Pete"—her dark eyes flashed a warning—"don't turn this into a joke."

"I'm sorry."

She stood up, clutching her elbows as if she was trying to stay warm, and stepped over to the window. It was the kind of winter day you only get after a major snowstorm—bright and sunny and beautiful—but I doubt if Elena saw any brightness or beauty in it. "This is the worst thing that's ever happened to me," she said, turning to face me. "One minute I want to cry and the next minute I want to smash things. One minute I hate him and the next minute I think I must still love him or I wouldn't give a damn."

I waited a long time before I asked her, "What are you going to do?"

"I don't know. Geoff is like a different person. I've never seen him cry before. He literally got down on his hands and knees and begged me to forgive him. And then one of the girls came down and asked us why we were crying, and we couldn't stop."

There was another awkward pause. Finally Elena said, "He's their father. I can't just walk away from that and twelve years of my own life without giving him another chance."

I nodded.

Elena sat back down at the table.

The awkward pauses had expanded to fill the conversation. Neither of us could think of anything more to say. Five minutes must have passed before Theresa finally broke the ice. "I thought all along that the two of you were making the whole thing much too complicated," she said.

"Mother—"

"I'm talking about the murder case, not your love affair."

Theresa stepped out of the kitchen and looked straight at me. "Which, by the way, even though it's none of my business, I think you ought to get on with in spite of her staying up all night talking to Mighty Mouse. Talk is probably all he can do."

Elena buried her face in her hands.

"By the way, I always figured it was the Viagra that killed Babylon," Theresa said. "Especially after I watched that videotape. The last thing that man needed was Viagra. But what I'd like to know is, how did you know it was Ernie?"

I was grateful to Theresa for changing the subject. The murder case was like comic relief compared to what I was going through with Elena. "It was that night I spent in jail," I explained. "There was a young man in there who'd just been convicted of something, and he was complaining that his innocence should have been obvious because there was too much evidence against him."

Elena poured herself another cup of coffee. The crisis had passed and for better or worse she seemed to be her old self again. "He was probably framed," she said. "If there's way too much evidence against a defendant, you begin to wonder if the police made it up."

"That's what I realized. There was way too much evidence pointing to everybody but Ernie, and he was the one who was giving it to me. The files, the emails, the search trail in Yvette's computer. His implication of Lockjaw and his sighting of Sproat on the night of the cocktail party. And finally his claim that Yvette had been in the building the night Neil died. That's where he went a little too far. It was something I could check for myself. I called building security and pretended to be from the firm. They didn't really have any record that she came to the building that night. Ernie made that up. That's when I was sure it was him."

"How did you know he was Babylon's son?"

"I guess I just put two and two together. Something had been bothering me about Irene Fluegfelter and when I suspected Ernie was the killer I realized what it was. She was so proud of her son but there were no pictures of him in her house when I went there. Only pictures of dogs. And then I realized I'd asked Ernie to help me find Irene Fluegfelter the night before I went out there. So they had time to change the pictures."

It was almost time for Elena to go back to court. When she stood up to find her coat I followed her into the living room and we shared a long embrace. "It's sort of ironic," she said, "but if you hadn't cleared things up, I would still think Geoff was involved in... much worse things than he was really involved in."

I forced a smile. "He deserves another chance."

"There's no justice in it for you. I know that."

"At least there's irony," I said. "Irony is a kind of justice."

When we turned around we discovered Theresa peeking around the corner at us with a puzzled expression on her face. Evidently our little soap opera had taken an unconventional turn. "Now what?" she asked.

"Now," said Elena, "maybe everyone can get on with their lives."

But there was one more loose end that needed to be tied up, and Elena and I both knew it. We couldn't all get on with our lives, at least not the way we might have hoped, if I continued my search for the surveillance tape. Finding it would mean serious trouble, not only for the Senator but for Tom Riordan as well—and in that event the Mists of Inverness would slide into bankruptcy, the partner guarantees would be called, and Geoff Goodwin a/k/a Mighty Mouse would lose his shirt, if not his cape. As she put on her coat, Elena couldn't help asking, "Are you going to keep looking for that tape?"

"Oh," I shrugged. "I don't know."

"It was probably destroyed long ago."

"Probably. But you know, if there's even a slight chance that it still exists—"

"Pete"—she squeezed my hand—"Do me a favor? Forget about the tape. You're only going to get in more trouble if you keep looking for it."

"But how can I just let them get away with something—"

"Sometimes you just have to accept what's already happened in your life and go on from there."

"Yeah. I guess you're right. It's not worth ruining your life over, is it?"

Before Elena left, she and I forced Theresa to surrender Babylon's homemade porno tape. We wiped it clean of fingerprints and wrapped it in a plain brown package marked "Confidential," which Elena was to mail to the Senator's office on her way back to work. She said she had to run—she had a trial at two o'clock—and we said good-bye at the door as we had done so many times before. And that was that. It was what Neil Babylon would have called a bittersweet occasion.

Back in my apartment, I considered my options. Which took about ten seconds because I didn't have many options to consider. There on the table stood my bottle of Jack Daniels, tempting as always, but I couldn't even decide whether it was half full or half empty. Another option, as I had been reminded the night before, was existential despair. But I had noticed that Brian O'Dolan, though a strong advocate of existential despair, always seemed to be able to find hope for himself, if not for mankind, by inflicting it on someone else. And was it possible that Bardahl was right? Didn't I really have the right to sing the blues?

The telephone rang and like a fool I answered it. It was Madison, and she wanted to apologize. I told her I was sorry but as far as I could tell there was nothing to apologize about. Our whole relationship had been a misunderstanding, if not a sham. "When you came into the Pickwick that night and gave me that first long kiss, were you in cahoots with him then?"

"No, I was trying to get away from him."

"But then later?"

"He threatened me if I wouldn't cooperate. He wanted to know why you were after him."

"He could have killed us both."

"I'm sorry. I was afraid. I wanted to tell you, but—"

"But what?"

"Most of the time I had the feeling you didn't really want to know very much about me."

That hurt, because it was true. "I'm sorry too," I said. "I'm sorry I was so blind and stupid that I didn't try to find out who you really were."

It wasn't a long conversation, and it ended with our accepting each other's apologies and agreeing that we could remain friends. I felt mean and sad, but that was the way it had to be.

A little later I fished in my jacket pocket for the cocktail napkin that Connie Liebman had pressed into my hand the night before, on which she had written her phone number. She was a lovely woman in every way. I picked up the phone and dialed, but of course this was Thursday and like most normal people she was at work. So I had no choice but to call her at the office. We had a nice chat, culminating in a dinner invitation which she eagerly accepted. By the time I hung up I felt that there was still hope for the human race.

On that optimistic note, I re-examined my Jack Daniels bottle and decided that it was half full. A couple of shots convinced me that my disappointments would not prove fatal if I could salvage some meaning from what had happened during the past week. In order to live, we need at least the illusion of justice—some chance of a happy ending even if deep down we realize how arbitrary life usually is. Poor Ernie's death didn't do much for the cause of justice. He paid the ultimate price but he did not take away the sins of the world. There had to be a reckoning, and it was up to me to make it happen. I knew there were some places I could not go. Tom Riordan deserved to be hanged, drawn and quartered, but his downfall would bankrupt the Mists of Inverness and its investors, especially Geoff Goodwin. I might have enjoyed the irony of seeing Mighty Mouse reduced to penury and disbarred for manipulating the loan guarantees, but I owed it to Elena and my own macho pride not to be the cause of his ruin. Elena had to find her own way—I was hopeful that it would lead back to me. In the meantime, if she wanted to give her husband another chance I would not be the one to pull the plug.

But I felt no such compunctions about the Rittenhouse firm. Thanks to Ernie, I had amassed a valuable archive documenting some of their more dubious achievements. It was all there in black and white: How Senator Lou Squires used the firm as a conduit for peddling influence on state contracts and approvals. How he'd rigged the State Banking Commission's proceedings on Third Millennium's acquisition of Harrison State Bank in order to line his own pockets. How the firm had placed its own interests ahead of its clients' in promoting the Senator's corruption. I suspected that my old friend Bardahl— whose heart, much as I hated to admit that he had one, seemed to be in the right place after all—would be delighted to receive an anonymous package containing enough smoking guns for a prosecutor's convention.

I spent a couple of hours putting the documents in order and annotating them with brief explanatory notes which I typed on a cover sheet, just in case a careless reader might fail to see the point. Then I went down to Kinko's and made two copies of the whole package. One set I mailed to Bardahl, the other to a reporter at the *Inquirer* who had previously authored a series lambasting Senator Squires. Bardahl's set would quickly find its way into the State Attorney General's investigation of Senator Squires. Within six months the Senator would be indicted and Art Valunos would be forced to step down as managing partner. A lot of newspaper readers would be shocked to learn what goes on inside a law firm, even though what they learned would only scratch the surface. They'd never learn the truth about Neil Babylon and all the people who wanted to see him dead.

That night as I walked over to meet Connie I couldn't help thinking about Ernie and his bitter farewell, that little speech he delivered right before slipping off to tie those electric wires around his wrists. Ernie was a killer, and he admitted it. But a lot of other people had played a hand in his crime or welcomed its result. Patsy by spreading the vicious rumor about Alyssa and her stepfather and then blackmailing Babylon about the sex tape. Valunos by wishing out loud that Babylon would die so the firm could repay its bank debt. Senator Squires, out of jealousy for his wife and an insatiable thirst for more money and power. And even me, in some metaphysical way—I'd been so thirsty for revenge over my disbarment that I probably would have sent Neil Babylon to his reward if I'd had a chance. As Ernie said, a lot of people wanted him dead but they didn't do anything about it. Only Ernie had actually carried out what everybody else could only fantasize about. And in the end he didn't want us—his unindicted co-conspirators—to think we were any better than he was.

Patsy said Ernie was "beyond crazy"—he was evil. And I suppose she was right.

But there was also some truth in what Ernie said. If he was a little crazy and a little evil, he'd been able to camouflage it by working at a law firm, where he could be sure that no one would ever notice.

It was the perfect cover.

THE END

About the Author

Bruce Hartman is the author of eight novels. *Perfectly Healthy Man Drops Dead,* his first book, was awarded the Salvo Press Mystery Novel Award and published by Salvo Press in 2008. It is presented here in a slightly revised Tenth Anniversary Edition. Bruce Hartman's books have ranged from mysteries (*The Rules of Dreaming, The Muse of Violence, The Philosophical Detective*) to comedies (*A Butterfly in Philadelphia, Potlatch: A Comedy*), techno/political satire *(Big Data Is Watching You!)* and a legal thriller (*The Devil's Chaplain*). A graduate of Wesleyan University and Harvard Law School, he lives with his wife in Philadelphia.

www.ingramcontent.com/pod-product-compliance
Lightning Source LLC
Chambersburg PA
CBHW030403180626
46812CB00005B/1907